THE GREAT SNAKE

JENNIFER MUGRAGE

ISBN: 978-1-7358354-4-0

First Edition Printing
Cover Illustration Copyright © 2022 by Jennifer Mugrage
VTC Goblin Hand font by Larry E. Yerkes, licensed under the
1001 Fonts Free for Commercial Use License (FFC).
VTC Goblin Hand font suggested for titles by Benjamin Ledford.

https://outofbabel.com

The Scattering Trilogy:

The Long Guest (Part 1)

The Strange Land (Part 2)

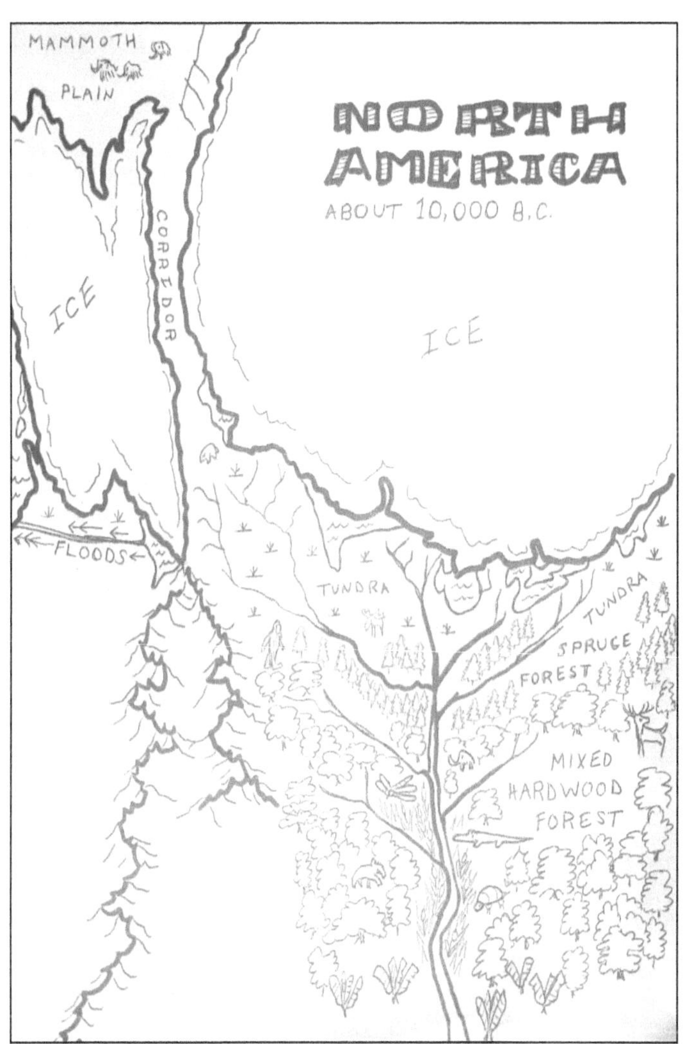

MAMMOTH PLAIN
NORTH AMERICA
ABOUT 10,000 B.C.
ICE
CORRIDOR
ICE
FLOODS
TUNDRA
TUNDRA
SPRUCE FOREST
MIXED HARDWOOD FOREST

ENDU'S SONS AND THEIR FAMILIES

Jai … *married to* … **Amal** (daughter of Hur and Ninna)

    Klee

    Kai

    Doon

    Mala

    Lana

    + younger children

Jabed … *married to* … **Magya** (daughter of Hur and Ninna; widow of Ki-Ki)

    Queet (daughter of Ki-Ki)

    Aki (son of Ki-Ki)

    Risa

    Inda

    + younger children

Ikash … *married to* … **Hyuna** (daughter of Hur and Ninna)

    Dumish

    Sira

    + younger children

Sha … *unmarried*

PROLOGUE

Behold, the people, the only known people. They are a group of between one and two hundred, with about half as many dogs. Watch as they journey south on a dark, cold winter's day, under a flickering sky. See them pull their sleds over the snow. See how tough and efficient they are. See how precisely they follow their leader, the one who has found the true path that will not crumble. They can make amazingly good time, better than you would imagine, for they are a strong people, an ancient race not yet weakened by disease and deformity. Above them, the sky flickers with curtains of blue and green, swaying as if in a distant wind. This they call the Grandfather Veil.

The elders know that they are not the only people. They remember a time when there were other human beings. When all the people of the world were gathered together in one place. But that was two generations ago. To the little ones, and even to their young parents, these two hundred are the only people in a wide, wide world. They will find wives and husbands from among their first and second cousins, and this will not cause them any problems. There is good blood in their veins. It is so free of disease, so much richer in a variety of traits than is our blood. Their blood can give rise to many tribes and races.

Even in this tiny group, not all the families are yet blood relatives. But in a few generations, they will be.

Every year, there are babies. These people love babies. Infertility is a rare and horrible curse. Children are a blessing. They grow up quickly and then they live for a century or more, learning new skills, innovating, contributing to the tribe. In the natural course of things, they could live for two hundred years and still be strong.

But there is another natural course of things. There is a current that flows another way, towards accident, injury, madness, and death. This is a land that eats people. Nearly every year, it seems, they lose someone to the cold, to miscarriage, to a predator, to a fall. Even to suicide. That is why it is important to go on having children. They need to keep ahead of the death.

Every so often, instead of blue or green the sky will flicker red. This is prettier and it gives a warmer feeling, but it makes the People nervous. It seems like a bad sign.

See them. There they go. They are different from you: better, cleaner, stronger. But their hearts are every bit as dark as yours. They are ignorant of many things which you know, and they know many things of which you are ignorant. Yet, they are you. They are your people.

And here we have a little girl, riding in a covered travois behind a pair of dogs. The wind blows under her, but she is cuddled in a warm nest with her brother.

Watch as she peeks out of the warmth to examine the arctic afternoon. Her round face is framed by dark wispy hair, colorless in this light, and the wisps are framed by the fur of her parka. Her eyes are black and bright and merry. See how the red light plays upon her face. She is a beauty. She is five years old.

This little girl is the hero of our story. She doesn't know her history yet, but she will find out exactly how she fits in to her people. Her people, the People, your people, they are the heroes of our story.

Welcome to their world.

CHAPTER ONE
BEFORE

Klee had four fathers. This was because of how the People reckoned kinship. Any brother of your father's was also called a father. Klee and Kai had a father, and their father had three younger brothers, so besides their own father they had three others.

Their own father, the one they were born from, was tall and thin, with a small, narrow, hawklike head. When Klee and Kai were little, they thought that this was part of being a father: you had to be taller than every other man in the tribe. When they were very little, he used to pick them up in each arm and they felt they were at the top of a tree. Then when they got a little bigger they began climbing on every high thing they could find. Klee could usually get higher because she was a few months older and so her legs were always longer.

Their other three fathers were as different as three men could be. Sha was young and fun and skinny, always ready to play with them. He was not really grown yet. He was seventeen and unmarried, still really a child though his body was as big as that of a grown-up.

Ikash was the tribal shaman. He was dark and quiet and still, with a calm black gaze that could pierce right through you. And he could sing. His young wife adored him, and all the little girls had crushes on him, except of course for Klee because he was one of her fathers.

And then there was Jabed, a big, round bear of a man, who managed to appear cuddly and soft even though he was in fact as tough as any man of the People. Jabed had a sweet, fat little wife (she was a "mother" to Kai and Klee, their mother's sister) and an ever-growing number of children. He was normal, established, stable, one of the fathers of the tribe.

Klee and Kai had grandfathers as well. Both of them were maimed, as older men tended to be after years of traveling through a dangerous world. One was missing a nose, one an eye.

Their grandfather without the eye was named Hur. He was a small man; fair-skinned, quiet, stable, soft-spoken. Hur was a bit hard to see because he seemed inseparable from mundane daily tasks. He was everywhere: hunting, healing, protecting, fixing, quietly guiding. He was everywhere, but he was nowhere obtrusive. In fact, he blended in so well that it would be a few years before Klee realized that Grandfather Hur was the People's chief. When she did, it did not seem to come as new information. It was as if she had learned a new word, *chief*, to describe what he was. He was to the People as the roots are to a tree.

Then there was the grandfather without a nose: Grandfather Endu. He was the sort of person that you noticed. He was tall, dark, dramatic, quick, and masterful. At night, when the People were setting up tents, he would stride around the camp with a part strutting, part hobbling gait, supported by legs that were unnaturally thin, stripped of their muscle, and a third leg, a snake-carved walking stick. He did no more work than Grandfather Hur – probably less, in fact – but whatever he did, wherever he went, he was visible. A charge seemed to hang in the air around him.

Grandfather Endu had been handsome once, but now he was frightening.

Klee and Kai knew that the People had always been traveling. They had vague memories of a journey eighteen months ago, when they were very small. What they didn't know was that this year was the first that the People had tried to make their annual journey by winter. The children were young enough that this one season of their lives had extended back and colored all their previous memories. It just made sense; the People had "always" waited for the snows to travel. Sleds worked better; there were no floods or falling ice. Predators hibernated; deer and mammoth came out to forage and were easy to spot and to spear. Travel days were cold and miserable, but in-between days were times to cuddle up in tiny tents, eat meat, sleep, tell stories.

The people stopped their journey and began to set up tents. This was the time when Kai and Klee would play "keep away," by which they meant, keep away from their mother.

Their mother was beautiful. She had a long sheet of blue-black hair and a round face that, during these winter months, seemed as pale as the moon. For some reason, she did not like Klee. She always wanted her to help out at times like this, young as she was, but she tended to expect Klee to read her mind, or to give the girl tasks that were beyond her capabilities. Sometimes, when pregnant, miserable, and driven beyond endurance, she would slap her daughter's face. Klee would cry loudly, and if her father heard, he would show up and harshly rebuke their mother.

But father was busy digging down through the snow. They would pitch their tent on the ground, and the snow would insulate it. Mother was sitting on the edge of the travois, hunched in miserable cold around her pregnant belly. She always wanted Klee to take care of Kai because she was a little bigger than her brother, so at times like this Klee was very cooperative. She and Kai stayed in their sheltered nest until they were called. She was taking care of him – and they were playing "keep away."

See the People set up their tents. They are experts at this. They can do it very quickly, without arguing, except in those families where arguing has become part of the set-up routine. In no time, there are two dozen little tents where before there were none, like a field of haystacks or a sudden range of hills.

The children's father helped their mother into the tent. Their family dog, Gobbo, hurried in after him, obediently shaking the wet from his fur *before* he entered. Then their father came and got them out of the travois. One by one he carried them, jouncing through the cold.

Their mother had built a tiny fire, using mammoth wool for tinder. The tent was filled with the powerful, bad smell of burning hair, but to the two children it smelled like home. The interior was still very cold, but it seemed warm after outside.

The children pushed back the hoods of their parkas. Klee's hair stood out around her head, flyaway in the staticky air.

Their mother reached out and tried to smooth the flyaways down. As she did, she pressed her lips together.

The People continued traveling south through the corridor of ice. Kai and Klee continued to grow. That spring, their mother had her third child, a son, Doon. She became even more short-tempered and preoccupied. Their father explained to them that they must help her out as much as possible. They became even better at chores and at keep-away.

There was a brief drought of babies while the People traveled south through the corridor. Most couples were making an effort not to have children. Conditions were too difficult, but they had been assured that this was temporary. Their shaman, who sometimes scouted out the land in his visions, had told them that the corridor would last only a year or two, and that south of it was a good land, a land that God had prepared for them.

In the meantime, there were catastrophes. Minor earthquakes were common, particularly in summer. Avalanches were easy to avoid provided the People did not venture up onto the ice, which they did not.

The ice had taken on a mythic quality, almost as if climbing up there would be akin to going right out of this world. Grandfather Hur believed that anyone who walked on top of the ice risked passing through the veil and ending up in the realm of the dead. But the People had no need of the ice, for there was plenty of game in the corridor.

Floods were harder to foresee. Local streams would overflow, unpredictably and disastrously. Several times, a family home or two was swept away; several times, heroism was called for. At last the People learned to build their summer camps on the high places, well away from sources of water, even though this was inconvenient.

The People did not know it, but as the glaciers melted, even more catastrophic floods were taking place miles away from their southward road. Far to the west of them, a lake was emptying itself towards the sea in a series of irresistible deluges, carving canyons out of the earth. Any one of these could have wiped out all the People in an instant. It was the end of the world over there. But they passed by, unaware, in safety.

The summer after Klee and Kai turned seven, the ice walls drew back. The People emerged onto a wide expanse of tundra. Everyone breathed a sigh of relief. They spent the summer relaxing and adjusting to the new land. Several couples became pregnant.

The chief organized a scouting party which ventured even farther south. They found that the tundra gave way to spruce forests. Besides the herds of deer, elk, moose, aurochs, and mammoths, which moved freely between tundra and forest, Grandfather Hur was delighted to discover a smaller shaggy elephant, a mastodon, which was more solitary and seemed to prefer eating the spruce-cones. And there were rabbits, groundhogs, and other rodents of every possible size, habit and marking. Some of these the People had seen and known, others they had never yet seen. There were the ring-tailed kind with tiny humanlike hands which loved to raid people's garbage. There were tiny hopping mice and large swimming mice. Along the rivers there were dog-sized beavers. Panic and hilarity ensued when the People – and their dogs – had their first encounters with skunks.

With the game came the predators. They had been lucky, when traveling past the ice, in that only cold-hardy predators threatened them; mostly wolves, bears, and the occasional huge, fanged cat which the People called a Great Lion. And these were enough. The People had a particular terror of the bear.

Further south, the scouts reported, it was a more complicated picture. There were cats of every size, including the Great Lion. There were dragons (both predator and prey varieties), giant birds, and a creature that the People had not seen in the flesh for several years: snakes. It might have been a terrifying picture. But Hur, who loved nothing more than to observe new animals, was in paradise. His excitement communicated itself to the rest of the People.

Grandfather Endu, who was a magical, spiritual person, dug himself a men's lodge. Or rather, he directed the digging of it. This was not the sort of thing that could be done by one man alone, especially a half-lame man. Klee remembered it, in later years, as the first exciting building project she had ever had a chance to observe. As there was no timber on the tundra, it featured no roof and was not nearly as impressive as the temples he would erect later. But to Klee and Kai, at the time, watching it emerge was unbearably exciting. They would watch the young men, bare-chested and digging, and would run between them as they worked, throwing clods of peat at one another and bringing it home for their mother's cooking fire.

Sometimes Kai would be given a mammoth-bone "shovel" and asked to help out. Klee was not allowed to do this, however desperately she wanted to. She would sit on the scrubby grass and watch as the round, sunken shape slowly emerged, and in the evening when they had all gone, she would climb down into it, walk around the rim, and vow to herself that one day she would build a *women's* lodge.

When the lodge was completed, the elders held a coming-of-age ceremony for the young men of the tribe. This year there were only three. Kor grandson of Melek was thirteen, Apik son of Melek was fifteen, and so was Malan son of Dusun. This situation, with an uncle and a nephew growing up the same age and even going through a manhood ceremony together, was not unusual among the People. At that time, women enjoyed fertility into their fifties or even sixties. Couples built their families slowly, spreading them out over decades. Often they were still having children after their oldest were grown and wed.

The manhood ceremony consisted of several days and nights spent in the men's lodge. The initiates would sleep there by night, and the days and evenings were spent in storytelling. A cycle of stories had developed which told the story of the world from its beginning, through a series of disasters, down to the present day. The tribe believed that every young person should know these stories because they contained critical information, deliverable in no other form, about how to be in the world.

Most of the information that the shaman would share with his young cousins was not secret knowledge. These stories were told, in a less formal way, as entertainment at feasts and to children around family campfires. But of course they had developed variations. During the manhood ceremony the whole cycle was told, straight through, in the standard form as it had been memorized. This was to be sure that no one missed anything. After the three days of storytelling, the initiates would go out on their own and meditate until they had a vision.

Although there were only three initiates and one shaman, everyone wanted to use the new men's lodge. Besides the three youngsters, the lodge in the evenings was packed with other men: elders, fathers, anyone who had a free moment. They lent their advice and their weight to the words of the shaman, who was himself only twenty-three years old.

Klee wanted badly to hear what was being told. But she didn't dare, because it was sacred. Also, her mother was pregnant again and miserable, and it was Klee's full-time job to watch over Doon, who was now walking and, if left unattended, would get himself into all sorts of danger.

So Klee sent her brother to listen instead. The ceremony was easy to spy on. Kai sneaked up the side of the hill into which the lodge had been dug. He wormed his way up the earth berm that had been built all around the pit with blocks of dug-out peat. He could lie comfortably on its rounded edge with just his black hair and bright eyes peeking over the top. He needed to do this. It was impossible to hear otherwise. The shaman had a quiet voice which filled the bowl but did not carry past it. At key moments he would lower his voice even further, and the initiates would all lean in.

Later, Kai reported on what he saw and heard to his sister.

"He told the gods-coming-down-the-mountain story. And he told some stories about the Blood-Eaters. And about the salvation tree and the flood."

Klee pushed out her lips in a pout. "I know all those stories already," she complained. "I don't see why it all has to be so *secret*."

"I know the stories too," said Kai. "But he told them really good, sister. Like I've never heard them told before."

"Not even when he comes over to our hut and tells them to us?"

"Well … I can't remember."

"Didn't he say anything really *scary*?" she persisted.

Kai announced eagerly that he had. "Whenever he goes to tell a sacred story he puts some smoke on the fire."

"Puts some smoke on the fire?"

It transpired that the shaman would smother the fire in sweet herbs of whatever kind he could find. Up here in the tundra it was mostly sage, but in later years he would add lavender and tobacco. A thick column of fragrant smoke would rise from the fire and would seep into the corners of the lodge. It would whip around and would even be brought to Kai's nose whenever a breeze made it into the depression.

Kai described how good it smelt. He coughed a bit, he said, but it made him feel calm and peaceful too. It put him in good mind to hear a story.

"Maybe that's why," he added, "I felt his telling was better than ever before."

"But how is that scary?" asked Klee.

"*Because*," said Kai. He dropped his voice in a dramatic impression of the shaman's whisper. "*Telling the sacred stories* – or doing the manhood ceremony or something, I forget which – *it attracts the Great Snake*."

Klee looked at him in silence, hesitant to speak. She had only heard rumors of the Great Snake, but a little thrill of fear was instant as soon as its name was mentioned.

"*He can control reality*," Kai continued. "That's what the shaman said. He can make it winter when it's summer. He can make you think you're naked when you're not. He can make you think you're healthy or in pain. He can make you think you can fly, and then lead you right off a cliff."

The two children looked at each other soberly. This was, indeed, as scary as anything Klee could have asked for. She could not think of a more frightening prospect than an entity that could control any aspect of reality, at any moment.

"How can you stop him?" she asked.

Her brother bounced excitedly a few times on the balls of his feet.

"*The smoke*!" he pronounced giddily. "The snake doesn't like it. It confuses him. He's a spirit who lives in the air, so when we put something from the earth into the air, it – I don't know. He doesn't like it. It hurts his eyes or something. Because it's a sweet smell. Anyway," he finished lamely, "the shaman thinks it might help."

"*Might* help?" said Klee.

"He says nothing is certain," said Kai. "Going on a vision is always dangerous. The main thing is to believe the sacred stories … and not to trust the snake. Oh, Klee, I can't wait 'til it's time for *my* manhood ceremony!"

"It sounds as though you know it all already," said Klee acidly, because she was jealous. But then when she saw the sad look on his face she added quickly, "But there's lots of exciting things you haven't heard."

"How do *you* know," he muttered.

And though the shaft went home, she swallowed her pride and said gently, "I'm sorry, Kai. It will be fun. I am looking forward to it with you."

What she was really jealous of was the *idea* … the idea of a loving older relative of the same sex teaching you how to become their kind of person. This was not something that Klee's mother seemed to want to do with her. Amal's instinct was not to usher Klee into womanhood, but to try and keep her out. But this was not a clearly formed insight in Klee's mind at the age of seven. All she knew was that she wished she had been born a boy.

After walking each of the initiates to the place they had chosen to meditate, the shaman would always go off by himself and do something or other. Fast, pray, patrol near the initiates to be sure – from a distance – that they were safe.

Klee approached him before he left camp. He was wearing a buckskin shirt that had fringes on the sleeves, as if to make him easier to grab onto. She plucked at these.

He stopped, turned, and looked down at her smiling.

"What is it, little one?"

Klee blurted, "Don't *women* ever have visions?"

She thought he might laugh at her, even if it was just a secret smile, but he didn't. Instead, his face immediately became serious.

"Yes, certainly," he said. "Grandmother Zillah."

Grandmother Zillah? Klee was not certain about her. She was the matriarch of the clan, tall, thin, and golden-skinned, the grandmother of Klee's mother Amal, the mother of Grandmother Ninna, the only adult in the world who had white hair. She had great power, no doubt. She was a healing woman. She was present at most births and was the first person to call whenever anyone was sick or injured. But everyone knew that Grandmother Zillah was a little strange. She walked around the camp muttering to herself. Klee had heard her father say that Grandmother Zillah was talking to the dead. She did not think that this counted as a vision.

"I don't mean a *crazy* woman," she said.

The shaman flinched. "Is that all you know of her? That is not respectful, little one." Though his words were a rebuke, his voice remained soft as usual. "I don't want to hear you calling her that again. Grandmother Zillah is not crazy. She knows many things." He paused, and then added, "You should ask her."

"Yes, father. I am sorry. I will ask her," said Klee.

But as it turned out, she never did.

Over the next few years, the People – your people – moved farther south. They spent a year on the tundra, then two years near the border of the spruces. The summer before Klee turned ten, Ikash's wife Hyuna had her first baby. Klee cried when it happened, running off where no one could see her. Hyuna was a nice aunt, only twelve years older than Klee. She was a younger sister of Amal, and of course she was married to one of Klee's "fathers." She had always been playful, cheerful, and – for a woman – relatively fierce and athletic. She was the sort of woman that Klee would rather like to be. Now that Hyuna had a baby of her own, Klee felt she had lost something. Perhaps she didn't want to be ousted, yet again, by a baby from anyone's affections. Or perhaps she feared to see the matronly changes that would now come over her beloved young aunt.

The People, your people, moved again. Through the spruces, to a forest of vast hickories, ashes, oaks. Things were different here: unpredictable. The weather was much warmer, so much so that the oldest people, people like Grandmother Zillah, said it reminded them of a distant place called Si Nar. There were all kinds of plants that might be edible, and the People set about testing them. They fed them to their dogs, then they licked them, then they nibbled, seeing which parts might be edible, which parts poisoned you or else had some other effect. Which ones were easy, quick sources of food on the go, and which could perhaps be cultivated.

Of the animals too, there was a baffling variety, more kinds than the younger generation had ever seen in their lives. The insects alone were enormous. It was a wild, surreal, risky land, but the People were brave explorers. They moved forward cautiously, but they moved forward.

Timber was plentiful, but obtaining it was difficult. It had been a generation since the People had seen forged metal. The elders remembered that it used to be plentiful back in mythical Si Nar. There was a process for obtaining and extracting it. It was a long, sometimes dangerous process, requiring skills that the People had forgotten. Only Grandfather Endu thought he remembered and might be able to re-create the process, if they came to a likely place.

But for now, trees had to be felled another way. The People did this with a slow-burning fire applied to the trunk. Then they would go to work with saws, wooden saws set with flint teeth. Their tools were inferior, but their skill was consummate. They had been building nearly every year for three generations.

The trees were average-sized here. The ice had been withdrawing for only a lifetime. In the years to come, when they went farther afield, they would find trees that were huge, bigger around the base than a good-sized hut or than the men's lodge. But that was later, when they were no longer one people.

The chief asked the shaman whether they had at last reached the land that God had for them. The shaman replied that he thought they had.

Grandfather Hur, who was sixty-seven years old and thus probably less than halfway through his life, declared that barring the unforeseen (which was almost guaranteed to make an appearance), he saw no reason to move again in his lifetime. It would take them, he thought, fifty or a hundred years to domesticate the plants, to learn to hunt the animals, to find the metal (perhaps) and the flint and water sources, to fully see the possibilities of this place right here. If the elders were agreeable to it, he thought they should settle. They should stay.

This speech proved once again that the old man was full of surprises. Hur was an accomplished nomad. He loved to explore; he loved to hunt. At moving times, he always did what was necessary without blame or complaint. If any older member of the tribe had wanted to keep moving forever, everyone expected that it would be Hur rather than Endu, rather than Grandmother Zillah. But Hur liked many things, and he had found them here. He declared his hands were full. Perhaps the younger generation would want to move off as the People expanded, and this would be a good base to move from. But for himself, Hur was content to stay.

The elders spent a year discussing this. The idea seemed alien to the younger people, but not to the older generation. Most of them remembered a more settled life from the days before the disaster. Endu, in particular, had long wished to abandon tent life for the comforts of a permanent home.

They spent a year; they talked to their wives about it, and they decided. This was a good place. They had everything they needed here. They would stay.

The decision had an energizing effect upon the People. Huts were expanded, winterized, made yet more comfortable. A new men's lodge was begun, this time to have wooden walls and a roof to hold in the holy, protective smoke. The ugly, electrifying Grandfather Endu, who was tired of dressing in skins, sent his wife out to look for wearable plants. They would stay! They would stay! Everyone was busy with staying-tasks. Everyone was happy with it.

Here, in the wooden complex between spruce and hardwood, was where Klee was going to finish growing into a woman.

CHAPTER 2
DURING, AND IMMEDIATELY AFTER

Things began changing the summer before Klee turned sixteen. But first let us get to know her as a young woman. She developed early; she was done with her growing before the end of her fourteenth year, an age at which many of the other girls still looked like children. Klee did not have many age-mates of the same sex. Only Neet and Dagwa were exactly her age. Gupet, daughter of Endu, and Risa (her sister born to her father Jabed) were two years younger. Then there were some older girls. Riba daughter of Melek and Queet daughter of Magya were two years older than Klee. Kit and Djila were four years older, which when Klee was in her early teens put them almost in another generation. When her body developed, she joined them as a peer, and they would have welcomed her as a fellow woman if she had been willing.

But these were all. There were more boys than girls in that generation.

Klee grew up tall, just as both her parents were tall, relative to the rest of the People. She was long-legged, broad-shouldered, flat-chested, with a squarish body shape not too different from a child's. Because of her build she continued to be venturesome and athletic.

Her hair was a problem. Klee had expected that as she got older she would become more reserved and ladylike, like her mother. This did not happen. She also, somehow, when she pictured herself as a young woman, had pictured her hair being blue-black, smooth, and straight.

Of course that did not happen either. It remained her own hair, which was to say reddish black and flyaway, with a tendency to be dry in the winter, and in the summer, unpredictably wavy. Even long as it was, reaching her waist, it stood out around her head like a bison-colored halo. Amal had a small, neat, oval head, but Klee's face was round and flat, adding to the halo effect.

This effect was worst just after combing, which was something Amal could never believe.

"Why is your hair so unruly?" she would say, as if this were somehow a choice that Klee had made. "Why don't you ever tame it?"

It was always like that. Her mother had to be better, or superior at something. At the time, Klee accepted this. Of course it was better, of course it was important, to have straight smooth hair that shone like the moon. It wasn't until much later that it occurred to her to wonder why it should matter so much whose hair was straight and whose was unruly.

Klee had never been able to discern how to please Amal, and at around the age of thirteen, she gave up trying. This led to a series of bitter fights about matters so small that neither woman could really understand them. These fights would always end with her father Jai stepping in, sometimes physically separating the two of them, sometimes slapping one or both to get them to shut up. Usually he sided with Klee, but as the misery went on, he became increasingly impatient with both his wife and his daughter. After nearly a year of this, they were known in the village as the family that was always yelling.

Kai had put an end to this, harshly one day, when he withdrew his friendship from his sister. He too was fourteen, stewing in his own misery, sleeping constantly, growing so fast his bones ached, passing through an intensely uncomfortable period as he got ready to grow into a man. He wished only to be left alone, far from even normal conversation, and he was sick of listening to his family fighting.

"It's all you," he told her coldly. "Do you realize that? They are fighting all the time because of you. Why can't you just stop?"

"Stop *what?*" cried Klee indignantly.

"Stop – stop fighting with her. Stop doing whatever it is that makes her unhappy."

"But I don't *know* what it is!" she protested. "I don't. You know that. You've always known that."

And her brother had waved his hands about his face in frustration, as if shooing gnats, and said, "I know. I know. I don't know either. But – it must be something you're doing, something you're being."

"It's not my fault! It's not!"

And he had shaken his head as if to snap himself out of this moment of residual understanding.

"It must be, Klee. I can't keep putting up with it – with you – anymore. I can't take it. Please just stop."

"I *don't know what to do!*" she had wailed, becoming teary, but her tears had panicked and disgusted him, and he had gone off by himself, as he did frequently that year.

That was the worst moment of Klee's life so far. Kai had always been her best friend, but after that, their friendship did not recover.

The thing was, there *was* something she could have done, Klee suspected, to win her mother's approval and affection. All she would have to do, she understood somehow, was turn her father against her. If she would behave really horribly, somehow – reject him, make him hate her, do some unknown and unspeakable thing – then her mother would be relieved and happy, and she would love her after all. Klee didn't understand why this should be her mother's requirement, but she had somehow always understood that those were the terms of the bargain.

But she wasn't willing to do it. It was unreasonable and unfair, and besides, she loved her father. It was wrong, she thought, wrong of her mother to ask for this, wrong of Kai to expect it, whether or not he understood what he was asking. Wrong of everyone to blame her for causing trouble just because she wouldn't do some unknown, monstrous thing.

As a boy, Kai was free to go off on his own, primarily on hunting trips with the men or even with the other boys. The year after their friendship ended, he participated in a manhood ceremony, and she lost him forever.

Klee was not a boy, so she had fewer excuses to go. She began to spend time at other houses, helping other women who had young children. She spent a lot of time with her aunt Hyuna, who now had two little ones. She went on fishing trips with the aunts and grandmothers. She spent time helping the tribal matriarch, Grandmother Zillah, with an agricultural experiment.

"Do you see this grass?" asked the grandmother. She stood near an upswelling meadow where the soil was higher and dryer than the surrounding area. The grasses that grew there were visibly different if one looked closely. Zillah's silver hair was stirring about her shoulders in the breeze. At that time she was still considerably taller than Klee.

Klee stepped forward and took a look. The head of the grass was about as long as a finger. It was packed with round, golden brown seeds.

Zillah twinkled her eyes at Klee.

"Go on, they are safe. I've tried them."

Klee took a nibble. It was dry, starchy, and good enough, but hardly worth a mouthful.

She looked at her grandmother in silence, not wishing to be disrespectful, but at the same time thinking, *How can we ever live by eating* grass?

"Ah," said Zillah brightly, as if she had discerned the question. "You will never have seen it, my child, but I remember that in the old place, where we grew most of our food, there was a grain called barley. It looked very similar to this. It was good to eat – in a stew, say, with meat –"

Klee cracked a slight smile, and Zillah noticed it immediately:

"'Why not eat the meat, then?' Well, there is nothing wrong with meat, but grains keep better, and you can do a great many things with them, delicious things which … which I see by your look that you cannot imagine. Never mind. You were wondering about scale. How would it be possible to produce large amounts of food by harvesting grass? Well, look you here."

She bent and, with some difficulty, plucked an entire stalk. It seemed to be very tough, and she had to pull up some of the shallow roots in order to do so.

"Look," she said, laying it out like a baby across her palms. "See how all down the stalk there are heads of grain? I believe this grass could be very productive. It could produce an abundance if we give it a little encouragement."

This was what Zillah believed about every thing and every one.

So Klee and several of her age-mates spent a few weeks that summer helping Grandmother Zillah harvest all the stalks of that particular grass that they could find – in that place, and in a few other high and dry places, between the oaks and spruces, that were open to the sun. It was good to be outdoors, enjoying the sun and wind, a basket balanced on one hip, doing some mindless work that sometimes brought her into contact with the other girls and sometimes allowed the mind to wander. Occasionally someone would start up a song, and they would sing together as they worked.

Grandmother Zillah always brought her spear, for there were predators in the area. She even asked a few young men to come along as guards whenever the harvesting women went any distance from the compound. On one occasion Kai was among these, and he stood resolutely staring off into the distance, occasionally flirting with the other girls, but neither talking to nor looking at his sister.

Klee's hair was too flyaway, and of too many varying lengths, to stay neatly in a braid while the winds blew. Once a gust came up directly behind her and took the whole mess and threw it forward over her head like a veil. When she thought of the untangling she would have to do, she nearly cried in frustration. She set down the basket and stood holding her temples.

At length she scraped the hair back from over her face, wadded it, and drew it forward over her shoulder. She had lost the battle; the tears were flowing.

Then a shadow fell over her shoulders from behind, from the same direction as the wind. She turned slightly and saw Grandmother Zillah smiling tenderly as if she had just witnessed a bird take flight.

"How unique you are, granddaughter, even though you may find it inconvenient." The old woman reached out with dry, capable hands and gathered back the mass of her granddaughter's hair.

"I once loved a man with curly hair."

Curly. Klee had never heard that word.

"I have at home some fragrant oil used in healing the skin," Grandmother Zillah went on. "When we return to the village I will give you a supply. I think it may help tame your curls."

Then she went away, because Klee was sobbing quietly although she didn't know why.

When they returned to the village Grandmother Zillah did give her a supply. And Klee and the other girls spent the next several weeks rolling the kernels of grass-grain in their hands, spreading most of them out to dry in the sun, saving the biggest ones so that they might be planted. Afterward, their hands were cracked and dry, and they all had need of Grandmother Zillah's healing oil. Klee surreptitiously rubbed a little of it on her hair, and though it did not make her mane smooth and straight, it did keep it from flying away.

The next spring they planted the grass-seeds using dibble sticks in an area that Zillah and some of the other grandmothers thought would make the grass happy, an area that was relatively high and dry. It was an experiment; they were not doing it out of starvation, but only to humor the grandmothers and their silly old-fashioned desire for grain. But every year the grass grew lusher, the kernels got bigger, and before long it had become an important crop.

Klee was always looking for excuses to stretch her legs. The tribe's new, settled life was easier on young mothers and little children, but the strong young men and women sometimes found themselves without sufficient challenges. One day early in the summer before she turned sixteen, Klee had taken a basket of laundry up the stream, past the women's and the men's places, to a small flat grassy meadow. Kai and Klee now had three younger siblings, with another on the way. In a house full of little children there was always washing to do, and as things had developed, that task usually fell to Klee. She liked it because it gave her an excuse to get out of the house and do something physically demanding. (Stomping and scrubbing heavy wet clothes, and indeed hanging them on bushes, took a lot of endurance; but it was wringing them that really built up muscles in the hands and wrists.) Often it meant she was with other women, and there would be laughing, talking, gossip, even water fights. Sometimes, as today, it meant some precious time alone. And though Amal might criticize how long the task had taken her daughter, still it was a contribution that she appreciated.

On this particular day, while Klee was standing midstream scrubbing and stomping, the nearby meadow became the scene of a pickup game of ball. The People loved wild, rough-and-tumble competition, and now that they had settled, hunting and travel were not enough to fill these urges. They had never in Klee's lifetime met any human enemies, so although the chief insisted that they still practice, there was never any real combat. But young men had a deep need to fight something, and so they had developed a number of sports.

The game they were now playing involved a fist-sized leather ball that the teams were trying to get to one end of the field or the other. There were very few rules: no biting, no eye gouging, no hitting below the belt. That was it. The teams were three on three. Kai was on a team with Kivaq and Kota, two sons of Shezer, son of Melek. On the other side was Klee's cousin Aki, joined by Watak and Ishak, two sons of Damai, who were older. These two resembled their father Damai. They had long, bony, diamond-shaped faces with rather prominent front teeth.

Klee got the laundry wrung and laid out (on the north bank, the side away from the ball game), and now there was nothing left to do but guard it and occasionally turn it. And still the game was going on. She needed something to do. She used to play this game with this crowd quite a bit when all of them were a little younger.

She called, "Can I join you?"

"No," said Kai.

But the others said yes.

She crossed the stream, lifting her skirt, which was only knee length. All of the other players were wearing loincloths and leggings.

It was decided that to make things fair, she should be on a team with Kivaq and Kota, because Kota was only twelve years old. Kai didn't want to be on a team with his sister, so he and Aki switched teams. Now she was playing against a seventeen-year-old, a nineteen-year-old, and her brother.

"I won't go easy on you," said Kai.

"I don't expect it," she answered.

Things went well at first. Klee was fresh, and all of the rest of them were winded. So for a while she was the champion of her team. Aki was laughing and saying, "Good job, cousin!" and "Not bad, eh?"

But soon things began to turn against the team of four. Kivaq, who was short, and Kota, who was younger, had started out especially winded. Watak and Ishak were both taller and still fresh … and Kai had a burning fear of being beaten by his sister. Before long, it was essentially Klee and Aki playing against three others.

Then there came a moment when Klee had a chance to block Ishak. He had his lanky arm raised, about to throw the ball over her shoulder to Kai, and she flung herself at him, arms up, with a war cry. She attained a great height, bowled him over with her chest striking his face, and both of them went down together.

Aki was yelling, "Get the ball, Klee!" when Ishak suddenly abandoned the game. He grabbed her about the waist, yelling, "Help me, brother!"

And before she knew it, Watak had come up behind and pinned her legs and two of them had flipped her over.

"What the hell are you doing!" she said, trying to kick him. But Watak only grinned and held her shins down harder, and the kicking action flipped her skirt up a bit and showed him something he shouldn't have seen. Klee couldn't put it down again because her arms were now being pinned by Ishak.

"How beautiful you are, daughter of Amal," said Watak, still grinning. He moved his hand up to her thigh and squeezed it.

She renewed her kicks, and he laughed and held her by the shins again, calling to the others to come and help, come and feel.

"Are you crazy?" said Aki. "Let her go!" His usually brown face had gone grey.

"No, it's harmless," said Watak. "Come and help me."

Aki flung himself at Watak, and then there was a moment when they were wrestling and Klee and Ishak were wrestling, but then Kai and Kivaq pulled Aki off Watak and some punches were exchanged, and then somehow Kivaq was helping to hold her down and also touching her, and Klee was crying with humiliation, and she was furious with them for having made her cry.

"Kai!" she cried raggedly. "Aki!"

But her brother, having broken up the fight, stood back and wouldn't meet her eyes. Aki had been punched in the stomach, but after a moment he struggled to his feet and went tearing off toward the village.

"*Coward!*" she screamed after him.

He wasn't running away, he was going for help. But by the time he came back with it, every single one of the other players had touched her, including twelve-year-old Kota. And Kai stood by and let it happen.

Klee took all the stored rage of her fifteen years – which was considerable – and began to call them the filthiest names she could think of. Most of these she had learned from her father, not when he was speaking to his own family but whenever he was angry with someone else. But they began to hold their hands over her mouth, and worst of all, Watak forced his great tongue between her jaws. She bit him, and he punched her.

And then Sha arrived like a storm with Aki in his wake.

Sha – the youngest of Klee's fathers – was gentle, funny, musical, the tribe's artist. He had never married. Klee had not known he was capable of violence. But he was. He was lanky and rangy, with large hands and feet, as tall as Watak but more muscular. His face was a dark reddish brown with indignation. Between them, he and Aki quickly broke up the rape. Kai shrank back; Kota fled; Sha broke both of Damai's son's noses and Aki broke some ribs on Kivaq.

When all of them were sitting on the ground wheezing and bleeding, Sha turned to Kai and struck him across the face as well.

"For shame!" he said. "How could you not defend her!"

Klee had flipped her skirt back down and stood. She was cursing as hard as she could to keep herself from crying again and because there was no adequate way to express her anger.

Sha looked impressed.

"That's good cursing," he said. He was still chestnut-colored and breathing hard through his nose. Furious, but not furious with her.

He began to herd Klee and Aki back toward the camp.

"You two are injured," he said. "I'm taking you to Grandmother Zillah. *You four*," he said over his shoulder to the others, "If the elders would allow it, I'd kill you. You've got no right to behave that way to any woman, but especially not to my sister."

"I am not your sister," Klee corrected him.

"Yes, you are," said Sha, still walking straight ahead, still red and huffing.

"You are my father!"

"I'm your brother. Let's talk about this later. I am taking you to Grandmother Zillah."

"No, don't!" she cried out, stopping still. Sha was surprised enough that he stopped still too.

"I have laundry to collect," she said.

"Oh, for goodness' sake. You can get it later."

"No. I don't want my mother to hear about this –"

"You mean Amal."

"That's what I said, my mother. She will blame me – I can hear her now – she'll say I shouldn't have joined the ball game –" Her voice began to wobble, and she quickly stopped speaking.

"If she says that, I'll kill her too," countered Sha. "Your evil stepmother. All right, have it your way. Go and get your laundry. Actually, I'll stay with you. Aki can send Grandmother Zillah out to us. I don't think we'll be able to keep this from Amal, though, sister."

It was the third time he had said it. Klee tipped her head and looked at him, but she didn't at that moment have the energy for puzzles.

He walked her back across the stream. She splashed her face and picked the grass out of her hair and washed out her mouth thoroughly. Then she silently started to turn the washing, which was still damp. Some of it was Kai's. His clothes, which she had been washing for him.

While she did this, she started crying again. She knew the facts; everyone by fifteen knew the facts. They had seen it done or heard of it. She knew what had almost happened to her.

She knew the facts, but she hadn't known it was possible for there to be so many *people* involved. It was awful. It seemed to confirm everything that her mother had ever said about her, every bad thing that Kai had ever thought.

Sha asked her about it. Had they actually forced her …?

"No," she snapped. "I suppose you'll say that in that case I shouldn't be so angry."

He was shocked. "I would not say that! I'd still kill them for you, if you wanted, sister."

"Don't call me sister," said Klee.

Sha fell silent.

The clothes were not yet dry when Grandmother Zillah arrived, not throwing punches but looking like a storm. She embraced her granddaughter and began to question her. Klee glanced at Sha, the youngest of her fathers who was now insisting he was not her father, and he took the hint and melted away.

Klee took Zillah through the incident step by step. Zillah examined her injuries, of which the punch on the cheek was the only one, and Klee spent some time sobbing in her grandmother's arms.

"… and Sha keeps calling me his sister," she finished as an afterthought.

Zillah drew breath, and then fell silent for a long time. Klee was so busy being miserable that it was some time before she noticed that the old woman was extraordinarily still.

"What's wrong, Grandmother?" she said, not bracing herself for blame, because she did not think that Zillah would cast blame like Amal.

"Do you mean," said Zillah slowly, "Do you mean that no one has told you?"

She was still holding her fine, expressive golden features very still.

"What?"

"He is not your father. He *is* your brother."

Klee shook her head. This made so little sense that she was not even thrown.

"That cannot be, Grandmother."

"Yet it is," said the matriarch. "Perhaps I should not tell you … but Sha has already told you … but perhaps I am not the best one. I will get someone to explain it to you.

Who would you best hear strange news about yourself from? Jai – I mean, your father?"

"Not my father," said Klee. She could only imagine Amal's jealousy if Jai were to share a secret with her.

"Who then …" said Zillah out loud to herself. "Sha is busy starting a tribal war, as he should, after what has been done today. Perhaps I should tell you … but I am not good at secrets …"

While she thought, Zillah began to gather up the pieces of laundry, and Klee began to help her. The old woman should have trusted herself and told the girl the truth on the spot, but she did not trust herself. She decided at last to bring her granddaughter to the person that many people went to with their troubles: the tribal shaman.

The laundry and ball game debacle had happened in the morning, and it was now noon. The village, now that the People were settled, was large enough, and enough spread out, that it was possible to bring Klee to the shaman's house without everyone seeing her. In the summer the People still often took their meals at a communal cookfire, but the two women found Ikash in his own back lot.

He had brought a bowl of stew from the common fire, and he was feeding his four-year-old daughter. His six-year-old son was running among the hardwood trees behind the dwelling, breaking branches and generally causing chaos. Hyuna, nine months pregnant, was sampling another bowl of stew, forcing bite after bite into her crowded stomach. Sha had made a curve-shaped basket chair for her so that she could arch her back in these late pregnant days. The family had it sitting outside, because in the summer time no one spent the daylight hours indoors.

Ikash was thirty-one years old. He was a young, handsome man, but as appropriate for a shaman, there were times when he seemed much older. He had a certain presence, as Hyuna had once tried to explain to Klee. He could make any room – or, indeed, any outdoor place – seem warmer simply by being in it. Space seemed to warp around him. When the two of them were alone together, the inside of a small hut would seem large. If they were alone outdoors, or in a large common room, the landscape would collapse into a small, cozy dome around the two of them. He was gentle, said Hyuna. Not timid. But considerate.

Ikash rose when he saw his grandmother; and until Zillah stopped her, Hyuna too started to struggle to her feet.

"What happened?" they both said. "We heard at the fire —"

"Much has happened," said Zillah. "I am here to ask you to tell a certain story. To your *sister*."

His little black eyes grew round, and he swung about and looked toward Hyuna.

"I will go and visit my sisters," Hyuna said, this time, in fact, struggling to her feet, though she had to put her hands on the ground at one point to do so.

"And I will take the children to visit the stream," said Zillah.

"Here, sit down," said the shaman to Klee as the two women faded away. "Are you all right? Are you hungry?"

"She can have the rest of my bowl," Hyuna, waddling away, called over her shoulder. "I can't manage it."

Ikash jumped up and brought his wife's mostly full bowl of stew to Klee. It was still warm, and she began to eat. She was suddenly ravenously hungry, but when the food hit her stomach it felt sour.

The shaman sat looking at her in a way that made her uncomfortable.

"I don't want to talk about the – ball game," said Klee. "I am all right, they did not really harm me, but Grandmother Zillah tells me Sha is not really my father. If he is my brother I want to know why no one has told me and why he hasn't been living with me and – Kai."

She could barely stand to speak Kai's name. But she felt that this new information was somehow connected to his betrayal. It might be the key to everything.

The shaman silently ran a hand over his face. Then he told her the story as they sat there in the summer woods.

It was a beautiful place to hear a story. His wooden house reared, well-constructed, well-decorated by Sha, overhead. On the other side of them were the humid hickory, the ferns, the oaks. Tree-frogs sang. Rabbits ventured near – the two humans were sitting very still – and flying squirrels and three-foot dragonflies glided among the trees around them.

Klee started out eating as the shaman told her the story, but before he got very far she had put her bowl down.

"Once," he said, using the People's formula for beginning a story that was true, "There was a handsome man who married a beautiful widow. He was the brother of the chief, and he thought she was very lucky to get him. He wanted her to be the perfect wife. He wanted her to do everything perfectly. At first, she did. But then things got harder. She bore him four sons, and with every child she had, it became more of a burden for her to be perfect.

"Her husband, instead of helping her, tried to make her perfect by complaining, punishing and chastising her. He became more and more impatient with her flaws. He became cruel. Every once in a while, not often but at predictable intervals, he would brutalize her. And if they crossed him, he brutalized his sons as well.

"After a time, this once beautiful woman was no longer beautiful. She was so beaten down by the handsome man's behavior that she wasn't able to carry out normal household tasks. She was stressed, unable to think clearly, and desperate for escape. But there was nowhere she could go. She tried staying with her relatives. This worked for a time, but it didn't work forever. Her husband always expected to have her back.

"No one knew exactly what to do. Not the woman, not her sons, not the grandmothers, not the husband's brother who was the chief. It was a difficult situation. But for the once beautiful woman, it was truly desperate.

"Then one day, something happened. The woman became pregnant. She did not feel she had the strength to raise another baby under the harsh rule of her husband. But she did not know what to do. So …"

And here he paused for a long time.

"… So she told no one."

Again he waited a bit, and then said, "At last the woman had her baby. And just as she had feared, it was a girl."

At this, the shaman stopped speaking and looked Klee full in the face.

"The girl was you," he told her. "You are the daughter of the chief's brother and the woman."

Klee knit her brows and looked at him. She did not know how this could be possible. She was the daughter of Jai and Amal. She was the oldest child in her family. This story he was telling sounded as if it came from another family entirely, and not from now but from a long time ago.

She tipped her head.

"Go on," she said coldly.

The shaman went on.

"After the woman had her baby, everyone was surprised. But her husband was pleased and pretended he had known about it all along. Only the woman was in despair. At night, when all were sleeping, she took up her baby and began walking away from the camp.

"She walked for many hours. She got far away before her family realized she was gone. When they woke, they went after her. Her husband, her sons, and her nephew, Ki-Ki, who was at that time the shaman.

"And one of those sons," he said, "Was me. I am the third son of the woman."

He met her eyes again.

Klee's eyes were still narrow.

"Are you saying …" she asked levelly, "That you also … are my brother, not my father at all?"

The shaman nodded, but held up one hand to forestall her questions: *all will be revealed.*

He was a good storyteller, and his skills had, so far, carried him through what was clearly not just another story. But as he reached his point, he began to swallow every once in a while. The story became interspersed with pauses, and moments of silence.

"We went after her," he said, "But we were too late. She threw herself into one of the scalding pools that were abundant in that area, for we were near a fire-mountain. By the time we arrived, she was nowhere to be found. The pool had swallowed her up.

"We never even retrieved her body."

Identical tears emerged from his eyes and tracked darkly, in parallel, down his brown cheeks. He bowed his head and passed a hand again over his face.

"We saved the baby," he said. "Or rather, the woman – your mother – saved the baby – you. She set you down in a safe place before she – jumped. And when we arrived, just a little too late, we found you. You were unharmed. We brought you back to the camp. And after a while, it was decided that you would be raised by your oldest brother."

He looked at her earnestly once again.

"Do you understand what I am telling you? Your father, Jai, is not your father. He is your oldest brother. You are our   sister."

        Klee opened her mouth to ask a question, but nothing came out.

She tried again. Her voice was creaky. "Why didn't you save her?"

He could only whisper. "We came too late."

"I had a mother? A mother who loved me?"

"She saved you from the scalding pool. And from your father."

"And who was my …"

She fell silent, dumbstruck.

"Do you mean that my father is the same one who is *your* father?"

He swallowed – the tears were still running freely – nodded, and got his voice back.

"That's right. Grandfather Endu."

Grandfather Endu, the ugly, electric, dangerous Grandfather Endu, who brought a cold tingle with him into every place he entered, *this* was her father?

A worse thought occurred to Klee.

"Did he … did he ever …"

She was spared from searching for words because the shaman intuited what she was asking.

"Did he ever do to her as they were intending to do to you today? I am afraid he did."

After that, the two of them could no longer stand to look at one another. Klee put her hands to either side of her face and let her hair fall forward. Ikash got up and walked around. Then he came back and sat down again.

"But why … how …" said Klee from within the fall of her hair, "Why is he married now?"

"He married again a few years later."

"Why didn't he raise me as his own?"

"We didn't think Mom would have wanted that. Jai had just married, and he wanted to take you in, so … we let him. We were trying to protect you."

Jai. By this he meant her father.

Klee was starting to feel anger now.

"You couldn't protect her, but you wanted to protect me."

"Yes."

She raised her face and blazed at him,

"But *why* didn't you protect her?"

He flinched. "We were children … but still, that is no excuse. You are right, we failed her … it's a long story."

"And you have not protected me even now!" she cried, her anger building by the second. Now she was the one who jumped up and paced about the clearing. "You haven't protected me from my mother. This must be why she hates me! She is my stepmother, not my mother at all."

"She *hates* you?"

"Of course," snapped Klee. Everything was revealing itself to her in terrible clarity. "And now I know why. She never wanted me. She wanted her own children and her own husband. That's why she doesn't want me to be pleasing to Father. She thinks I am taking his love away from her."

Then she rounded on him and cried,

"I cannot believe that none of you told me the truth. I can't believe you left me with *her!*"

The shaman was normally very stoic of face, but now he looked flat-out horrified. Klee waited for him to defend himself, but he did not. At last, she stormed away in tears when she realized that he was not going to speak.

That was the summer that Klee ran away from home.

After her conversation with the shaman, she went directly home. That is, to Jai and Amal's hut. She supposed she must still call it home, though now the color of everything had changed and she felt as if it had never been home at all.

As she stalked past the houses, people stared at her. Some tried to run up to her and ask questions or offer sympathy. Klee brushed them off. She did not care that they were curious. She had more important things on her mind.

Her father was not at home. (All was confused. She had forgotten to think of him as not-her-father.) Actually he was somewhere else in the camp, being restrained from taking revenge on her attackers. Kai, too, was elsewhere. He was being chastised, defending himself. Dealing with the aftermath of that morning.

But Klee had no time to spare. She wanted to be gone.

When she pounded up the wooden steps, across the porch, and through the door, her stepmother (Klee had no problem demoting Amal) looked at her anxiously. She had always had a startled, unlined look about her, like a deer.

The two of them were alone in the lodge. Amal, when she saw the storm that was her stepdaughter, had quickly ushered the younger children outside to play. She knew both parts of what she had to deal with: she had heard that Klee had been attacked, and had been informed that she was at this moment off being told the truth.

"Oh, my child," she said, holding out her arms as if to give comfort.

It was all that Klee could do not to scream.

"I am not your child," she said. *Keep control of your voice.* "I had a mother. A mother who loved me." *Don't cry in front of her. Don't cry.*

Amal dropped her arms. "*I* love you," she said, looking more frightened than ever.

Klee flung her head to one side and spat on the floor. The gesture was marred because some of the spit landed in her hair.

"Don't spit in here, it will smell," said Amal automatically, before she remembered to whom she was speaking and looked panicked again.

"Who is my real father?" Klee demanded.

"What?"

"Tell me the truth! Is Grandfather Endu really the father of … of your husband, or is he someone else as well?"

Amal looked at the floor.

"He is the father of my husband," she said.

"So he is my father? He is the man who beat his wife until she killed herself?"

"That is what they tell me," said Amal almost inaudibly. "I myself never saw it happen."

"So I am not your daughter. I am your husband's sister. So the whole story as the shaman told it to me is true."

"It is true," said her stepmother.

Klee stood in silence for a moment. The shaman had told her the truth – and she had not doubted it – but it had been too big to take in. There were too many parts to it, too awful in their variousness. She could not swallow the whole truth at the time he told it to her, not until she had chewed on it. As she was chewing now.

Grandfather Endu – *Grandfather Endu* – was her father.

This would bear some thinking about.

But she could not stand thinking about it here. The longer she stood in silence, the more vulnerable she became before her mother. Before not-her-mother. She did not want to give Amal an opening. She needed to go someplace quiet and think about all this. In fact, she needed to go someplace quiet – forever.

"I am leaving," said Klee.

"You can't," said her stepmother, "I need your help with the children."

"You are not my mother!" cried Klee.

She bustled past Amal – who was heavily pregnant, just like Hyuna; who would indeed be needing help – and began to gather up things that belonged to her and things that she thought she could get away with taking. She took the family's second-best knife. She almost felt guilty about this, but then remembered that they owed her *everything*. She packed it all into a carrying-basket of the kind that strapped across the forehead. She headed for the door.

"Don't do this." Amal was crying. She stepped timidly in front of her stepdaughter. "Don't do this. Oh God, it will kill Jai."

"Perhaps he'll finally hate me," said Klee. "Isn't that what you wanted?"

"What? No … no …."

Klee was lit up by righteous anger. She felt, somehow, that it was all one thing. That if all of this deception had not happened, then neither would the attack have happened. Neither would Kai's rejection of her. That it was all traceable back to Amal and to the people who had abandoned Klee to her.

She drew herself up and looked as fierce as she could.

"Step aside, Mother. I mean, sister-in-law. Step aside. You never loved me. You've got no right be crying now."

Amal stepped aside.

"He will find you!" she called after Klee, almost before she was out the door. "He will find you, my daughter! You can't hide your tracks from a hunter like Jai!"

He did find her, of course. He caught up to her before she had even selected a place to camp. She was striking out through the spruces, intending to head north for the tundra. She would find some place high and dry and make her home there. She was good at fishing and was a decent shot with a bow, enough to catch rabbits and things like that. If no predator attacked her, she could live comfortably forever. If something *did* attack her … well, at this moment, she did not much care.

Klee was tall for a woman, but Jai was much taller. He was the tallest man in the camp. He came striding between the trees, which were kept rather open by the grazing of the mastodons. Klee could hear and even glimpse him coming well before he caught up with her. She did not run from him, wishing to preserve some dignity, but kept walking resolutely.

When he caught up to her, he seized her right wrist in the hard, engulfing grip of his own right hand.

Klee stopped walking and looked at him with her lips pressed together. Behind him, between the grey spruces, clouds were piling up in the east, already going golden in the afternoon light. Her life had already been changing for a day, for a whole horrible day.

The winds were whipping her flyaway hair about below the tump line of the carrying basket. Tears were smarting her eyes.

He – Jai – pleaded with her. (She could not stop thinking of him as her father.) He was crying; she had never before seen him cry. It made her uncomfortable. It was as if all the rocks in her world were crumbling, were avalanching as suddenly as the ice, and all on the same day. Jai had a hatchet face, large almond eyes, and a reddish complexion. Like most people, he did not look good when he cried.

Klee asked all the same questions, and he gave her all the same answers. She chewed on her truth a little more. She did not like that it should be *her* truth; she had not chosen it. But it certainly was hers, for they had made it so. It sounded, now, terribly true, coming from a man she had always trusted.

"You lied to me," she kept saying.

"We were *protecting* you," he said.

"You should have told me."

"Oh really?" He shook her wrist, which he was still holding, back and forth a little in frustration. "When? You have just now grown up. Do you think you were ready for this knowledge as a child?"

"Let go of me, please, brother."

"I *was* protecting you!" he insisted, not letting go. "I have always loved you."

Klee started crying again. Her tears had run out, so it was a dry sob. Then she sobbed harder in frustration with herself. She squealed like a wild boar and stamped her foot. And all the while, the man who had been her father looked horrified, stricken, but still he did not let go of her hand.

At last she got control of herself and managed to say, "Your *love* is the very reason you did not protect me. The more you loved me, the more your wife hated me. She has made my life a misery. Did you not see?"

He was silent, and she knew that he had seen.

"You saw," said Klee, happy to have found a way to hurt him, "But you continued in your way because you wanted me near you. You did *not* protect me from *her*. I would have been better off anywhere else. With someone I knew was not my mother. With – with the shaman. With my *real* father."

"You think that, do you?" said he, getting angry in his turn. "Do you think his wife would have treated you better? My God, Klee, if you knew how much you look like our mother! You were the queen of our house!"

"Not to Mother," said Klee. "I mean – not to *Amal*. I was an evil spirit that she wanted cast out. Well, now I am cast out. Let go of me, brother. Or do you mean to drag me back by the arm?"

Jai dropped her arm as if it were hot.

"Look, you don't have to leave the village," he said. His edge of panic was gone and he seemed unsure. "Even if you don't live with us anymore. You can find some place to live. We have already punished the evildoers –"

"Even Kai?"

His hatchet face became very grim, and she knew that things had not gone well between father and son. And that consequently, Kai was now going to hate her forever.

"I won't live in the same camp with him," she said.

"We can keep you safe."

"You have already shown that you cannot. Besides, I don't want to be kept safe, I want to stop being lied to."

He then began to tell her that she would not survive on her own. She began to tell him that she would. But she prevailed, because he was not willing to resort to force.

"You cannot stop me from following you," said Jai, and his sister replied cuttingly,

"Yes. That is what your wife said."

"Why, that little pup!" said Hyuna. "How dare she talk that way to you!"

Hyuna had been Ikash's wife for twelve years, almost since they were children. She was short and slight, with long flat hair of the ashy brown of a mink. Her temperament was warm, changeable, and fiercely protective of her husband. He had always been deeper than she was, and he had lived through considerably more tragedy.

After his conversation with Klee, Ikash had gone immediately to see his brother. He had a feeling his sister was going to storm off and confront one – or both – of her stepparents. It was possible she would beat him to it, but it was also possible that first she would go off for a private cry.

So Ikash had to try to see Jai. It was only polite to give him a warning.

It was a little difficult to get his brother's attention. This was right in the middle of the elders' investigation into the near rape, which was the worst such incident that had happened in more than a generation. Jai was in the thick of it, lit up with indignation. In his mind, the only question was whether the sons of Damai and Shezer should be tortured to death or merely executed. He had been told that Klee had learned the truth about her parentage, but the likely impact of this had not yet dawned upon him.

Eventually, Ikash was able to get his brother's attention, draw him aside, and with one hand on his upper arm, look up (Jai was six years older than the shaman, and even now that the two of them were grown he was still considerably taller), and speak to him and be heard. He strove to make clear that these new revelations loomed bigger, in Klee's mind, than the attack.

"She is very angry," he told his brother with emphasis. "Angry with me, with Amal, and I imagine she will be with you. Prepare yourself."

Jai tutted.

"Perhaps I should have told her myself, after all."

Ikash raised one shoulder. Things might have gone better if Jai had been the one to tell her; they might not. Who could say?

"What do you think she'll do?" asked Jai.

"I don't know," said his brother.

After this Ikash had returned to his back lot, which was still empty. He sat down again in the very place he had sat to be yelled at by his sister. He had rested his forearms on his knees, hands clasped together before him, and drooped his head.

Hyuna found him like that when she came hobbling back from a frantic visit with her sisters. She had been forced to bend rather far forward in order to get her belly out of the way sufficiently to give him an embrace. With a series of questions she had gotten the story out of him. And now, her pregnancy giving her an even quicker temper than usual, she was ready to demonize Klee.

"She has had a shock," said her husband reasonably. He did not stand to speak to her, nor even raise his head. "Two shocks, really. And – I did not realize – it seems she has been hurting for a long time. Apparently she has suffered at your sister's hands."

"And how is that *your* fault!" Hyuna cried. She turned away from him, clenching and unclenching her hands.

"It's not. I was the one who happened to be here when the storm broke."

"But she blames you."

"Oh, yes. I think she blames all of us. And perhaps … you know …" His eyes traveled back and forth, and fixed on the dappled, sunny leaf-bed. "Perhaps she's right. We may have failed her just as we failed Mom."

"No." Hyuna turned back towards him again, her yellow eyes blazing. She stepped into his range of vision and put a hand on his cheek.

"No," she repeated, "You did not. What were you meant to have done? Look, I love Klee, but she's behaving like a selfish little girl who can't see beyond the end of her nose. When you told her, she went directly to her own pain, you said? Did she even stop to shed a tear for your mother?"

"Well, no. But then … Mom isn't real to her yet. She's only just found out that she existed. Also, she's just survived an attack. Of course she isn't thinking clearly."

"… You are right," said Hyuna after a moment. "I am sorry. That poor girl." She sniffed a little, and then added,

"None of this is your fault, and it isn't hers really. And even Amal … I don't like to think that she could be so wicked, but yet, at the same time, I do believe it. I've seen her be sharp with Klee.

"But even her, she didn't start any of this. It's all the fault of your father!"

Ikash let this pass. They had long ago worn out the discussion of Endu's faults.

"I, I just …" said Hyuna shakily, "… I am sorry you had to go back over all this. I am sorry, love. I'm sorry."

"Thank you," said Ikash helplessly. He rose wearily to his feet and planted a kiss in his wife's hair. And then, he just held her for a moment. Her physical presence had always been calming, one of the best gifts she could give him.

Then he straightened up and added,

"But this isn't over, I'm afraid. It's going to get worse. It is just beginning."

CHAPTER THREE
KLEE'S VISITORS

Klee slept out. One night, two nights, among the spruces. Jai kept following her. She kept ignoring him. In between, she walked. When the opportunity arose, she would shoot herself a meal: a rabbit. A ptarmigan. A large snake. (Snakes were tastier than you would expect.) She did not offer any of this food to her brother, but when he snuck some, she did not stop him.

She didn't sleep very well during these nights. She had bright, confusing dreams, dreams that mixed old memories, recent events, and things she wished would have happened instead. She would spend half the night, as she thought, awake, thinking about things … and then she would wake in earnest and see his tall lean figure, standing guard over her, spear in hand. Which was incredibly annoying, but on some level she also appreciated it.

On the third day she came to some hills. She hadn't reached the tundra, but she had at least put some distance between herself and her family. Perhaps it would be enough.

She spent several hours poking about in the hills until she found what looked like a good enough place to live. She had hoped for a cave, but this was not that sort of place. These were smooth-scraped hills, left behind by the retreating glaciers not that long ago. They had stands of trees upon them (aspens, Jai said), but they were thin, shortish, brushy trees, not like the kind that grew around the village, the kind with huge girths and a thick roof overhead that had taken many years to grow.

But she found a hollow near the top of one of the hills: high, well-drained, prettily framed by the young trees. It was east-facing, so that in the morning it would catch the light and quickly warm up. She would be able to sit there, she thought, and watch the sun rise. On the north side of the hill was a spring that ran down to a little creek, which then meandered out eastward toward, eventually, the great river.

"I have found a place to live," Klee told the man who until a few days ago used to be her father. "You can go home now."

Jai didn't want to go.

"You cannot stay here forever," she told him. "You have your *own* wife and children, remember? Your wife is going to have a baby. Perhaps she would like you to be there for that event."

He stayed through that afternoon, watching with silent approval as she selected a site and built herself a hammock. She made it fairly high off the ground, cutting little wedge-like steps into one of the trees that bore it. When she got hungry, she ground up, and then ate, some acorns from her campsite's single oak, as well as leftover meat from the day before. She did not offer any to her relative.

Jai stayed one more night. He slept on the ground; Klee slept in her hammock. All that night, every time she woke and sensed him still there, she would yell out,

"Go home!"

On one of these occasions, after she yelled at him, she heard a distant answer, an odd percussive whoop that sounded humanlike but in a lower register. Then she lay still, not scared exactly, and listened. That was probably an Older Brother. Older Brothers were a large, bipedal primate that resembled oversized hairy human beings. This was why they were called Older Brothers. She was a little surprised to hear the voice of one this close to the tundra. They liked the great forests. They liked to make nests in the trees.

Sha was the one who had first encountered the Older Brothers. They were his totem. He was the only member of the People who had ever been close enough to touch one. Klee would like to tell him that she had heard one of them call ... oh, but then she remembered. Sha was not her father anymore, he never had been her father, but he had recently come to her rescue, but in doing so he had also witnessed her greatest humiliation, which was why she must stop thinking about Sha, which was also why she intended never to see Sha again.

Somehow she got through that first night at her campsite.

When she got up in the morning, Jai had obeyed her oft-shouted commands. He was gone.

Now at last, for the first time in her life, she was left alone. It was delicious, and it was also hellish.

It was delicious because it was restful. No Amal to nitpick, to tell her to smooth her hair, to ask why she had not yet finished this or that. No brothers, fathers, uncles to tell her she was beautiful and to look at her as if they hated her for it. No curious, chattering cousins to *look* at her.

None of that. Space and time, at last, to breathe, to think. Space and time.

It was hellish because she was left alone with her thoughts. And her thoughts were merciless. She might have had space to breathe, but still she couldn't breathe because her thoughts would not let her.

She spent her days working, and while she worked, thinking. Sometimes she set down her work and stared blankly, lips moving as she worked out her thoughts. Once, she gathered a great armful of pebbles from the creek and laid them out on the bank in varying configurations … first, every person she knew as she *thought* they had been related to her; secondly, as they actually were.

Grandmother Zillah was still her grandmother. That part was unchanged. But it was almost the only thing that was. Klee had jumped up a generation. The more she thought about it, the more she wondered how she hadn't seen this before, how she hadn't asked any questions. The most obvious clue was that she and Kai were supposedly sister and brother, but they were only three months apart in age.

Her younger brother Doon and her little sisters, whom she loved in a maternal way, were actually her nephew and nieces. She was the sister of their father. The odious Kai was her nephew too.

But she still could not think about Kai.

She moved some more pebbles. The shaman was her brother as well. That made his children her niece and nephew ... and it made Hyuna, whom she had always thought of as a likeable younger aunt, actually her sister-in-law.

On the other hand, she had lost her blood relation to the chief. Hur and Ninna, who she had thought were grandparents, were now no relation. Or, wait (another pebble found its place) ... Ninna was the sister of Endu ... who was Klee's *father* ... so Hur was no blood relation, but Ninna was Klee's aunt.

And this meant she was also a cousin to Gorman, Ezra, Peres, Megal and Koret ... and to the little boy Meren ... for all of them were nephews to her real father. They were children of Enmer, the former chief who had died when she was small.

It gave her a headache, but she ran through it again and again until she had re-jiggered her entire family tree. When she was done, she felt she had grown up in earnest. She was no longer the little girl who thought of them all as her uncles and aunties and so forth. She was their peer.

Besides thinking, Klee built her camp. She could not make a tent until she had hides, but she piled up an earthen platform in the sheltered part of the hollow (stamping and tamping it was most satisfying) and covered it with a brush roof patiently and expertly woven. Upstream, she found cattails, which the People used for any number of things. Soon she had woven cattail mats over her brush roof, which shed the rain. She had a woven mat for a bed on the earthen platform, padded underneath with cattail fluff. It was late in the summer, but she was still able to find some cattail shoots for vegetables. And the roots could be processed to make a starch which thickened her stews. Because she was cooking for one, all her hours of work seemed to be multiplied in their effects. Everything was done on a smaller scale than it had been done previously, when she was helping her brothers and sisters and father and mother. Stepmother.

There were not many big rocks just here, but the glacier had dumped a few medium-sized ones. She carried them up from the creek bed and built herself a hearth. She'd kept a fire going from the live coal she had brought from home …

from the old place, rather … and now she tried to keep it smoldering all night because re-starting it was such a chore. Having a fire constantly going would give away her position, but Jai already knew where she was camping and there were no other human enemies that she knew of.

One thing she did not think about was the future. She did not ask herself in any serious way whether she could truly survive here, by herself, through a winter. She knew the answer was that with luck, yes; without it, possibly not. But facing this took too much mental energy. Perhaps she could ease into winter. Or perhaps something would happen before then: something would happen at the camp, for example, and all the people she hated would be found, miraculously, dead.

Klee might not have been thinking of her future, but her extended family certainly were. They began to visit: to try to apologize, to win her over, to get her to change her mind.

It was odd to be made so much of. For most of her life, she had been ignored. Of course, all small children were ignored in some sense. Their status was low; they were taught and cared for, but otherwise let be. Usually this was fine, unless someone was being treated cruelly. In that case, they would like someone to notice their plight. And no one had noticed, or if they had, then apparently they'd felt it was no one's business but her family's.

Klee had grown into a woman, but in her mind she was still a little girl. She was, consequently, surprised that a whole tribe would mobilize like this to woo back one lost member. A part of her couldn't help feeling that it was too little, too late. But this feeling seemed ungrateful, so she was confused.

The first delegation she received consisted of the tribal chief accompanied by the wizened, leathery Damai, father of the two leading rapists. Klee did not dare to yell "Go away!" at these two as she had at Jai. Short, slight Damai, with his long, ugly, toothy face, seemed so *old*, and the chief had a quiet dignity about him, besides which he was the chief and her uncle by marriage.

Neither of these men was a big talker. They stood in silence outside of her shelter for a long time, and she let them stew. Then she came out and greeted them and offered them mint tea, which was just basic human decency. They sat down in the exact same spot where they had been standing.

Eventually, somehow, the conversation started. Damai had come to apologize for the actions of his sons. He explained that Sha had given them exactly what they deserved when he broke their noses, and furthermore, that Damai himself had told Sha so. Damai said he would do whatever was needed to make it up to Klee and her family. One of his sons would marry her, if she liked (Klee snorted), and he would give whatever gifts Klee or parents demanded. Shezer and his sons were making similar offers.

"What about Kai?" Klee asked them.

Hur gave her to understand that Kai was being dealt with by his father.

At that, Klee suddenly felt so bereft that it was all she could do not to burst into tears. She shivered and hugged herself.

"The problem," she told the two of them, "is not what happened. I – accept that you are doing all you can to make it right. Indeed, everything would be settled already if I were a normal girl with a normal mother and father. But I am not. The problem is, I do not have a family."

"Am I to understand," said Damai after a beat, "That you are living out here not because of what my sons did but because you found out you were adopted?"

"Yes, of course … Uncle," she blazed.

She still used the honorific title, trying to answer respectfully despite her anger. After all, they were elders.

"My father is not my father. My mother is not my mother, and she hates me for it. My brother …"

She trailed off, still unable to talk about it.

Hur was nodding as if none of this surprised him.

"I think they still want you, niece," he said.

"No, Uncle, they do not. My presence there sets the whole family fighting. Even now … I am not even there, and I am still causing … still causing my brother to be at war with his son."

"So you do not want to go back."

"I am determined not to."

The chief met her eye with his single, grey-yellow one. Then he nodded gravely. He took a sip of his mint tea. He pushed up the headband that covered his empty eye socket and wiped the sweat out of the socket, then returned the headband. He had gotten into the habit of doing this, particularly on hot days, showing people his empty socket when he was relaxing or thinking. He did not seem to realize he was doing it.

"We will think about this," he said at last, meeting her eye again. "We will try to find a solution for you. Is there anyone in the camp you have had your eye on … any young man you might possibly marry?"

"No, Uncle," said Klee.

This was true. She had done her share of flirtation and had stolen a few secret kisses, but she had not lost her heart to anyone. This was because she had not really thought of herself as a woman, certainly not as a woman anyone would want to marry. All her energies had been taken up with becoming a person. As, indeed, they still were.

"Well, if you like, until you marry you can stay with us," said her uncle Hur. "Ninna would love to have you. You won't remember it, but she cared for you for almost a year, before your – before Jai adopted you, when you were a baby."

Klee looked at the leaf litter as a strange feeling blossomed in her chest. She was embarrassed, but also warmed. She hadn't known that Ninna had taken care of her. And perhaps Aunt Hyuna had as well ….

"I don't like the idea of you spending the winter out here alone," he continued, "but it is a few months before we must worry about that. Go on living here, niece.

Perhaps you need the time to think. It is like being out on a hunt … or on a vision quest."

She looked up, startled, remembering suddenly how she had once wished to build a woman's lodge and to go through something analogous to a manhood ceremony.

The two old men left before dark. They had gotten a pronghorn on their way out to her, and before departing they helped her get it spitted and roasting over a wide, low fire. It would keep for weeks if she roasted it very dry.

That conversation made Klee feel better, but it had a bad effect as well. She hadn't intended it, but the way the word got back to the camp was that Klee was looking for a family to live with other than her own. Apparently, many people were willing to fill this role, and it became a sort of contest as to who would solve the problem by winning her. Meanwhile, Jai was furious that he had lost her, and his fights with Amal became fiercer than ever.

About seven days later, Grandmother Zillah arrived, traveling as if in state, accompanied by Jabed and by his stepson Aki.

Jabed was the only one of Klee's brothers who had not had a chance to speak to her since she found out they were her brothers. He did not know exactly what he ought to say to her – things had not gone well, after all, for Jai – but he felt he ought to apologize, or explain, or possibly just allow her to yell at him. So he offered to be one who accompanied Grandmother Zillah.

Jabed was a big man: barrel-chested, taller than his brother Ikash, and just as smooth, round, and red-brown. He was married to Magya (a sister of Hyuna, a daughter of the chief) and the two of them had a large houseful of children. His older children were big enough now that he could go off for a day or two like this and not worry about leaving Magya and the young ones alone.

He had brought along Aki, who also wanted a chance to apologize to Klee … though Jabed didn't think any apology was necessary. If anything, Aki had been a damned hero. He had dealt with the situation as a male relative ought to do.

Jabed knew that Damai was not a monster. He was a good man. And he had not raised monsters for sons, either. Watak and Ishak were merely idiots. No, not idiots … an idiot cannot help being stupid … no, they were fools. Each of them was, basically, a very small moral sense being led around by (Jabed assumed) an average-sized penis. The moral sense had no chance, really.

Jabed understood. That was what he had been like at that age. That was what he was like now, in fact, if you came down to it. But now he was older. You needed a very strong will to control your urges at eighteen or nineteen. Jabed, by now, had branched out, matured, developed other interests. There were, for instance, the needs of his stomach.

He had been fortunate, when he was the age of the young fools, to fall into marriage to a woman whom he found very sexy, but who already had four children by her previous husband. Marriage to Magya had tied his sexual urges to his responsibility to take care of her and of those children. It had steadied him. And then she had gone on having children, and Jabed had gone on becoming steadier. He took care of her and the children, and she took care of his stomach and his other parts. It was a good arrangement.

What Watak and Ishak really needed, he thought, besides their noses broken, was to find wives. But they had hurt their chances with their recent behavior. None of the young girls of the tribe were going to go for either of those two now that they had revealed they were inconsiderate moral idiots. A woman wanted to think that her man was good. That was what Magya was telling him all the time: that he was good. He wasn't. He was steady. But that was only by an effort of will, and because she treated him so well, and because, with all the children and everything, he was tired. He would never be *naturally* good, not like her first husband Ki-Ki.

Ki-Ki, Magya's first husband, had been the shaman before Ikash. He had been a really, really good man. Smart, too, smarter than Jabed would ever be. But the trouble with being married to a saint was that he was likely to throw himself away on any tribe member who needed help, and that was exactly what had happened. Ki-Ki had died, horribly, the same horrible year that everything else had happened. He had died while trying to stop Jabed's mother from committing suicide.

She had gone into the pool, leaving her baby lying beside it. They weren't sure why – about anything – but they thought that she must have known the pool was deadly, or she wouldn't have left the baby.

Ki-Ki had arrived only a minute or two too late. He had been so bent on saving her that he had gone into the pool, too. He had gotten severe burns over most of his body.

Jabed and Ikash found him like that, a little later. He told them the pool was death. He told them not to go in.

He told them they couldn't save her.

Ki-Ki had caught up to their mother before Jabed and Ikash did, because his legs were longer. But perhaps it was also because his heart was kinder.

Jabed had wondered, many times, why he hadn't run faster that day. The surface reason was that he and Ikash never dreamed they'd be unable to overtake a middle-aged woman who had just given birth the day before. The deeper reason was that Jabed never dreamed she would commit suicide. The reason under that was that, in those days, he was a teenaged moral idiot. His whole mind was taken up with proving himself, with eating, with chasing girls. He hadn't been paying attention to what was going on with her.

Jabed thought that Klee knew there had been a Ki-Ki, father of Aki, and that he had died. He was fairly certain she didn't know how Aki's father's death tied in to her own story.

And, now, here was Aki. Jabed glanced at his stepson as he strode beside him.

Aki was *good*. He was like his father. He thought of Jabed as his father, of course – Ki-Ki had already been gone when Aki was born, and Jabed had been the first to hold him – but he *looked* like Ki-Ki. The dark skin, much darker than Jabed's; the long, narrow dark eyes; the lean build and square jaw and black hair that seemed to give off a silvery light. Jabed wasn't sure why Aki needed to come on this expedition. He hoped it wasn't to throw himself into some boiling pool, so to speak.

They arrived in the evening. Klee welcomed them grudgingly. She couldn't let her beloved grandmother sleep outside on the ground, so she invited Zillah inside and gave up her own pallet. But she *could* keep out her brother and his son, and she did. All night she treated them as she had Jai, poking her head out of her shelter to shout: "Go home!"

Crickets and tree frogs, but no Older Brothers, answered her.

Finally, near morning, Aki called out,

"Let us sleep, cousin!"

And Klee yelled back: "I'm your *aunt!*"

In the morning, they talked. Zillah did not have much to say. She had come to listen to her granddaughter and to answer any questions she might have.

And Klee did have questions. She directed them, however, mostly at Jabed.

She hated having to ask him for anything, especially information about something so important to her, but she couldn't help herself. Jabed had seen Klee's mother and knew what she was like. He had even seen more of her than Sha and Ikash; he was older than either of them.

He told her, in response to questions, that their mother had been round and soft, built like himself. She was not beautiful exactly – not as he remembered her – but she was comfortable. She was quiet, not bold; she liked to cook. She would break up her sons' fights when they were little. She sounded nice. She sounded, to Klee, like the perfect mother.

"Do I really look like her, or was my – was Jai only saying so?"

"No. You look a lot like her in the face," said Jabed.

"Was her hair like this …"

"Curly," supplied Zillah.

"Was it curly, like mine?"

"I … don't remember. I don't think so. She kept it in a bun most of the time."

Then Klee asked a question that she felt tempted to whisper.

"What was her name?"

And he told her: "Sari."

"Is that why your daughter is named Risa …?"

"Yes. And why Ikash's girl is named Sira."

Klee did not know it, but supplying all these details about the mother he had ignored in life was for Jabed a heavy penance. After half an hour of this, brother and sister were both exhausted. She walked up the stream, and he walked down the stream, and each was trying to hide their tears from the other.

Zillah and Aki raised their eyebrows at each other and began to prepare some lunch.

Later, they ate. Jabed's fears about what his son might do were unfounded. Aki wanted only to apologize for not being able to get the mob off Klee. She apologized for having called him a coward, not realizing he was going for help.

He also said that Kai had given him a message: Please tell my sister I am sorry.

"He'll always think of you as his sister," Aki told her, while she stood with her back to the three of them and her hair hanging down to hide her face. "That's what he said. And he's sorry he blamed you for everything, and your mother and father are fighting like crazy even though you are not there."

Klee made a tight sound that sounded like, "Not – mother – father –"

"His words," said Aki gently. "Anyway, he says they are crazier than he realized, and he is going to get married and get out of the house as soon as he can."

"Still can't face him," said Klee.

"He feels like shit," put in Jabed helpfully.

"Not my problem."

"No, it's not, daughter," said Zillah soothingly. "You didn't create this mess, though you found yourself in the middle of it. I am going to live with them for a while and see if I can keep things calm. I'll help to watch the little ones and to deliver Amal's baby."

"And you are free to live with Magya and me, if you like," said Jabed. "She would love to have you."

Klee did not answer him right away, but before the delegation left, she explained to her older brother that, no, she could not live with him. He might have meant well, but he had been one of the four "fathers" who had lied to her. She wanted to live with someone who had told her the truth.

"I understand," said Jabed, "And I sorta thought you might say that. But … well, can I at least leave you a dog?"

Sniffy, the young bitch who lived with Jabed and Magya's family, had had puppies, and he had brought along two of them. They were a few months old by then, old enough to leave home, and the People did not believe that anyone should live on their own without the company of a dog. Klee picked out the one that suited her, a wolfish grey male who was already showing promise of becoming lean and scruffy. She thought of naming him Ki-Ki, having heard that the former shaman, Aki's father, had had a wolf for a totem and had seldom gone anywhere unaccompanied by his dog. But she didn't dare to shock and hurt her guests by picking this name, right in front of them. So she decided to call him Guide.

She was doing more guiding than the dog, however, in those first days after her relatives left. She had to train him where to sleep, when to do his business, and not to destroy her things or get into her food. She gave him a bath (which he thought was a great game), and combed his fur for pests and thistles daily. In the lonely evenings, when he curled up at her side, she allowed that perhaps her older brother hadn't been entirely ignorant of what she needed.

Her next visitor came alone.

He was the one she had been waiting for without realizing it: her real father, Endu.

And he had come precisely in order to start being her father again.

The weather helped him. On the very afternoon that he arrived, there was a terrific summer thunderstorm of the kind that often stalked the land in those days. Often these storms were small, and you could watch them from a long way off, approaching at a walking pace, stalking along on their lightning legs. This one was huge, covering the entire region. It was soaking. It brought cold and dark and lasted for hours.

So, though it was still a long way from sunset when Endu arrived at the hills that were Klee's home, he arrived hobbling, dripping, shivering, under a changeable patchwork of roiling grey cloud and cold, fleeting blue.

Of course she could not keep him out as she had her brothers. She had to invite him in, in that condition. What girl could resist her long-lost father, when he shows up on her doorstep soaked and shaking, seeking reconciliation?

As soon as he entered her hut, the atmosphere changed. There was already that thunder-smell, but the storm by breaking had drained some of the charge out of the air. Endu, by taking one simple step forward, charged it again.

He also, by his presence, created a multitude of tasks. Klee had been sitting still, watching the rain, existing in a kind of peace. Now she took one look at his black locks plastered to his neck and forehead, and offered him one of her blankets. While he was drying himself, she rose and built up a small fire. Her coals had gone out, and with the damp air it took a long time to get a spark to catch. While she was doing it, she kept asking herself why she was going to all this trouble for the man who had killed her mother. Yet, she couldn't help herself: she was excited.

Endu looked spooky in the dimness of the retreating storm. His left eye, the skin around which had once been ripped, sagged and gleamed whitely. His missing nose was a horror until he turned his back and politely blew it. His hair, being wet, failed to hide as it usually did the tiny, pink nub of his left ear.

He saw her looking and said,

"Are you afraid of me?"

And she said, "No," with defiance.

"No, I am not afraid of you. I am angry with you, just as I am angry with all of them. You are the one who destroyed my family before I was born and left me to be raised by a woman who hates me."

"May I sit down?" said Endu.

He flashed a smile that was as white as his gleaming eye.

Permission granted, he spread the damp blanket and lowered himself onto it. His method of sitting was different than most people's, there being fewer muscles in his thin, wasted legs; but he had developed a way of doing it that was quick and had its own grace.

Guide came near, sniffing and growling a bit, and Klee sent him to a far corner, which was in fact only a few feet away. He lay down at her command, but he did not settle. She was feeling ambivalent about this visitor, and the dog had picked up on that.

Once he was seated, Endu looked at Klee, obviously waiting for her to sit. And, though later she would wonder why, she found a little stool she had made, pulled it up on the other side of the fire, and did.

What he said next surprised her.

"I have never lied to you."

Klee opened her mouth to protest that he had done so. Then she thought about it a little more. No, he never had said, *I am your grandfather and not your father.*

Endu pressed his advantage.

"Think about it. Have I ever called you Granddaughter?"

No, he never had.

"All right," she said finally, "but you *participated* in the lie. You didn't raise me. You let me go on thinking I was Jai and Amal's daughter. If you never lied to me with your lips, that has been because you scarcely spoke two words to me."

"They wanted to keep you from me," said Endu. "It has taken some time to discern how to get you back. Do you have anything to eat around here, daughter? I have been walking for many hours."

There was plenty to eat: berries and grain and cattail shoots and cold venison. She got up and fetched some and gave it to him cold, and had some herself as well. And the act of taking care of him warmed her toward him a little, as acts of caring will. Already she felt half on his side. More than half.

Then she remembered why this was wrong.

"But what about *her?*" she protested, more uncertainly than she had intended to. "What about the things you did to her? My mother?"

Her father set down his food. Clearly this was too serious a topic to be eating over. He had already put away enough to take the edge well off his hunger, but Klee did not notice this.

He sighed, bowed his head, and put one hand to his forehead.

"It was tragic about her." His voice was filled with pathos. His face appeared strikingly handsome for a moment from this angle, because his ruined nose was hidden behind his hand.

Klee's eyes filled with tears. For a moment she was in the presence of a handsome widower grieving over his wife.

"I admit I sometimes lost my temper with her, when she lived," her father went on, still hiding his face as if this were too much to contemplate. "She was a hard person to live with. She was strange, changeable, a little crazy. But I loved her."

"Did you?" asked Klee.

Endu raised his eyes over his hand, met hers, and nodded.

Then he pulled his hand slowly down his face and sighed again. He set the hand on the floor beside him, still not touching his food.

Klee had almost forgotten all the things her father was supposed to have done. Then she remembered.

"They – all of them – they said you drove her to suicide. That you brutalized her. Raped her."

He slowly shook his head.

"I never raped her, daughter. We had hard times – sometimes she was not feeling well – but these are intimate details …" He shook his head, his smooth, dark brow furrowed in frustration. "Am I supposed to explain this to a fifteen-year-old girl?"

"Sixteen next month."

"To my own daughter? It's crazy that I should have to explain this. I don't want to ruin your innocence. Sometimes things go wrong between a husband and wife … but rape? No. I never raped her."

"Yet, she killed herself."

He nodded, looking sad. "She did. It was tragic. But nobody really knew why. She never explained to anyone what she was thinking. I think, by that time, she was *very* crazy. Perhaps she didn't have enough mind left to explain."

Then Klee shared some information with him, and hated herself for it immediately afterward.

"The shaman says she killed herself because she was desperate. Because she couldn't face, being in a house with you, raising a girl baby … me."

He looked at her very sharply for an instant.

"He told you *that?* As if to blame *you* for her death? That was a very cruel thing to do."

"No … I don't think that's what he— "

"My third son hates me," said Endu. "He always has. I am sure he believes what he told you, but we cannot trust his version of the story. Your mother didn't tell anyone what she was thinking. She didn't even tell anyone that she was pregnant."

Klee nodded. The shaman had admitted that much.

Her father smiled at her.

"I was so happy, though, when she delivered you. We had a few hours of happiness before the madness finally took her."

She tried to remind herself, *Don't believe him.* But it was a faint reminder compared to the warm feeling that smile gave her.

"And then you gave me away," she said.

But there was no bitterness in her voice.

"It was a chaotic time. Nobody knew what to do. Sari had died, and Ki-Ki – he was the son of my brother, and our shaman at that time – he was dying too, because he had gone into the boiling pool to try to save her. You see, her madness cost another family their father. Oh, and we were fleeing from a volcano."

She cocked an eyebrow at him skeptically.

"I know it seems like too much," he admitted with a humorless chuckle. "And it *was* too much. But it was happening. If you don't believe me, ask any of the older generation. It's part of our history."

She *had* heard stories of the fire-mountain. And come to think of it, the current shaman (whose motives were now suspect) had mentioned it as well. But she had not until now understood how this volcano fit into her own personal history.

"It was a terrible time." Endu paused, and took a sip from the clay cup of spring-water she had given him, sighing deeply as he did so. "Anyway … during all this horror … I didn't know how to care for a newborn baby. So my sister Ninna took you in for a time, until everything settled down. She had always loved your mother," he added, giving her a flashing sidelong glance from his good eye, which was almond-shaped, charismatic, obsidian-black. "She had tried to help her, but Sari was beyond being helped even by Ninna."

Everyone knew that Ninna was the kindest mother among the People. Klee thought it spoke well of her father that he spoke well of Ninna. And she was happy that someone had been kind to Sari during her troubles, whatever the exact nature of those troubles had been. Of which, Klee was now not exactly sure.

"After that …" he said, "Jai had just been married …"

This agreed with the shaman's story.

"He was really grieving for his mother, and as a sort of service to her, he wanted to raise you. And the others, some of them already hated me and blamed me for Sari's death. They thought they understood what she would have wanted." He shrugged, and then added sadly, "Which was to keep you away from me. I had no wife to help me care for you, and Jai seemed to be in a better position to do it. So I let them take you.

"I did the best I could, my daughter. Perhaps I was wrong. I am sorry. But remember, I have *never* lied to you."

He reached out with a long, well-formed brown arm, and briefly squeezed her hand.

Endu made several such visits to Klee during the month before she turned sixteen. He always came alone, and Guide always responded to him warily. Endu allowed he did not much care for dogs. But he was making great strides in winning his daughter's trust. With each successive visit, his version of the story seemed to her to make more sense. This was doubly true because she received few other visitors during that time. No one was telling a competing story.

She found herself looking forward to his visits. The longer she listened to him, the more she was able to see past his deformities, and soon he appeared in her eyes as the darkly handsome man he had once been. She flourished under his attention. He really seemed to want her as his daughter.

Added to this was the pleasant sensation of growing clarity as she accepted his story. He offered her a complete, sensible, sad but also beautiful picture of her family history. It was a relief after the panic and confusion of the previous months.

She began to sleep more deeply at night. When she did dream, her dreams were not of things she wished had been done, but of what had actually happened.

On his second visit, among many other things, he told her how he had come to be maimed. He had been mauled by a bear.

Even the phrase "mauled by a bear" sent a little thrill of fear through her. The People had a deep, spooky fear of bears, even greater than their fear of other predators in that world that included Great Lions, tigers, and various kinds of dragons. The People had had a few bad experiences, and these were burned into their collective memory. Also, their paths had crossed with the bear more often than with the other dangerous creatures. Bears were omnivores, eating many of the same foods that people craved. Though huge and powerful, they were a bit more human in scale and seemed to understand people's thinking in a way that could be unfortunate. And, at least this far north, they were more numerous than dragons.

This is the story as Endu told it.

His son, Ikash, who was at that time newly the shaman, had gone off on his own for an irresponsibly long time to seek a vision. Ikash's dog, Frost (now an old bitch; then, still practically a puppy) had come back alone, and the tribe had become concerned.

"Because they were all still blaming me for my wife's death," Endu told her, "Grandmother Zillah insisted that I be the one to go out and find my son. And of course I wanted to, though I didn't know how he would receive me."

He had come upon Ikash all alone, interrupting him in the middle of a vision. The boy had been in an altered state, perhaps a little crazed with what he had been seeing. He had attacked his father. The two of them wrestled – Endu was trying not to hurt him – when suddenly, Ikash fainted.

"He's a strange, delicate young man. He is brilliant, of course, but weak and unstable."

And as Endu crouched over the unconscious body of his son, there had come a great she-bear to attack.

"I had left my spear back where he attacked me," said Endu. "I didn't know if he was alive or dead at that point, but I tried to fight the bear with my hands. I tried to draw her away from his body."

He had succeeded, and Ikash had emerged from the experience unharmed except for his injuries from their wrestling match. A rescue party had arrived after only a short time, and it had taken all of them, working together, to subdue the bear. By the time they finished, the beast had mauled Endu and had killed his older brother Enmer, who at that time was the chief. Zillah had been obliged to do surgery on Endu. They had had a funeral for Enmer.

"Hur became chief after that," he told her, his wide mouth twisting a little, bitterly. "I was not considered for it, I was too busy recovering from my injuries. Also, they all blamed me for the bear attack."

"What – ? How – ?"

"Because I supposedly attacked Ikash – "

"That's so unfair!"

"… And because they thought it was sent by Sari. The bear was our totem, mine and hers, during the years we were married."

"It was your *totem?*"

Her father nodded. "And perhaps it *was* sent by her, too. However I may have failed her, daughter … I have paid. I have paid."

He ran a hand gingerly down his thin, mangled legs, and she saw crystal tears on his black lashes.

"It was never my totem after that," he muttered. "I took one that may kill, but will not maim. It strikes only once." He groped about on the ground and found his short walking-stick, on which Sha had carved a sinuous shape. "My new totem is the snake."

On his third visit, Endu laid a serious proposition before his daughter.

"Several years ago," he said, "My older brother promised me that when the People stopped traveling, I could go off and build a city."

"Don't we have a city *here?*" said Klee.

"Oh, child." Endu flopped his head forward for a moment. He used to throw it back at moments of exasperation, but he had learned that since his mauling, this presented an alarming view to his interlocutor. He shook his head, and chuckled – exasperatedly but not, she thought, unkindly.

"How can I explain to you what a proper city is? It's not your fault you've never seen one. None of your generation have. You were born after God's judgment on the world."

For some time he spoke, endeavoring to give her an idea of streets that were paved; of buildings in unimaginably large numbers; of fountains, canals, temples, towers; built of brick or even stone, faced perhaps with gold; like a range of perfect mountains made by man: polished, gleaming. The pictures that all of this created in her mind were dim, because she had so little frame of reference, but she could get some idea of what he was saying by starting with their wooden village, Sha's carved and painted eaves and freestanding, sculpted tree trunks, and expanding upon that. The vision that he planted in her mind was wondrous. Later, when she had seen at least the beginnings of a city, she realized that she had imagined it pretty well, but that she had pictured it floating as if in the clouds instead of planting it in the midst of fields and forests.

Endu explained. Now the People were settled, and they were getting almost too numerous to keep track of. There were certain individuals, such as Klee and himself, who for reasons of their own wished to leave the People. And Endu had been made a promise by his brother.

He had spoken to the present chief about it. The chief had agreed. Endu was welcome to take his immediate family and travel, find a new place, build a city if he wished. He could bring along any who wished to go with him. He would, himself, be the king of the new city.

"And you are my daughter!" he enthused. "You will be a princess. You can run all kinds of things. You have so many abilities, but you don't have any scope for them here. There are too many people, and all of them think of you as a little girl."

"What about your wife?" said Klee. "What does *she* think of all of this?"

"She is for it, of course, but she is busy raising the little ones. She doesn't have the time or energy that you do. She has no desire to run a city."

And when would all of this take place?

It transpired that autumn was a good time for traveling. Endu meant to leave within two months. The People were so adept at traveling in the snow and ice, and this southern land was so much softer than what they had been used to, that he did not think they would have much difficulty finding a suitable place and throwing together some decent dwellings before winter. That would be the beginning.

"This is very sudden, Father," Klee said.

"It's a great opportunity! Don't you want to get away?"

She did. She was already thinking of building a women's hut ... nay, a women's temple!

"Think about it," he said. "I will give you some time, and then I will come back and see if you are desirous to go. And if you are, I will come back a third time and get you when we are ready to depart. Oh, and everyone knows that I am inviting you, or will know soon ... so you may get some more visitors."

Contrary to Endu's prediction, Klee's last visitor that month was not one of her relatives urging her to do this or that. It was instead someone who was an age-mate of hers but whom she hardly knew. It was Hur-kar and Lien's son, Setiq.

Setiq had blue-black hair and creamy, light-golden skin. His face was angular: his cheekbones seemed to poke forward from it, and he had an aggressive, pointy, forward-thrusting chin. It looked as if, were he to smile with that face, he'd have no skin left to spare.

But he was not smiling, not at first, when he arrived at her camp as she was taking the washing up from the creek-side, just before the dew fell, of an evening. He came from a shy, quiet family, and he was soft-spoken and hesitant. He came without a dog, and he stopped afar off and called to her.

Setiq was no blood relative of hers. Klee *knew*; she had just spent several weeks memorizing her clan's family tree. He was the grandson of the present chief, the son of Hur-kar, who was Hur's son by a previous wife from the old days. His mother was Lien, who was also not directly related, though she too of course was descended from Japheth.

Klee now knew that laundry and teenaged boys didn't mix, so she let him cool off while she brought armfuls of blankets up to her shelter. Then she came out and greeted him from a short distance.

"You may approach the camp," she said, "But only as far as the cookfire."

It was not practical to cook indoors every day, especially in fine weather. She had a cookfire built next to a large river-stone in the clearing just downhill from her shelter. This she kept smoldering most days, except in heavy rain. Now she bent and built it up, not turning her back to Setiq.

Her visitor edged gratefully into the smoke. There was still plenty of light in the air, but the evening chill was falling and the mosquitoes were coming out, and the smoke helped with both.

"Now," she said, "What are you doing here?"

"I just came to tell you, I am sorry about what happened to you, and I hope you'll come back to the People. That is all."

Klee narrowed her eyes for a second. He hadn't mentioned her leaving with her father, so he likely didn't know that was an option. She decided not to bring it up.

Instead, she said, "*Which* thing that happened to me? You know, the sons of Damai are not the reason that I'm out here."

He looked uncomfortable. "They say you are angry because your relatives lied to you."

"Did you lie to me as well? Did *you* know who I really was?"

Setiq held his body very still. "I did know, but I didn't think much about it. I figured *you* knew."

Her eyes flashed with frustration, and she asked him sharply, "When did you find out?"

"I don't remember. I don't always pay very good attention," he admitted, "when they are gossiping about the family."

Hur-kar and Lien were both so reserved that Klee hadn't imagined they gossiped at all. But perhaps they did their talking in private.

She thought about all of this for a little while. Setiq stood there patiently. Finally she said, "You hope I return? You came all this way just to tell me that?"

The golden skin turned darker. There were two spots of brown on his protruding cheekbones.

"Nobody knows I'm here." He gestured toward his equipment, which he had set down. "I'm on a hunt."

"Oh … they'll know," said Klee. The village information machine was a terrible thing to behold.

"Look," said Setiq. He straightened up a bit and met her eyes. His had dark lashes and startling light-brown, almost golden irises: eyes that had come from his grandfather Hur.

"I like you," he said. "I didn't know all this was going to happen. It's a mess."

"I didn't cause it."

He waved off this distraction. "I didn't say that. I just said it's a mess."

"It *is* a mess," agreed Klee.

"What I'm saying," Setiq persisted, "is that for some time I've – hoped to get to know you. And I – still do. Hope."

Klee looked at him – at the black-rimmed, light eyes, at the pointy golden chin.

"Would you like to kiss me?" she said.

He leaned forward and did. It was nice. The pointy facial bones were no problem.

Setiq put his hands on her shoulders, lightly, not like Ishak. But still she wanted to be unfettered. She spread her arms out like wings. He ran his hands lightly down her arms, reached her hands, and intertwined her fingers. He had long, ropey, golden arms and his fingers were thin and hard.

He squeezed and released her hands. The kiss ended.

Setiq smiled. It turned out it didn't break his face, after all. It was a surprisingly sweet smile, buried deep between his nose and chin. It transformed his face.

Klee felt flushed. "You can't stay," she said.

"I won't stay," Setiq was saying at the same moment. He added, now a little cocky, "I can walk in the dark. I've been through the ceremony."

"Did you have a vision?" she blurted.

He paused and looked over his shoulder. He was already in the act of picking up his equipment.

"Sort of. I saw a marmot, or something like it. It's my family's totem." He shrugged one bony shoulder. "Not a very hard animal to spot."

Klee wanted to say something encouraging at this point, something about the effort he had just expended to see her, something perhaps about his skill as a hunter. But all the things that sprang to her mind sounded too sarcastic. So she was silent.

Setiq went away. Klee wanted badly to call after him, "Come back!" Or at the very least, "Come back some day!" But she did not.

Things might have gone differently if he had come to visit her a little earlier, but by that point she had already decided to go south with her father.

CHAPTER FOUR
THE SHAMAN AND HIS RESPONSIBILITIES

It was a strange, unsettled early autumn.

Klee had been living away from the People all summer. And the ripples from that disturbance had far from settled, when Endu had dropped another stone into the pond by announcing that he was going off with his family to found a city. This was something he had been talking about for years, but it had been delayed by various crises like his getting mauled by a bear and then getting remarried. Ikash had been expecting his father to make this move for a few years, now that the People were in a good land, but the sudden, rushed timing of it seemed strange.

A few weeks later, the reason for the timing became clear when Endu announced that Klee was going to come with him.

This announcement created panic among the people who knew Endu best: his younger sons, his mother, and the family of Ninna his sister. Everyone felt strongly that Klee must be convinced not to go this route, but no one felt that they should be the one to speak to her about it.

No one was more worried about her than the shaman. Klee was being courted by Endu, who, Ikash knew from experience, could be gallant and persuasive. Especially with women. Even with his ruined face. Perhaps *because of* his ruined face, though he'd been that way before his injuries. Now, though, with the scars and the pity angle, he tended to try even harder.

Endu just had charisma. Ikash himself had felt it. It was insoluble to ugliness, and to any amount of bad behavior.

Like everyone else who had spoken with Klee recently, Ikash had little hope that he could make her see sense about Endu. Nevertheless, he equally knew that it was his obligation to go and try. But he could not go and try just now. His father had pulled off this move, like every one of his moves, with either spectacularly bad, or brilliantly strategic, timing.

Ikash had to stay in the village because Hyuna was right on the verge of delivering her baby. Her mother, Ninna, who was going to be her midwife, even thought she was past due. Ikash could not go on a seven-day jaunt to find his little sister's hideout. He had his wife to take care of.

It was unsettling and frustrating, but he was not going to abandon Hyuna. This was her time of difficulty.

Hyuna, like her mother and like her older sister Magya, did not suffer pregnancy and birth gladly.

"I am *never* doing this again," she had said, late in the process, during the births of each of their previous children. He had been worried the first time she said it. Then, six months later, when Dumish was teething, growing hair, and rocking back and forth on his hands and knees, Hyuna had gotten teary-eyed over the fact that her baby was going to grow up and had started wondering out loud when they could safely have another one.

It had still been another year before she became really interested in Ikash again. That had had to wait until Dumish was mostly weaned. It was all or nothing with Hyuna, he had learned. There were periods, like the early days of their marriage, when she wouldn't leave him alone, when she was always pouncing on him. Those were the good times. And then, like now, when she was pregnant or recovering, there were these times of drought. More than drought, it was not just a matter of what he could or couldn't get ... they were times of positive need, when she needed him supporting her the way he supported the initiates every few years on their vision quests.

That was how it was with women, he thought. They were like the weather. Summer and winter, and then spring again. It wasn't their fault, it was the way they were made. If you wanted children (and everyone wanted children), you just had to put up with it. You just had to be patient. That had been the mistake, thought Ikash – one mistake of many – that his father had made with his mother. Wanting her to be the same all the time. *Demanding* that she be the same all the time. And, by the end, she *was* the same all the time: withdrawn. Wary. Dead-eyed. Not available to Endu or to anyone else for that matter.

Ikash had had plenty of practice waiting for Hyuna. He had loved her since they were children. There had been several years when it looked as if he would never be able to have her … when he had even wondered if he would ever marry anyone at all. But what he had always loved about her was her cheerfulness and energy, the contrast her nature presented to his own. He never wanted to see that light grow dim.

Now he was sitting in their wooden lodge, looking at her fondly, and the two children were climbing all over him. Dumish was six years old, a chunky brown boy who looked just like his father. Their four-year-old daughter Sira, meanwhile, was a miniature Hyuna. It was funny, and rare, when children looked like exact copies of their parents. But even when that happened, they were very different on the inside. The soul did not come from the mother and father. It came straight from God.

Ikash was a self-contained sort, but just as he was used to waiting, so also he was used to being climbed on. When he was a boy, his brother Sha had wrestled with him constantly. Now he had Dumish on his back and Sira making a frontal attack. He was fending off one of them with each hand as he thought that, as Hyuna looked unlikely to rouse herself, he had better go off to the house of some relative or other and see if he could find some food.

At that moment, his mother-in-law arrived with dinner.

Ninna creaked up onto the porch and then bent through the leather door-flap, bearing in her hands a huge wooden bowl of stew. She did not look much like her daughter – she was curvier and much darker of face and hair – but she had the same cheerful nature. The harmonious quality of the home she shared with Hur, Hyuna's childhood home, had been one of the many things that had first attracted Ikash to his wife.

"Oh, thank you, mother," said Ikash.

"Grandma! Grandma!" cried the two children, jumping from their father to run and buffet Ninna about the knees.

She stood firm, swaying slightly like a tree in a breeze, until they had completed their greeting, and then she came forward and set the bowl down beside the large stone bowl in which, when indoors, they built their fire.

"I thought you might have a lot on your mind," she said, "And could use some supper."

Ikash had risen to greet her.

"I have not even built up the fire yet," he told her with a sheepish grin. "As you see, mother."

"I doubt I can manage to eat anything," said Hyuna. She had been lying on one of the low bunks; now she swung her legs about and rose, groaning, to a sitting position. A moment later she whimpered and said, "But I am so *hungry!*"

"It will be over soon, wife," Ikash told her.

"Will it?"

He appealed to Ninna with his eyes, and she winked at him.

They fed the children, somehow, and somehow got Hyuna fed. And Ikash must have eaten, himself. He didn't remember eating, but at some point he stopped being hungry.

In the night, she was up frequently. This was normal – but then he heard her moan.

"Hyuna?"

"I'm all right," she said indistinctly, as if holding her breath.

He hated that. His mother had often claimed to be all right when she clearly wasn't. It had made it difficult to help her. He was glad Hyuna couldn't see his face in the dark.

He said, "You certain?"

"I don't want to be wrong …"

"Be wrong."

"Well. It really hurts."

He went to get her mother.

"Oh … all right …" Ninna murmured sleepily when they roused her. "I don't know why these things always happen in the middle of the night."

Then she added, "Do you want to be here to welcome this one too?"

Ikash nodded.

He had been present at the births of both his older children. With Dumish, the older one, he had just been curious. And when he had requested to be present, his mother-in-law (and Zillah, the camp's most experienced midwife) had asked him, "Are you sure?" And at that moment he had become more certain, not less.

"This will be one of the biggest things she ever does," he had told them. "Of course I want to be there for it if possible."

And the two older women had not forbidden him.

But Ninna had said in surprise, "You are a very unusual man," and when he looked at the ground in shame, she had cuffed him affectionately on the back and added, "That was a compliment, dear."

Ikash knew he was not a typical man of the People. Certainly he was not as manly as his father would have liked him to be. You needed to be like that in order to be shaman. You had to have man plus something that was somehow woman in you. He was not insecure, however. He was a husband and a father. His masculinity was not defined by qualities he kept out of himself, but by qualities that he had. Giving birth was a women's mystery, but it was not something that they did all on their own. It was something that men and women did together.

As it turned out, it did not ruin the birth process for a man to be present. Of course, there was good reason that most men preferred not to be. The process was earthy, tedious, and slow. It was surprisingly mundane for everyone who was not the mother. But for Hyuna, it was her great deed, and he wanted to witness it so that he could praise and appreciate her properly. And when it came to the point, despite the earthiness, he had seen glory. He knew then that he did not want to miss the births of his other children.

"What about Dumish and Sira?" his mother-in-law whispered to him during the dark walk from one house to the other.

Ikash said, "I will take them to my brother in the morning."

By his brother he meant Jabed. He and Magya had a house full of children who would be happy to play with their cousins.

"Perhaps the baby will come before morning?" said Ninna.

"I think I will still take them."

"Good idea." She clucked her tongue, and reached up to squeeze his shoulder.

Father, mother and baby would need some time on their own to rest and heal. Ideally, they should have a month. He knew Jabed wouldn't mind watching his children for that long. It was the sort of favor that the People often traded.

The baby did come in the night, with glory, and Ikash was the first to hold him. It was a boy this time, coming out with a chubby square face, red-brown skin, and tufts of fair hair that seemed to resemble Hyuna and her father. But his eyes quickly darkened after birth. All three of their children had dark eyes, even Sira, who other than that exactly resembled her mother.

"How is he?" asked Hyuna. Ikash, grinning, brought the child close where she could see him. He rubbed a cloth over the baby's head, and Hyuna gasped when she saw the downy tufts of hair stand up, the color of autumn grasses.

"You made a good one, wife," he told her.

She laughed weakly. This birth had brought her some unique indignities. Among other things, she had vomited.

"Well, he is delivered, anyway," she muttered. "And you and I are still friends, somehow." Her eyes were already falling closed.

"I will show him to my mother at the Solstice," said Ikash, and he gave the baby to the two grandmothers, who were eager to clean him.

Winter solstice was the time the People believed that the dead came near to visit. The long night caused the boundaries of the other world to shrink down closer to the walking world, like a leather bag shrinking as it dried. The cold and dark made the dead feel comfortable, and they would venture near. During the ceremony, the People built a great fire, and the edges of the firelight became the very boundary of the walking world. No one was to venture outside the range of the firelight … but within it, they would drum and play music and speak to their dead. It was a spooky time, especially for children; but it was a happy, poignant time for the older ones, those who had lost someone. It was the only time of year that they could speak to those they longed for. Then they would show them things, like Ikash showing his mother the baby, and they would burn fragrant smoke to keep wicked spirits away and to make the beloved dead feel welcome.

The next morning, Dumish and Sira were shown their baby brother and their mother – both sleeping – and then, *quietly*, were let out into the sunshine, where they immediately began yelling. The two of them were like puppies: as soon as you set them down, they took off running. Ikash walked behind them, laughing to himself at their antics, on the way to his brother's house.

Jabed and Magya seemed determined to double the size of the People all by themselves. They had two children grown and married already (these were actually Magya's children from Ki-Ki). Then at home they had Queet, a teenaged girl only a few years older than Klee; Aki, who had gone with the delegation; Risa, a girl now thirteen; three little girls, and a baby boy. Magya seemed to become pregnant every year or two, and though she sometimes miscarried, usually the baby lived. Queet, Risa, and the eight-year-old, Inda, were always at work helping manage the younger ones, bustling about with as much cheer and command as their mother.

Jabed's house was not built up on stilts and steps like his brother's. He had wanted it flush with the ground, so that toddlers would not fall from heights and dogs could walk easily in and out.

As soon as Ikash and his two charges arrived, pandemonium reigned. Ikash's four-year-old daughter Sira started calling out that she had a baby brother. Several large dogs came charging out of the house and knocked down Dumish, who began wrestling with them. Three little girls appeared from behind the house and began dancing and giggling with Sira.

The noise drew Magya, who had one-year-old Ash on her hip. Short, plump, dark and pretty, she was an older sister of Hyuna. She congratulated Ikash on the successful birth, asked a few polite questions, and gave him a sisterly hug with the arm that was not holding her baby. He averted his eyes; she had apparently been nursing the child and had forgotten that her wrap was hanging open down to her belly. He asked her whether the children could stay with her for a month or so, and Magya replied that it was all right with her, but "Don't run off," because Jabed would want to say hello.

After just a moment, sure enough, Jabed appeared. He too had been in the back, building up the family's outdoor cooking fire. He congratulated his brother on the child, thumping him on the back a little harder than was necessary (this was a habit from their childhood).

Jabed grinned when the thump on the back caused Ikash's knees to flex.

"You look tired, brother. Go home and get some rest."

"I will, but first I have a favor to ask."

Ikash explained that after spending a few days with Hyuna and the baby, once he knew they were healthy, he needed urgently to go and talk sense to Klee. Would Jabed and Magya watch his children for a long time, perhaps for more than a month?

Jabed's face fell when Ikash mentioned their sister. He was a big, rounded man, taller and thicker than Ikash, and when he was troubled his smooth brown face looked like a child's face puzzling over a difficult problem.

"Do you think you can convince her?" he said in an undertone.

"No, but I'm going to try."

"Would it really be so bad, do you think, to go with Dad and found a city?"

"I do think. That's why I am willing to leave Hyuna and the baby."

"Yeah … you must think it's important."

"Mom will be with them, but still."

"As you say – still."

When Ikash said 'Mom' in this context, he meant his mother-in-law Ninna. In the days after his family fell apart, Hyuna's parents had become his own.

At that moment, Magya's daughter Queet poked her head around the building. She looked very much like Klee, but she was slighter, with straight hair. She said she had been cooking breakfast. It was a porridge of the wild grass that Grandmother Zillah had tamed, which the People were calling maize.

"Do you want some, Fathers?" she said to the two of them.

Jabed did. Ikash thanked her, but he was not hungry: he needed sleep. He went home and took a nap with his newborn son lying on his bare chest, the baby's legs drawn up like a frog's, molding his little body to his father's.

Hyuna and the baby throve, and after a week Ninna said that they were out of danger. Ikash could go off and visit his sister.

He was dreading it.

Early in the morning, before he left, he approached Hyuna to see whether she was asleep. The family slept on benches along the wall covered by curtains, but in the early days after a birth, husband and wife did not share a bed. Hyuna's curtains were back. She was sitting up with her back against the inner wall of the house, child in her arms, eyes open but drooping. Her silky hair, which she had braided to keep neat, was falling out of the braid, making a shaggy halo around her face and ears.

Ikash sat down on the edge of the bench, leaned forward, and brushed a strand from her forehead.

She looked at him with her honey-colored eyes, which at this moment had deep circles below them.

"Thanks," she mumbled. And then, "Are you going?"

"I'm really sorry," he said quietly. "I have to go and see her."

She beamed at him gently. She was so pretty, he thought. Of course she had always been pretty, but this post-baby time was special. There was something extra that was present with her – with all women, really – whenever they sat happy and holding their baby. They looked so serene and beautiful.

"Of course, love," she said beatifically. "We've discussed this. Mother will take care of me, and you will go and convince Klee."

He didn't remember discussing it with her, but perhaps she had it from Ninna.

"We've discussed this?" he asked, checking.

"Well … good as. You see the condition I'm in, I can't be around for every discussion."

He laughed and kissed her, but she did not want to be kissed, as she was falling asleep. So he said goodbye and went out into the morning.

As soon as he got well away from the village, he felt his spirit soften and expand. He loved the people he lived with, but there was something about the wilderness – outside the camp – that was relaxing. Whenever it wasn't trying to kill you, that was. Coming home at the end of a long, hard day, or of a long, cold hunting trip, the village with its haze of smoke was always a welcome sight. But in the same way, those first few steps out into the grasslands on a bright morning brought an equally welcome feeling.

Anyone familiar with the People's history might have expected them to be terrified of setting off thus, alone. Several notable tragedies had begun with someone striking off by themselves, failing to return, and having a party sent after them. But actually, these were rare exceptions among thousands of trips that usually proved uneventful or even profitable. The men liked to hunt together, particularly for big game, but neither was it unusual for a man to go on a solo hunting trip. Some men, like Hur, actually seemed to need it. Scouting trips composed of smaller groups were also not uncommon. Stakes were higher, of course, whenever someone ran off in distress – as Ikash's mother had once done – or went on a questing type of ramble, as with the young men's vision trips. But not every trip was a quest. Most of them were relatively safe (or as safe as anything could be in that world), particularly when they were routine.

This trip felt like a quest to Ikash. At least, he was nervous enough for one. He remembered when, after months of procrastinating, he had finally gone off to seek God … or to *face* God, more like, for the dark presence had been tugging at him for a long time by then and he had grown weary of avoiding it. He had been worried about what he would find, about what the presence would be when it finally rolled over him. He had worried about whether he could go through it without disintegrating.

What he had *not* feared was that nothing would happen. He had known something was there.

It had come over him in a cloud.

That was fifteen years ago. This trip felt a bit like the beginning of that one. His sister might not be a great spirit; she might not overwhelm him with her very presence, but nevertheless the situation felt just as opaque to him. He couldn't remember feeling this antsy since that day.

He tried to calm down. He tried some slow breathing, felt his shoulders relax, and focused afresh on his surroundings. It was three-day, two-night walk to her campsite, those who had visited it said. He had some traveling ahead of him. He would need to shoot his dinner.

He was planning on something small, such as getting a couple of ptarmigans, one for himself and one for his dog. A hare or groundhog would do as well, though those were larger and would take longer to roast.

These woods were strange. They looked like the sort of place there ought to be mammoths. There had been plains back in his boyhood, before the People came through the ice. Those had been *crawling* with mammoth. Ikash, and every man in his generation, had had their eyes trained to expect that when they started scanning a landscape, it was not a question of whether they would see a mammoth herd but when their eyes would light on it, and of where it would be, north or east, far or near. Sometimes it was a question of which of several herds to pursue.

These woods, now … the People saw a mastodon occasionally, but it was always an event. And the herds were much smaller, so much so that the People felt reluctant to kill any of the beasts. So any man who, like Ikash, was no longer a youth, always experienced a sensation of disappointment when he looked for mammoth and *all* he saw was a herd of elk, or of aurochs, or a family of mule deer, or a solitary pronghorn. All of these things were fine to eat, and some, like the aurochs, were certainly dangerous, but they did not have the mammoth's clumsy, terrifying splendor.

His dog, now … she was perfectly happy with the day and with the game she was seeing. She was no longer young enough to dash off after every winged thing that they flushed. Frost was a blue-eyed older bitch, on the small side for a dog; white-faced, comforting and fluffy. She had been with him a long time, since well before the ice. She had, in fact, been a gift from his older cousin Ki-Ki during a difficult time in Ikash's adolescence when a puppy was exactly what he needed. She was walking a little slower these days, but not enough for him to dream of leaving her behind.

He reached down and scratched the dappled fur on her ruff, grinning.

Suddenly it became difficult to breathe owing to a sharp pain in his left collarbone. He stopped walking and found a sheltered place inside the cave of a giant spruce. He stretched out on the fallen needles, flat on his back, putting as little pressure on his shoulders as possible. It felt as if it were broken, but it was not broken. He would wait for the pain to go away.

Ikash was subject to occasional pains such as this one. Sometimes they were so real that he honestly couldn't tell, say when on a jaunt like this, whether he had actually broken a bone out of nowhere, whether he was actually going to be disabled. This one, for example: it felt as if his collarbone were freshly broken, but he knew exactly what this was. It was a return of the moment when it *had* been broken, by the pounce of a Great Lion, when he was fourteen.

So it would go away. He need only wait.

Frost understood about these things. She sniffed at him, verified that he lived, and then settled herself near his head, facing outward, ears alert.

He kept taking breaths that were as deep as he could manage.

This is what these pains usually were. They were memories of old injuries, of old fears. Sometimes they were not even his own injuries. He had felt an ankle-break once – excruciating but, in his case, brief – that he was sure belonged to Sha. Other times he couldn't tell whose pain he was feeling. He was bearing them for the tribe, perhaps. He didn't know why. Someone had to suffer for them, he supposed. Someone had to bear their pains. This despite the fact that each person also bore his or her own, and in fact the shaman hadn't seen any evidence that the People's troubles were lightened because he also felt them.

His breathing was becoming deeper. The collarbone was starting to feel more like a break a few weeks old. Frost licked his face, and he smiled.

At other times, a pain would come that was completely inexplicable, not resembling any injury or sickness he could think of. He thought he knew the source of these as well, but in practice it wasn't always easy to tell the difference between suffering that came from someone else and that which came from a malevolent spirit.

Breathing. Glad to be able to breathe. He would get up and go on his way soon.

Sometimes his breathing was disrupted as well. This always happened at night. He would wake with the sensation of something putting pressure on his chest or on his windpipe. Sometimes he thought it was his father – a memory of his father – but, if it was, it would always fade when he woke.

When it didn't fade. Well.

It was the Snake, he was certain. Shoving its big, muffling white muzzle against a person's nose, tightening its glistening coils about his chest. Causing the heart to pound faster in panic, which was a natural human reaction whenever a snake was near.

It was just showing its power at those times. That was what he guessed. *Look*, it was saying, *what a simple thing it would be for me to kill you. I can stop your breath at any time as easily as this.*

It never did kill him, though. He didn't think it actually had that power. Yet the body always believed it during the awful moment.

His secret fear – so secret that he didn't allow himself explicitly to think it – was that the Snake might turn its attention to one of his children. That it might stop their breath. He had a vague idea (again, unexamined) that the Snake did have the power to kill babies, especially the very little ones. Occasionally a baby would be found that had stopped breathing and no one knew why. Ikash wasn't sure what the rules were. One would think the Snake would kill all of the People if it were able. That it would already have done so.

He had realized that the Snake hated babies. It hated babies, and it hated for women to bear them.

And speaking of babies, there was one girl child who had been saved, at the age of a day, from a terrible death sixteen years ago. And now that he was breathing better, he had better get up and go to see her.

And what, he wondered, was the particular pain that his sister was now feeling? And why, much as he wanted it, was it not being given to him to bear it for her?

CHAPTER FIVE
THE SHAMAN AND HIS SISTER

Now that she had decided to go with her father, Klee started to feel anxious. It wasn't as bad as when she had been in complete confusion about everything in her world, but she felt nervous, the way she had felt a few years ago when her body started changing. As if something was going to happen. Which, of course, it was. But she was not certain exactly how it was all going to fall out.

She was going to be leaving everything she had ever known. Even though she had hated everything she'd ever known, still she couldn't feel entirely happy about leaving. She wondered whether it was really true that her father had talked to the chief and the chief had agreed to split the People like this. She wondered whether her family were really going to let her go that easily. She wished she could – not talk to them, not most of them anyway, but be near them so she could see the way they behaved and gauge their reactions.

She had been alone for a long time, and had liked it. Now, though, she was starving for connection, for information. It was here, in this small, isolated dale, that she had first learned from her father the real truth that had helped her decide to go with him. Yet somehow, because of her isolation, she felt that she was making the decision blind.

She kept thinking someone would come to try and talk to her about it, and before very long, someone did. Unfortunately it was the one person that her father had warned her she absolutely could not trust.

The shaman's arrival was a little like the arrival of his father, but less dramatic. It was drizzling, not raining; he was damp, but not bedraggled and limping. He came accompanied by his dog, an elderly, white-faced female. Instead of dragging himself right up to the mouth of her shelter, as his father had done, he stood at the opening of the valley and let the dogs find each other.

Guide barked joyfully and went bounding out to greet Frost, who Klee was certain was some older relative of his. He danced about her, and the two of them spent some time sniffing one another. Then Guide sniffed at Ikash as well, pronounced him acceptable, and butted up against him. The shaman reached down and scratched the puppy's head. As he did so, his face softened. Despite what she now believed about him, Klee almost smiled.

"Come on, older brother," she called. "Come to the fire."

Summer was at its very ending. During the last few days, Klee had begun to keep a fire going, even during the day, in the clear space just downhill from her shelter.

The shaman bowed his head politely and advanced to the fire. Klee had seats there, seeing that she had been receiving so many visitors, but he did not sit down immediately. He drew up close to the warmth and spent some time drying his back and his front.

As soon as he got within range of Klee, she felt the atmosphere change. It wasn't as electrifying as with Endu, but with his presence, the air felt different.

"Happy birthday," he said before seating himself.

Klee was surprised. This was indeed the time of year when she was born. She had recently turned sixteen. She was always surprised when people outside her immediate family (what *used* to be her immediate family) remembered or cared about it, even the shaman, who was technically her brother. She had imagined that his only concern would be to justify himself and denigrate his father.

She could not bring herself to thank him, but she inclined her head enough not to be rude.

The young shaman sat a long time in silence, waiting for her to speak. Klee stayed stubbornly silent. *He* was the one who wanted to talk, so why should *she* do all the work?

She was just beginning to think that she ought to get up and do some of the tasks she had it in her mind to do, when he apparently decided he had been there long enough to risk speech. "Is it true that you are considering joining the party that goes to found a city with our father?"

"Not *considering,*" said Klee. "I have absolutely made up my mind to go."

"Why?"

"Because I can no longer live in the village among people who have lied to me and used me. He has good plans, he needs people to help him, and he wants me to come along. It sounds like a good life."

The shaman glanced up at her once, quickly; his eyes were smaller than his father's and not as flashing. Then he looked down at the flames and said in a soft voice, "I beg you not to, sister."

"Why? Because he is such a wicked person?"

He glanced up again, startled.

"Oh, yes," said Klee. "I know what you think of him. He has told me."

"What has he told you?"

So she told him the tale as she had it from Endu. How Sari was crazy, and no one really knew what she was thinking, so they filled in their own guesses. How her husband had certainly never raped her, though he had lost his temper a few times. (The shaman started to speak, and then stopped.) How happy Endu had been when Klee was born, but the tribe was suffering a series of disasters. They needed someone to blame, and they chose to blame Endu for everything, including his wife's death. He had many enemies among the People, and many people hated him, but none more so than his third son Ikash.

"… And how could you accuse *me* of being the cause of her despair, when no one really knows?" she finished. "That's just cruel!"

The shaman's small mouth fell open. His little black eyes got wide. He closed his mouth and stared without speaking. In fact, he was stunned at his father's audacity. But to Klee, it looked as if he were dismayed at being caught out.

"So you admit it?" she said. "You admit that his version of the story is true?"

He put his elbows on his knees and stared downward. At last he came out of his hunch and said faintly, "Of course I don't admit it. He is lying to make himself look better. It's something he always does. I guess I should have known all along what he would tell you. He always maintained that Mom was crazy."

"He said you would say that. He said you hate him."

"Well, I certainly don't *like* him, but I didn't make all this up. He is dangerous, Klee."

She shook her head. "He is misunderstood. He's been mauled, so now he *looks* dangerous, and everyone is against him. But I've spent many days talking with him, and he is a good man. He loves me."

"I knew him before …," the shaman started to say, but then he checked himself, perhaps realizing that this would not convince her. Instead he asked, very gently, "So, you are determined to go with him?"

"I am. I have thought a lot about this."

"I can see that." He heaved a sigh. "Has he talked to you about what sort of a city he wants to build? About his god?"

"His god?"

"The great snake."

"Oh, yes … his totem. Yes, he says it is his special spirit and that it will watch over the wanderers and help us when we go to found our city. But he says that you have no totem because you have no respect for the spirits, and that you will say the snake is evil."

Once again the shaman sat and blinked at her, apparently thrown at being outflanked.

"I do respect the spirits," he said slowly. "I don't have one particular totem because I need to be able to talk with all of them, and because my loyalty is to the great God. I suppose my father told you that because I don't respect him, I don't respect *any*thing."

She was silent. Endu's words had been uncannily like that.

Her brother nodded a few times.

"The snake is a true power. It is in rivalry with the great God for the rule of this land. My father wishes to honor it, but I do not trust it. This disagreement goes back several years."

"I suppose you rejected it just because you don't like *him*."

"It's understandable you would think that, but no. I have had a few encounters with it —"

His eyes searched around, as if even here in the daylight he should not be speaking of this. His opened a pouch among his clothing, withdrew some sweet, dried sage, and sprinkled it on the fire. His voice became lower, though it remained matter-of-fact. "It has tried to woo me."

He began to tell her about the snake, how it could alter reality. Klee stopped him.

"I know some of this, brother," she said.

"How? Have others told you of my visions?"

"I sent Kai to spy on a manhood ceremony when we were small. And then to come back and tell me."

"Did you now?"

For the first time on this visit, her brother cracked a grin.

"That sounds like something Sha and I might have done when we were little."

She was surprised he wasn't angry. Talking to him face to face like this, he didn't seem like a bitter, hate-filled person.

"I will tell you," he said, "About my first encounter with this snake."

But first, more sweet smoke went onto her fire.

It was a strange story. He had been out on a vision quest. He and his dog had been attacked by a Great Lion in the snow. The snake had appeared in a blaze of light which drove away the lion. It had *levitated* Ikash – hard as that was to believe – and had begun to heal his injuries.

"It asked for my loyalty," he told her. "It *demanded* that I serve it. And I almost gave in, it was so beautiful. But I asked it to heal my dog, and it ignored me. Then I turned it down … and it dropped me like a stone."

Everything had gone away: the warmth, the light, the music. The healing which had begun, had stopped progressing.

"It was right here," he told her, placing his right hand on his left collarbone. He hitched the left shoulder up and rotated it, as Klee had seen other men of the People do many times with their old injuries. "Grandmother Zillah said, when she saw it, that it had a few weeks of healing on it. But after that I was on my own. I still feel it sometimes."

"You rejected a great spirit because it stopped healing your collarbone?"

"No. Because it wouldn't heal my dog."

"What happened to the dog?"

"He died."

"But … it must be a very great spirit if it could heal you even part way."

"Oh yes. I don't doubt it could have done more if it had wanted to. Perhaps it could even have brought my dog back from the dead. Though I don't know what kind of a life that would have been for him. But yes, it is certainly real. And *that*," he said, looking at her earnestly, "is why I am so anxious about you. Klee, *please* do not go off and live in a city that is founded on the name of this snake! I cannot tell you how much it is *dangerous!*"

Klee felt a moment of doubt. She cast about in her mind for reasons not to reject her father and his totem. Then she seized on one.

"But *you* can alter reality, too!" she cried. "You can make a room bigger or smaller, you can warm it up. Your wife told me."

"I …"

The shaman stared at her, clearly bewildered.

"But that's not …. What … what are you talking about?" he asked.

Klee realized she had made a mistake. Her face grew hot. She stared into her campfire.

Ikash looked hard at her for a long moment, waiting for an explanation. But there was no explanation she could give that would not embarrass them both.

Finally he said, "Are you saying *I* can alter reality?"

Klee thought it might not be best to repeat that this information had come from Hyuna.

"You can," she whispered. "I felt it, when you arrived. Things felt different."

He was silent another minute. The sun shone (drawing towards twilight now); the fire crackled; the smoke rotated playfully and blew across their faces.

At last the shaman said slowly, "Look, I'm not sure what you mean, but ... of course the atmosphere changes whenever another person comes near us. Our spirit bumps up against their spirit, sort of like beasts in a herd ... and we feel it. Of course that happens. Is that what you meant?"

Perhaps it was what she had meant. Klee nodded.

Her brother exhaled. "All right. Yes, that happens. But that's not a ... power I have."

It was, but he didn't know it.

"I can't alter reality in that way," he said. "I can't alter it nearly enough. What I am talking about, with the snake

… it can change things *completely*. It can overwhelm your senses."

"It can show you what is real," said Klee.

"No!" He made a passionate chopping motion. "It can *change* what's real. It can show – what *it* wants to be real."

"What if that *is* real?"

"It isn't."

"But perhaps it is. I cannot trust anything that you, or any of my other brothers, tell me. You have lied to me all my life. The only one who has told me the truth is my father."

The shaman sighed. He pulled his small square hand down over his eyes. Then he began speaking in a slow, stilted manner. "He waited until you found out the truth from others. From me, in fact. Then he jumped on it and took credit for it. He's like that, he likes to be right. He likes to – overwhelm. Just like that serpent. He – he –"

Suddenly his breath seemed to cut off. He made gagging faces as if choking.

Klee was first shocked, then repelled, then concerned. "Are you all right, brother?" she cried.

She got up and thumped him on the back.

After a few thumps he took an explosive inhale. Then he gasped for a while, leaning down again with forearms on knees, wheezing.

"Thank you, sister," he said at last, voice still creaky.

"What the hell was that?" said Klee.

"It happens sometimes."

"But what *was* it?"

He wheezed a little more. "Perhaps I inhaled an ash from your cookfire."

"You didn't." She cursed. "You tell me the truth!"

"You won't believe it."

"That's my business. Tell me, brother!"

"All right. I think it was the snake."

"Shit."

"You see, I *told* you –"

"How could it be your snake?"

"Sometimes I feel as if it's wrapping about me … or putting its face against my mouth …"

Klee had been standing over him, insisting, but now she collapsed to her haunches. "… *And thrusting its tongue into your mouth?*" she whispered.

"Yes. Perhaps. Doing something so I can't breathe."

"I know that feeling."

"You do?" He met her eyes finally, with a look of dismay.

"Yes. Watak did it to me … when …"

"My God," he muttered. "I never thought of it as …"

His thoughtfulness deepened.

"Have you felt this feeling since, sister?"

"Yes. I thought it was just a bad memory."

More silence while the shaman considered. "That is probably all it is," he said at last. "Do you ever feel anything else that's hard to explain?"

Amal slapping her face. Ishak holding her down by the arms. Watak's hand on her thigh.

These were not hard to explain.

"Not really," she said.

He looked at her sharply.

"Just memories of people touching me. I don't like to be touched … why am I telling this to *you*? I don't even *trust* you!"

He had recovered from his coughing fit, and now he looked at her sadly. "I am sorry, sister. About those memories. I know what you mean, believe it or not."

Now it was her turn to glance sharply. "You *know what I mean?* You are accusing Gr – our father?"

The shaman was silent.

She pressed, "You are saying he put his hands on you?"

He looked irritated.

"Look. I don't want to go into details, but of course he did. Of *course*. That's what I've been trying to tell you. He can be great sometimes. Even most of the time. But when he doesn't get his way, he gets frustrated. And then ... he gets cruel."

Later, Klee would wish that at this moment she had asked him, unwilling or no, to go into details. But she was on the defensive.

"He says he never did the things you say."

"You have to choose who to believe."

"I have! I believe *him!* Everyone else has lied to me!"

Her brother jumped up and towered over her. There was a fire in his eyes, and she realized that if he was as Endu said, perhaps she should not have provoked him.

He made a frustrated gesture and stalked off a little ways among the saplings. It was well into evening now. She could see his long black queue twitching and bouncing on the pale buckskin that covered his back. After a moment he came back, still clearly frustrated but moving more slowly. He did not take his seat. Instead, he crouched by his sleeping dog and began to stroke her fur.

He looked up at Klee when he spoke to her. His round face had spots of flush on the high, sharp cheekbones. "Suppose you go with him and only later find out we were right. You'd be trapped, just like our mother was. You'd wind up living in some – hellish city. With him, his wife and children, and that snake."

"I'm not going to *marry* him. Anyway, suppose I don't go. I'd stay here and never find out whether you were right. And I'd never believe anything anyone told me ever again."

He stared at her for a moment. Then he did the pulling-the-hand-over-the-face again.

"Sister. I understand that you want to know the truth. That is admirable. But you do not know what you are risking. If you go on this … journey … the cost will be your life. There must be other ways to find out truth besides the way that destroys you."

"Perhaps there would have been other ways, if I had been told about all this earlier. Then I could have observed him and the rest of you and taken my time deciding who was the more trustworthy. But all of you have taken that chance from me. Now he is going away. If he goes and I stay, there will be no way for me to discover the truth."

The shaman sighed deeply, and Klee saw that she had won the argument.

"All right," he said. "I see that you are determined to go with him. I cannot dissuade you." He shook his head. His hands continued to move slowly over the soft fur of the dog. "But listen. At least let me give you some advice about how to handle him. I've lived with him, so I know a little bit about this. He likes to be right. If you want to travel with him and his family, then you'll have to let him have his way."

"I can do that," said Klee.

"Can you?"

It sounded like teasing, but her brother did not crack even a slight smile. After a moment, she realized that the look on his face, now dimly lit by twilight and campfire, was a look of fear.

"I am not sure you can," he said. "You haven't done that with any of the rest of us. Not even with Jai when you thought he was your father. But if you want to survive, you will have to try."

"Father is different. He is not the person you describe."

"Let us hope that is so," said the shaman.

The hand wiped the eyes for a third time.

"Night has fallen," he said. "I did not bring any meat with me. Do you have some here?"

"I caught some fish earlier. Before you arrived, I was going to dry them."

"Well, shall we eat together?"

They did. The shaman did not eat much. That night he slept in the doorway of her hut.

The next morning they had the same conversation again, but shorter.

Klee woke before her brother, visited the stream, and then began to build up the cookfire. He had brought her some uncooked maize, and she was making porridge of it. The smell reminded her of Grandmother Zillah.

Then she looked over her shoulder and saw him standing on the ledge in front of her hut, wrapped in a blanket, blinking and looking frowsy.

"Good morning, brother," she called, and added, bantering, "Did you dream of your snake?"

"Nope. I kept breathing all night."

They ate in silence – the People did not talk while eating – and then Klee asked, "Is it true what Aki says, that my par – that my brother and Amal are still constantly fighting?"

The shaman nodded. He swallowed his last mouthful of maize. High in the air, over the two of them and their dogs, it was a clear morning. The sun wasn't yet high enough to reach them through the canopy, but the whole sky was glowing white behind the branches.

"The chief has tried to talk to them about it," he said. "Tried to get it stopped. For the sake of their younger children."

The chief was, of course, Amal's father, and besides his duty to keep the peace among the tribe, he was always meddling in his daughters' marriages. Klee could imagine him, with that devious look that she now imagined on nearly all her relatives, saying to Jai, "Don't blame my daughter. Klee isn't gone forever. Hang on. We will get her back."

But she *was* gone forever.

"He told Jai," Ikash went on, "That he has to let you go."

Klee was shocked.

"Let me *go?* The chief said that?"

"Yep. He said you probably will never come back to their household, and that my brother should get used to it and work on caring for the wife and children he has."

"But … if he said to let me go … then I am free? I can go wherever I like?"

"Of course you are. You could go with our father. No one can stop you."

"Then why aren't *you* letting me go?"

"I am trying to convince you to stay in the area. That doesn't mean you would have to go back and live with my brother. There are plenty of other places you could live."

"So I am free to go where I please," she said bitterly, "As long as it is not with my father."

So their discussion began all over again.

He pleaded; she resisted. Before long he saw that his pleas were hardening rather than softening her. He stopped pleading and said that he would return to the People.

"Hyuna had her baby. It's a boy," he told her. "I can't be away from her for very long."

And Klee, who still loved Hyuna, told him to pass on good wishes from her.

It wasn't until later, after he had gone, that it occurred to her to wonder whether the whole choking routine had been faked. But if it had been, it was the most convincing performance she had ever seen.

So Ikash started back. He did not stop to hunt; he did not stop to eat; he just walked. He really didn't know what to do about anything, but he knew that he needed to get back to the People. He wanted to get back to Hyuna, he supposed. At this moment he didn't really want much of anything. There were no thoughts in his mind.

Once or twice during that first day, Frost, who was a competent hunter, caught some small animal and ate it, and Ikash came out of his daze long enough to note that he had not been feeding her, but that she had now taken care of herself, so they could go on.

That night it was different. His mind came alive, and he could not club it back to into numbness. Round and round it went, arguing with all the arguments that Endu had presented to Klee. He hadn't been able to oppose them strongly because he was being gentle with his sister, who was mouthing them. He wondered if he should have opposed them strongly anyway. He wondered, also, about other past events, whether Endu had discussed them with Klee, and what sort of a construction he had put on them. Had Endu mentioned the bear that mauled him – which was clearly a judgment from his family's totem – and, if so, how had he managed to make that Ikash's fault?

After wearing out these topics, his mind turned to regrets. He had warned her about the snake, the one who came with shining, but he had not talked about the one who came in darkness. Perhaps he should have. He was not very adept at it, which was why he had not tried, but now he wondered how he could possibly have talked to her at some length about the snake, and yet said never said one word about God.

After many hours, he fell into a kind of sleep. Then, in the length of the night, the temperature dropped. His dog Frost backed up to him to for warmth – he was under a tree, near the edge of the shelter, well away from the roots – and they enjoyed a little more sleep curled around one another.

Then the thunderstorm broke.

It woke the man and the dog. It terrified them with a series of confusing, complicated gusts and even some hail. The water came so thick, and so much from the side, that they were quickly soaked even inside their shelter. The fine soil under them became a series of rivulets carrying tiny rafts of needles.

At first, the water was too omnipresent to make getting up practical. Ikash sat, cradling Frost, who had never liked storms and was whining, both of them getting completely soaked and miserable, all of their energy going toward withstanding this onslaught on their senses. As the noise of the storm slackened, somewhere they could hear wolves howling.

Eventually conditions changed from Waters of Judgment to Ordinary Rainstorm. Ikash had long since realized he would not be getting more sleep that night, but neither should he start to walk again while it was still dark. Visibility was low; streams would be flooding; certain nocturnal creatures would be out, stirred up, doing their thing. He wondered whether Klee, back at her camp, was taking this opportunity to fish.

By predawn, the storm was gone. Ikash rubbed Frost vigorously to fight the chill. He himself was shaking, but that would mend if they got up and moved about.

"Come on, grandmother," (for his dog was a grandmother), "Let's hurry," he said.

They ran for a while. The sun came up. His body started steaming. He stripped off his buckskin shirt and leggings, and worked them in his hands. They were probably ruined, but perhaps if he got back to camp quickly enough, they could be salvaged. The only bit of clothing he retained was his loincloth. As the sun climbed higher, it started to warm him, patchily, through the trees. It would have been a beautiful morning to run in for anyone who hadn't just suffered a sleepless night.

Then he remembered everything he had been thinking about before that storm. His mind went blank again. He kept walking.

About noon he was trotting along, considerably slower than before, one wet, flat legging slung over each shoulder and still working the buckskin shirt in his now-aching hands. He sensed someone coming from a distance. When you belonged to the People, if ever you saw someone coming from a distance it was guaranteed to be someone you knew. He kept watching the figure for a while, through a couple of turns of the landscape that hid, and then revealed, it. Soon it became clear that the person was his father-in-law, accompanied by a dog.

They drew near. They approached each other. Finally, in a small swampy clearing, they stopped walking. The dogs commenced their mutual sniffing ritual.

Hur would have looked like a wild man to anyone who did not know him. In recent years he had stopped constantly wearing the woven headband that covered his empty left eye socket. The scar was old and seamed, and everyone had gotten so used to the sight that it was no longer horrifying. It was just Hur. Unlike most of the People, Hur was hirsute; his beard grew and had to be shaved or trimmed regularly. Today, he had about a month's worth of growth on it, so his face was framed by greying brown hair above and greying brown hair below, blending in to his browned summer skin.

But his clothing was neat, and he was not wet or bedraggled.

"Looks like you got rained on," he said, not unkindly.

Ikash shrugged. The leggings continued to adhere to his shoulders. "Looks like you didn't, Uncle."

"I built a shelter."

"I – didn't," said Ikash, feeling foolish.

"I guess you had other things on your mind."

That was Hur. Always practical, never judgmental.

"I came," said the chief, "Thinking you might still be out at her camp, and I'd join you. Now I find you have left already. Should we go back there, do you think?"

Ikash shook his head.

Hur said, "Is she – "

Ikash shook his head more sharply. He was fairly certain that if he opened his mouth, what would come out would be a dry sob.

It would not be the first time he'd made such a sound in front of his father-in-law. There had been one other time, thirteen years ago, when the chief had drawn him aside to tell him he was free to marry Hyuna. But the way he had put it was, "You are welcome in my family." Ikash had found himself, somehow, sobbing his heart out on a patchy hillside on a sunny autumn day very much like this one. Something had happened, in that moment. They had never discussed it, but both men would probably remember it for the rest of their lives.

But, back to *this* autumn day. At length Ikash managed to squeeze out, in a rather strained voice, the words, "He has told her a pack of lies. About me, about – Mom – "

Hur made a sort of grunt that sounded like, "'Course he has."

At that moment, a huge shadow passed over the clearing. All noises, except for the wind, fell silent.

They would not be able to tell, without a deal of squinting, whether it was one of those giant birds or whether it was a dragon. Either way, it was predator, and they were prey.

There were no tall shrubs nearby, but both of them dropped into the rushes facedown and lay still. The sun baked their backs; the grasses rose above them. Their buckskin shirts would blend into the grass in color. Hur's hair was a light brown, now going grey, and should not be very visible, but Ikash's was a rich, shiny black. Nothing to be done: the important thing was to avoid movement. The dogs, too, had flattened themselves in ways that in other circumstances would have been comical.

The two men were curious about what the creature was, but they could not turn over onto their backs. It would be unlucky to show it their faces, however much they might want to. Their clothes were growing damp with the soggy ground, and as for insects, the two of them were getting eaten. This new country had all kinds of pests, including tiny ones that would burrow into the skin and stay there, for weeks, itching, beneath your loincloth. But better to be eaten by pests than by a dragon.

Still they stayed.

Ikash felt a small hard hand pat his back. He knew it wasn't a signal that all was clear, because the shadow was still circling. Then he realized that he was sobbing after all – and not dry sobs, either. He was weeping with frustration and helplessness, weeping over his sister, weeping beside his father-in-law as they hid in the midst of a bright day with the shadow of a predator sweeping back and forth over them.

The hunter got bored and went away. Still they stayed. Ikash finished his cry. He began to be able to speak. "I can't protect her, I can't protect her," he kept saying. Hur remained silent. Eventually the small animals tuned up again – rodents rustling, ptarmigans chuckling in relief. The flying shadow was truly gone. The two men got up immediately. Both of them would be itchy for weeks.

They began walking back towards the People. They walked some way in silence.

Then Hur said, "Tell me about it, son."

Something happened to the shaman's face whenever the chief called him "son." It seemed to blossom, like a flower. It happened now, briefly, before his face collapsed again.

He told the chief the bare facts. He did not mention details, such as the question of whether his mother had truly been raped. He didn't mention the snake.

"She believes that my father is a good man and that all of us are against him. He has convinced her," – his pulse speeded up with the injustice – "that Mother was crazy. Klee does not trust me, nor, I imagine, anyone else but *him* ... and she is determined to go with him and found a serpent city."

Hur asked a few questions. Was there no way they could save her?

Ikash thought not, except by force.

What, asked Hur, if she did go with him, was the worst that might happen?

Immediately, Ikash's mind went to very dark places. Endu had seduced his daughter's mind. What if he did the same with her body? Would anyone do that, even Endu? Ikash didn't think so, but he couldn't be sure. His father's mind was opaque to him.

Then there was the snake to consider. It, too, liked to violate minds … and perhaps bodies as well, if he was right in his suspicion that Watak thrusting his tongue into Klee's mouth, and the snake thrusting its tongue into the shaman's mouth were the same thing.

There seemed to be no bottom to his mind. There was no limit to the horrors he could imagine. But he couldn't distinguish actual danger from his own fears.

"I don't know, Father," he said helplessly.

"Come," said the chief.

So the shaman spoke the worst of his fears.

Hur was dismayed. If things were really that bad, he thought, they would be justified in using force. Even in killing Endu, perhaps.

But Endu had not done any provable wrong. You couldn't kill a man for having a particular totem, or for talking to his daughter. Hur had never liked Endu, and deep down he did believe the man was wicked. But a chief could not go about killing people he disliked, especially when they had wives and children. Also … Endu appeared to feel real affection and pride for Klee. Leaving aside the snake, it was hard to believe he would really harm her.

The chief did not voice these doubts. He knew they would neither convince nor comfort Ikash. After all, these same things could once have been said about Sari.

Instead he said, "Are you certain?"

"No, Father, I am not. I have a feeling."

"But you haven't had a vision, or anything like that."

The younger man sighed so deeply that it tore at Hur to hear it. "No, Father. Just a feeling. I hope it may not be true."

They walked a little farther, and then the chief said, "We will think what may be done. There may be no way to stop her from going with your father's party."

Ikash nodded. "I am going to fast every day for her."

"You cannot fast *every day*, son," said Hur reasonably.

The other looked up as if waking from a daze, realized what he had said, and gave his father-in-law a brief grin. "Right. Well, I'm going to fast as often as possible."

Twilight started to come, and they shot a couple of ptarmigans. They roasted them, both of their stomachs growling, but when it came to the moment, Ikash said he wasn't hungry.

Hur said, "You have eaten nothing for two days. Your dog is crying for this food."

Indeed, she was whining eagerly.

"You have a wife and a new baby at home," the chief went on. "If you don't eat this, I will feed it to you bite by bite as if *you* were a baby."

So Ikash forced himself to eat. As soon as he started, he devoured the soft meat. Afterward, when they lay down, he felt nauseous.

He couldn't stop wondering "what if." What if the snake were back in Klee's little hollow, right at this moment, smothering her? What if it were thrusting its long tongue into her mouth as she slept? He felt an impulse to grow to giant size and dash back there. It would only be a few huge strides over the land in the starlight.

Of course, if he did such a thing, he wouldn't be able to see the snake, nor to do anything directly against it.

Father God, he prayed silently, *Protect my sister.*

Almost right away he felt himself wilting and sliding towards sleep.

The first night after Klee's visit from the shaman was the night of the storm. Klee had no trouble sleeping that night, for storms always soothed her. But the second night was another matter. It was cooler, which was good sleeping weather, but Klee could not sleep. Her thoughts were so loud, and the night was so still.

She tossed and turned in frustration, furious with her brother for having come and planted doubts again just when she had gotten away from all the confusion, just when she had made up her mind. But then her own mind whispered to her, *What if he were right to plant these doubts? What if I were, at this moment, actually wrong about everything?* Then she felt as if the very earth was dropping out from under her. Fingers scrabbling at the edge, she tried to think.

The things her father had told her sounded true. The things her brother told her – well, it was as if he wanted to make the worst out of everything. Everything he said had sounded paranoid by daylight … but, now in the dark, it all seemed terribly true. True by the very fact that it was the worst.

What was true? Her father's reasonable explanations, or her brother's insistence that she face the darkness?

It was not fair that two opposite things should both have the ring of truth, that she should be all on her own to figure it out; that if she got it wrong, her life might be required of her.

But it was only the shaman who thought that her life might be required of her. That was because he loved to make everything into a spiritual drama. No one else thought this a matter of life or death.

But her mother had actually died.

But that was due to her own sick mind, not to the Snake.

Something rustled. It sounded like it was right in the wall of her shelter, about to drop down upon her. She tried to roll out of the way, but she couldn't move. It was as if the bones of her shoulders were stuck to the cattail mat and the cattail padding beneath, as if rods were holding them to the pounded-earth floor.

She began to panic. She breathed faster, but each breath brought her no oxygen. She began to see stars.

It's the Snake, she thought. *If it lets me go after this, I will stay. I will stay. I won't go with my father.*

But after a few moments her breaths became deeper and more productive. By the time she was breathing well again, she wasn't certain that anything had been constricting her throat or threatening her at all.

And by the time she woke the next morning, she had revoked her revocation and was trying to pretend it had never happened.

CHAPTER SIX
... AND INCREASE ON IT

Hyuna was sitting outdoors on a blanket with the baby. Everyone knew that babies needed sunning. She was lying beside him, half dozing, every once in a while opening her eyes in sudden panic to check that he was still there.

These early days after a baby were always a matter of surviving hour to hour.

They hadn't named the child yet. So many unlucky events were happening just lately, and they wanted to give him a good name, not an unlucky one. But the baby had been lucky so far. He nursed well. He changed visibly from day to day, his eyes growing brighter, his skin healthy and peeling. Already, in the few days since his father had been gone, he had developed a little rounded belly. His fair hair had not fallen out, but it was coming in darker at the roots.

They would name him some time after Ikash returned, she supposed. After they found out what was going to happen.

She was not expecting Ikash and her father back at least until the moon had become full, but when someone came and stood over her,   she opened her eyes and there was her father.

"Your young man," he said, "is back and he needs you."

Of course Ikash was not so young any more, but Hur had always called him that – *your young man* – ever since shortly before the two married. Before that he had been *the son of Endu*, which in Hur's mouth was a much less flattering description.

Hyuna groaned and peeled herself up off the blanket. She felt as if she had to move every part of her body consciously. Sleep was still in her limbs.

The baby was sleeping, his huge head turned to one side, arms splayed out around it, framing it, bent at the elbow.

"Will you stay with him?" she asked her father, and the chief replied, "I would love to stay with this young man."

"Where is he?" she asked, meaning Ikash.

"He is at the meeting-fire."

So she dragged herself in that direction.

The central firepit was not lit, but it was still a place for gathering, news, and meetings, and a place where people would check in when they returned to the village. Ikash was there, seated on a low stool. Grandmother Zillah was seated beside him and had given him some sort of drink. Grandmother Zillah had all kinds of concoctions: for sleep, for pain relief, for heart's ease.

He saw her coming, set down his drink, and stood. He had splashed his face with water and he was wearing an old woven tunic of her father's.

When she saw the look of extreme weariness on his face, she knew it had been very bad.

She could see that he had spent some time working on it, on his own, as he walked, and that he had spoken to her father about it, whatever it was, as well. That was good, because she had not the energy to be the first ears to hear whatever it was, something about Klee apparently. She had been up all night with the baby. She was barely keeping herself together.

She walked up to him, however, thinking the whole time that she didn't have the strength to do it, and offered an embrace.

Ikash stood still and held her very tightly. He was a hard hugger.

She squirmed around a little, not enough to make him think she was trying to break away. The front of her wrap was wet where her new-mother's breasts were leaking.

That was inconvenient, but unimportant. Moments like this didn't come along often, thankfully, and in a moment like this she didn't want to let him down.

He was shaking – oh God, this was rare. What was she going to do if he collapsed? She stood there, breasts leaking, hips and back aching, and bore his embrace, because that was honestly all she could do.

Suddenly he said, "Shit. I'm sorry. I'm squeezing you."

His voice was almost his own normal voice. He stepped back and looked at the wet spot on the front of his tunic – rather low down because he was so much taller than she – and gave a quiet laugh.

"Sorry," he said.

Hyuna stretched her sore back and shook out her arms.

"Not important. It'll wash."

It was true. She was seldom free of a mess of some kind or another in the early days with a baby.

Then she said, "I take it she is still angry?"

The weary look came back. "She is determined to go with him."

She wondered how many hours of fruitless argument were summed up in those few words.

"Oh, love," she said.

She drew near again and leaned on him – sideways this time, with plenty of room to wind an arm around his waist without getting squashed. As she did so, she suddenly felt an overwhelming urge to sleep. She was so tired that she could not bring herself, at that moment, to care about Klee for her own sake. She cared about Klee's fate only as it affected her husband. And even for that, she had nothing to give him. Never mind making everything right, which was what she would like to do. With a newborn to care for, she was barely hanging on to sanity. She couldn't sit for hours (or even minutes) and listen to him talk. She wasn't ready to resume making love yet. She was giving everything she had to staying alive.

All of a sudden, to her horror, she realized *she* was going to cry. This was all backwards. It was selfish of her.

She couldn't stop it; she started weeping.

Ikash repeated his earlier curse in confusion. He had put an arm around her shoulder when she cuddled up sideways a moment ago; now, charmingly, he lifted it slightly so that it hovered. "What is it?" he said. "Is it Klee? Is it me? Is it because I've been away?"

"No, no …" Hyuna said weakly, and wept. "It's nothing. It's everything. Y-you remember … I always … get like this after a baby. And I'm so *tired*."

Then she added, "Don't look at me, it's not a pretty sight."

He laughed a little – she had always loved his almost inaudible laugh – and leaned back, giving her space.

"I am sorry," she said, "But I don't have anything to give you."

He exhaled. The arm came down again, gently, around her shoulders.

"You don't need to, babe. It does me good just to … when I come back to the house, and you are there in it."

Grandmother Zillah had tactfully disappeared during this conversation. Now she materialized again, this time offering Hyuna a drink too.

"I think," she said, "the two of you need to get some rest."

"The baby will need me soon," said Hyuna, looking up from her tea. She had been so thirsty that she'd finished it at one go.

"If he does," said Zillah, "I will bring him to you."

But as it turned out, Zillah kept the infant occupied for several hours. And Ikash and Hyuna went back home, and they did rest. They didn't talk, they didn't make love, they merely slept and slept.

Later, when they were stronger, he was able to summarize the situation as it stood with his sister, and Hyuna was able to listen.

"Perhaps we should name the baby Kel, after her," she suggested.

And her husband's face became hard, and he said, "I'm not going to name a baby for her. She's only going away, she isn't *dead.*"

Ikash went to see his children.

They were not at Jabed's house. Magya, who was there, told him that her teenaged daughter Risa had taken the little ones to a particular meadow so they could run about. Ikash knew the meadow. He made his way to it, walking the paths along the edges of the maize gardens, beside the irrigation ditches.

He got to the meadow, and not only his own and Jabed's children, but about half the children in the village were there. It was hard to sort them out with his eyes;

while he was still doing so, his daughter Sira noticed him and shrieked,

"Daddy!"

Ikash went down on one knee, held out his arms, and the two of them came rushing toward him and knocked him flat.

There had been a very brief period in his life when no one regularly knocked him flat. It had been after he moved out of his childhood home, but before he married Hyuna. His wife didn't actually weigh enough to knock him down, but God knew, she tried. The young Hyuna had been an enthusiastic pouncer. Now that she was older and more tired, that duty had been taken over by his children.

Six-year-old Dumish was sitting on his chest, bouncing. Ikash grunted, said, "That's enough, son," and tossed him off to one side. He bounced up like a ball, laughing hard.

Little Sira was sitting on his legs. Ikash sat up carefully, and she stopped attacking and cuddled up against him.

"Daddy," she said, "When can we come home? I miss you and Mommy. I don't like living in another place."

Her voice started out whiny, and by the end of the sentence she was sniffling.

Here is a little girl who needs her father.

"You can come home," he said.

Dumish said, "I want to stay a few more nights with the cousins!"

"That is fine too," said Ikash. "But for now, both of you come with me to see your mother and the baby."

Sira was four years old. It would never be this easy again to fix things for her.

When they got home, Grandmother Zillah was sitting cross-legged on their front porch, head propped against the side of the house, enjoying the sun.

"They are asleep," she said quietly.

So Ikash took his children in to see their mother and brother – quietly, quietly – and then back out again. And then Dumish took off with a passing cousin to return to the meadow, but fair-haired little Sira, who wanted to cuddle, sat on her father's lap as he sat and leaned against the wall beside his grandmother. And he and Zillah had a conversation about Klee that was very indirect, so that it would pass over Sira's little brown head.

Ikash had had conversations, before now, with Grandmother Zillah about the snake. Zillah was the only one of the People who really could be said to remember what the world was like before the earth's many nations were scattered. There had been a city, and a tower, and so forth, and these were remembered by all the older generation: Damai, Melek, Endu, Hur, and even faintly by the younger adults such as Rumi and Ninna, who had been teenagers at the time of the disaster. But there had also been other things, things that a person had to experience as an adult in order to know fully: a society, a culture, people other than the People. Important stories of things that had gone before; members of the very oldest generation who remembered what things had been like before the Flood. Although Endu thought he remembered all these things – and, indeed, he had imbibed them – he had been a very young man when, as they liked to say, "the Tower fell." Little as he might like it, most of his life had been spent as a nomad. Among all the People, only Zillah had grown to full adulthood in that world. She had married, borne and raised children, and lived to see her oldest son marry and begin to have children, all before the fall of the Tower. Only she could be said to have that older world in her bones.

Thus, Ikash had had conversations with his grandmother about the dark presence and about the snake. Though he knew they were real (this was confirmed by his own experience and by myths and teachings from Ki-Ki), yet he had wanted to make sure they were *really* real things, things that had belonged to that older world as well as to this one, things that the ancestors also remembered. If not, then they could be mere residents of the new lands that the People had traveled since the scattering. And if that, then they could be deceiving; they could be anything.

He did not think that either the Snake or the Presence was a merely local god. He had his reasons. Still, he felt blind, as one always felt blind when groping about in the spirit world, and he had wanted to know anything that the grandmother could tell him.

As it had turned out, she was able to tell him a great deal. She had been, after all, the source for the stories that Ki-Ki had codified.

Grandmother Zillah was not a particularly spiritual person, and she claimed never to have sensed the presence of either the snake or of God. However, there was plenty of information about both which had been common knowledge in her girlhood. The snake, she said, was "the shining one," and had been the king of the gods who had come down to earth, once, upon a mountain. Everyone knew the snake was associated with that mountain, with the stars, with fertility, with ancient mysteries only partly revealed. With the giants. Some, in her girlhood, had become very interested in this and had sought to study and develop these connections. They sought snakes for healing. (Ikash had started when he heard that.) They tried to find out which god belonged to which particular star or stars. There had even been rumors – "only rumors, mind, grandson" – that the Tower itself was intended as a gateway for these gods.

But Zillah and her first husband, Golgal, had paid little attention to mysteries and rumors and these had *not* been the reason that *their* family was working on the tower. They had understood it to be only a place of refuge, of safety for humanity, a point from which to observe (not worship) the sun, moon, and stars. And, of course, a temple for the worship of the great God.

Everyone knew, Zillah had told him, that there was a great God who had made the heavens and earth and everything in them. He dwelt in darkness (again, Ikash had started, then nodded slowly). He did not, and perhaps could not, as the snake and the other gods did, reveal himself openly to men. Still less would He do as they did and mix with people promiscuously. But occasionally He spoke, and when He did, those to whom He spoke heard His voice. He had spoken to Father Noah, instructing him how to get inside a … and here came a word with which Ikash was unfamiliar. He knew the story, though, having learned it from Ki-Ki. The way they had always told it to the children was that Noah and his wife had taken refuge inside the bark of a tree when the waters came.

But God had spoken to Noah even after this, Grandmother Zillah said. He had given the following instructions (she still had the words memorized): "*You must not eat meat that has the lifeblood still in it. And for your lifeblood I will surely demand an accounting. I will demand an accounting from every animal. And from each man, too I will demand an accounting for the life of his fellow man.*

Whosoever sheds the blood of man, by man shall his blood be shed;

for in the image of God has God made man.

As for you, be fruitful and multiply and increase in number; multiply on the earth and increase on it."

When God spoke, in the old stories, it was so often in poetry.

"Some people do not wish to follow the great God because He hides His face from us," said his grandmother. "They grow impatient, I think, and they wish for gods that will come and shine and dazzle. You know, gods that will *do* things. But I do not feel that way. I don't think He owes us any revelation of Himself. It is very rare that He speaks to people, grandson. Very rare. I have had the privilege, several times, to meet Father Noah. But since then ... out of all the people in the world ... I have never yet met another person to whom God spoke."

Ikash had let this statement stand. He thought it was true. He had had at least one, very vivid experience of the dark presence, and it had brought great comfort to him. But it had not done what he could call *speaking*. There had been no words: no assertions, no predictions, no commands. And as far as he knew, this had also been true of all of Ki-Ki's visions.

"I think," Zillah had said, "That with the words of Noah, He has given us enough to go on."

All of this background was sitting quietly between them now as they talked about Klee.

"Grandmother," said Ikash, very quietly, very casually, so as not to attract his daughter's attention, "You know the true story of my mother."

Zillah nodded. She was still resting her silver head against the wall of his house, eyes closed to de-emphasize the conversation. When the sun shone on her face, she looked like a young woman. She was 105 years old, but the skin of her neck was still firm.

Zillah, in fact, could probably have told details about Endu's abuse of Sari that even Ikash didn't know. Zillah had spent the years of her son's marriage trying to stop the abuse: rebuking her son (always with temporary success), examining and supporting and providing refuge for Sari. She did not feel responsible for Endu's hard heart, for each man was responsible for his own heart, and Ikash didn't blame her for it either. She had tried. But although she hadn't been able to save Sari, she had an impressive store of medical knowledge. As the tribe's most experienced healing woman, she wielded what could be called professional opinions.

"My sister still trusts you, I think," whispered Ikash, almost inaudibly.

Zillah paused for a long moment, and then replied, "Perhaps."

"So – forgive me, grandmother – why haven't you been to talk to her? You can convince her if anyone can."

"I have not been to talk to her," said Zillah immediately, "because I think that going with her father is something she needs to do."

Ikash felt his stomach drop when she said that.

"Are you saying – it would be a *good* thing?"

"I won't go *that* far," said Zillah.

Another pause, to break up the conversation. Little Sira became very heavy. Ikash looked down and saw that she was asleep.

"If I have learned anything," his grandmother went on, "It's that I am a very bad judge always of what course of action will be *good*. I don't know how this may turn out. Of course there are bad things about it. But what I mean is that she has set her heart on it. She *needs* to go with her father and find out who he is. And who is to say what will happen if we imprison her here? I would think that her hatred for all of us would only harden."

He remained silent at this, but he felt a hot turmoil inside him.

"Surely –" he began, getting agitated. Then he remembered his sleeping daughter and started over again more softly. "Surely she could find out who he is from you and me, Grandmother, without putting herself at such … at such *certain* risk."

"But I am not sure that she can," said Zillah gently. "If I speak to her now about your mother, all my words will be only so many stones that she must climb over in order to get to her goal."

"What is worse?" muttered Ikash. An imprisoned and bitter Klee, or a ravaged and abused Klee? And were those really the only two options?

It was at times like this that he wished God *would* speak to him, and that very clearly.

"Perhaps the worst need not happen," said Zillah. "Let us say that she is running madly, and none can call her back or cut off the path of her flight. Very well, but perhaps someone can run alongside and at least keep her from going over a cliff. I don't think this is the time for my words, but for my presence. I have resolved I am going with her."

CHAPTER SEVEN
I WILL CARRY YOU

It had been arranged that Klee would return to the village for a few days before the planned date of her father's departure. She was going to help his wife, Dira, with the arrangement of the family's caravan. She was going to see the rest of the People and say goodbye.

Klee was not looking forward to this visit. She wasn't certain that she would know how to be when she was around people again. At the same time, she felt excited about making the decision final, about getting started. It had been many years since the family had traveled, and she itched to see new lands. All in all, she spent her last day in her solitary camp restlessly, a bundle of impatient hopes, fears, and reluctance.

A distraction arrived. It was Setiq, son of Hur-kar and Lien.

This time, he stayed.

Setiq wasn't much of a talker. That was fine with Klee, who was sick of talking and explaining herself.

He did speak, but – on that night – only in short sentences.

"Your hair," he said.

"I hate my hair," said Klee.

"I love it," said Setiq, and he scrunched it up and released it.

Later, when they had been kissing for a long time as the autumn twilight purpled around them, Klee interrupted to warn him, "I don't know what I'm doing, you know, Setiq."

"Nor I," he murmured.

"I cannot have a baby. I am leaving on a journey."

"All right."

When they finally came together, her only regret was that it was so dark she could no longer see his golden eyes.

He was a little more talkative in the morning.

It transpired that he had sounded out his parents to discover how they would feel about his joining the pioneering party led by Endu. He hadn't said that Klee was the reason, but he expected they knew.

"You're coming along?" asked Klee in surprise. "As my – as my – "

His eyes were rather narrow, and when he smiled, they nearly disappeared.

"As your husband? Well, why not?"

"I just … did not expect this," she said.

"I didn't either," said Setiq. "But – I hoped. My future, you know, it depended on how things went last night."

"But … I didn't realize … I didn't think you would leave the People … well, at all, really, but especially not for *me*."

"Why not? Did you value yourself so lightly?"

"I … don't know," she said, but she felt a great joy welling up in her heart.

Her dog, Guide, had accepted him, anyway, and indeed had stood guard all night outside the hut.

But Klee was confused about whether they should return to the village separately or together. She very much wanted him to go back with her, for she had been dreading that dramatic, lonely entrance. At the same time, she realized that returning as couple would double the amount of talk and stares. Not wishing to embark on a life of guessing games, she decided to be direct.

"Are you planning to go on a hunt, or to come back with me?" she asked.

He looked confused. "With you, of course."

"You realize that will be an announcement. They'll know …"

"They'll know anyway," he said, "as soon as they see you."

Indeed, they knew.

Klee had never intended it so, but nonetheless every move she made seemed to cause pandemonium among the people in her world. They had all run about like mad things when she went away alone; they did the same when she returned accompanied.

Jai was livid, and Klee was livid with him in return. Then Hur intervened, putting his small square hand on the much taller man's arm.

"I seem to recall," he said evenly, "That *you* seduced *my* daughter before you married her."

Jai's head jerked backwards slightly as if he had run into a branch. Then he flushed, nodded, and cracked his small, wolfish grin.

Endu, like Hur, was calm. He seemed, if anything, proud of his daughter. He only asked her whether she liked

Setiq, and whether this would change her plans. Did she aim to stay or to leave him behind?

"He wants to come along," she said.

"All right. I'll have a word with him."

Endu seemed to glow now that he was leading an expedition and screening suitors for his beautiful daughter. 'Having a word' with the young men, just like the chief. His satisfaction overflowed into consideration, and he looked tenderly at Klee and said, "Is there anything I can do to help you?"

"I'd like a place to be alone," she said.

Endu laughed. "You have just spent a summer alone, my daughter!" Then he became arch and added, "Or … *nearly* alone."

But he offered, and she accepted, a curtained alcove of his home that was dark, comfy, and surprisingly quiet. She'd have preferred to be up a tree somewhere, but she did not feel that she could turn down an offer from her father and his wife now that she had thrown in her lot with them. Besides, her solitude here would be safe. That would not be the case at an outdoor location where anyone could seek her out.

Beyond the heavy woven curtain, Endu's wife Dira tiptoed about the house, making preparations. Klee knew somehow that although she was meant to be helping her, Dira would never ask. She would wait until Klee was ready. It was a delicious feeling, so different from Amal. It made Klee want not to take very long before she went to help her … but she just needed an hour to collect herself after the chaos of returning to camp.

"Was he good to you, my daughter?" Endu had asked.

And Klee had nodded, silent and shy. He was indeed good.

"Lie back," Setiq had said. "This will not give you a baby."

She lay back, and he had taken his golden, wedge-like face – perfectly shaped for the purpose – and buried it between her legs. And Klee had floated away.

She shivered in the dark, remembering him.

"She was definitely blushing," the shaman told his wife.

He said it with a happy smile. This new development was surprising and a bit confusing, but on balance he thought it a good thing.

"Just like you," said Hyuna.

"I do not blush," said Ikash, blushing. He and his sister both had brown skin that was light enough to show red on the cheeks.

"You are doing it this moment," said Hyuna. Her husband laughed and she leaned over the baby, who at this stage she was still constantly holding, and kissed him. "Oh," she said, "I am happy for her."

"So am I. I think. They are awfully young …"

"Older than I was when I married you."

"That's true … but you were so … so wholesome and stable."

"I was a child who had no idea what I was getting into."

He shot her a dark, worried glance, and then saw that she was teasing.

"Besides," said Hyuna, "It will mean one more person near Klee whom she trusts and who actually wants the best for her."

"If Setiq really wants the best for her."

"What do you mean?"

"She has been all that people have talked about this summer, and he is fifteen years old. Perhaps all he wants is something unique for himself and a bit of reflected glory."

"Oh, no. It's not that," said Hyuna immediately, with a confidence that surprised her husband.

"How in the world can you know?"

"I have heard that he's a had a crush on her for some time."

"You have heard that?"

"Hur-kar told Mama, and Mama told me."

This made sense. Hur-kar, father of Setiq, had been raised by Ninna, Hyuna's mother. Nevertheless, Ikash found himself staring at his wife with disbelief. She was not a malicious gossip, but it never ceased to amaze him the way she seemed to know everything.

"You have just been confined for three months with pregnancy and then with a newborn. How can you know all this? When did your mother tell you … was it to pass the time while you were giving birth?"

"Oh, goodness no," said Hyuna. "It was only after the two of them came back to camp. Hur-kar wouldn't allow Mama to spread tales about his son until Setiq was ready."

"In other words, it was since this morning."

"Yes."

She seemed to think the conversation over, and resumed clucking at the baby.

They had a double wedding and a feast to say goodbye.

Ikash could not bring himself to eat heartily, and he noticed he wasn't the only one. There was a pall over this feast. Because of the size of the party that was leaving, nearly everyone in the camp was losing someone.

He could remember a number of weddings before that had also felt awkward. He and Hyuna had been married in the late winter, and that was to avoid having a double wedding with his father and Dira. Hyuna's parents had insisted that their daughter's wedding not be overshadowed just because dangerous, glamorous Endu had to marry his mistress.

Before that, there had been the wedding of Jabed and Magya. Again, a number of things had made it awkward. Endu and Hur, the fathers of the groom and bride, had stood looking daggers at one another, for one thing. Also it had been, at that time, just over a year since the deaths of Sari and of Magya's first husband Ki-Ki, and all of the People were still whirling about in a confusion of grief. But Magya had desperately needed help with her children, and Jabed was mad for her and needed to be headed off before he did something foolish.

And a year before *that* was the wedding of Amal and Jai. Amal had been pregnant. Hur had been, if anything, grimmer than at Magya's wedding. Ikash hadn't realized at the time what a fateful event it was, but it soon became clear because just a day after the feast, Sari had gone into labor and … well. There was little need, at this moment, to go back over the details of all of that.

Now, at this wedding, Ikash finally knew how Hur had felt. Now it was he who was losing a loved one while at the same time desperately hoping things went well for her. And he was losing other loved ones, too. Grandmother Zillah was going. Everyone had been dismayed to hear this, none more so than Ninna. But Zillah calmly pointed out that she had trained both Ninna and Ninshi in all her medical knowledge.

"The last time I left this camp, it was by force," she said. "This time, I am going of my own free will."

And then there was Sha.

Sha, Ikash's younger brother, had been his companion all through their childhood. They had hidden out from their father, wrestled, and hunted together. Sha had been there through the many twists and turns of Ikash's quest to marry Hyuna. The two brothers had gone together to the sulfurous, glassy pool to retrieve their mother's body. Sha was unlike Ikash in build and personality. He didn't have visions. He didn't immediately understand the things that Ikash said, nor did Ikash always understand him. But because of their shared history, the two of them were somehow one person.

So it had brought on a tearing sense of loss when Sha had come to his brother and told him that he intended to go with Klee, to keep her safe from the snake and from their father.

Ikash, who was never quick with his replies, had stood still for a moment to wait for the ripping sensation to subside. It was similar to the way people plant their feet and stand firm when they meet a particularly strong current.

Then he bent his head again over the poles he and Sha were lashing together. They were, at the moment Sha chose to tell him, in the midst of constructing and loading a travois for the party that was preparing to depart. The two of them had always talked best together when working, or playing their instruments, or wrestling, or lying in the tent just before sleep.

Ikash was not completely surprised by Sha's decision. His brother was loyal to family. Nor did he think that presence of Setiq obviated the need for an older male relative to go along and protect Klee. Both of them knew that Setiq was young, inexperienced, and likely to be no match for Endu.

At last, all he said was, "I am going to miss you, brother."

Sha punched him lovingly on the shoulder.

At that moment their father approached them with his curious, commanding, half-hobbling, half-galloping stride. He was bare-chested, as usual in the summer, and was wearing sandals and a knee-length woven skirt with a diamond pattern.

Endu did not have any teenaged boys in his household, which was why his grown sons were helping with his travois.

The work was taking place in the edge of the woods behind Ikash's house because that was where the timber was. This part of the forest was relatively safe. The larger animals had mostly been kept away by the presence of people, and the canopy protected them from the huge predatory birds. The forest was no longer humid and insect-infested, but beginning to be dry. Nuts were ripening and creatures preparing for winter.

Endu inspected their work and pronounced it solid. He cautioned them not to make the travois too heavy. The group would be traveling light. Dira, as a woman, was not a strong puller, and Endu didn't have the strength he once had before his mauling.

Sha straightened up from his labors, tossed back his floppy black hair and told his father that he, too, intended to join the expedition.

Endu was delighted. He beamed. The smile pulled open his gaping nose-holes horribly.

Then he clapped Sha on the shoulder and said how glad he was that a grown son of his was coming along.

"We will build a city together!" he said.

He seemed to grow taller by the moment as his plans found more and more support. He was so happy with himself that he glowed. His smooth hair gleamed blue-black, and his dark skin gave back from the forest's edge the white reflected sunlight.

Then he said, "But what will you do for a wife?"

Ikash had been wondering the same thing. Sha had not had good luck with women … or, rather, he had had trouble finding a woman that he liked. He was twenty-eight and still unmarried. Back in Sinar this might have been normal, but these days it made him stand out. He had had an affair, several years ago now, with Sassa, daughter of Lamek, who was five years older than he was. But things had not worked out for some reason, and she had married someone else soon after that … her marriage brought on, in part, by the truncated affair with Sha.

Ikash's little brother was the sort that older women tended to warm to. Of all of Endu's sons, he was most like his father in build, with a square face and a lean, broad-shouldered figure. He was a little fairer skinned than Endu and a little less handsome than his father had once been, but he had a puppylike appeal that made women want to mother him.

As for the husbands, Sha made them nervous.

From that point of view, it was perhaps good that Sha was going away, though the very words "Sha going away" caused a little stab every time Ikash thought them.

Now Sha smiled, spread out his lanky arms, and laced his fingers together behind his head.

"I have *found* a wife, Father," he said.

This caused a sensation. Endu gave a startled bark of laughter; Ikash, who had been working on the travois, jumped to his feet.

"Who? Who?" they wanted to know.

Sha gave his brother a brief, apologetic glance. He had intended to tell Ikash this part first and alone, but they had been interrupted by their father. "Wana, daughter of Damai."

Wana was what might be called an *interesting choice*. She was twenty-four years old and still living in her parents' home, her three older sisters having married long ago. Her face was pleasant but plain, her build sloping and comfortable rather like Sha and Ikash's mother had been. She was competent, as far as anyone knew, at household tasks, but was shy to the point of being mousy.

And she was the older sister of Watak and Ishak, the two who had assaulted Klee.

The shaman and his father looked at one another, thrown, while Sha grinned at them. Then, after a second of being taken aback, both of them started down very different mental paths.

Ikash was thinking that the more he thought about it, the more Wana seemed like a good choice for Sha. She was unassuming and wouldn't boss or dominate him. She would probably be glad to get out of her household, which was good if marrying Sha was going to mean leaving the People forever. While not beautiful, she was pleasant, healthy and strong. She had the motherly aspect that Sha seemed to like, but she was a little younger.

"You talked to *her* yet?" he said to his brother.

Sha nodded, still grinning. *Oh, yes.*

"She's willing to go with you?"

Yes again.

"Is she sweet?"

Yes, yes, a thousand times yes.

Sha was looking so pleased with himself that Ikash began to wonder if he'd done a little more than talk. The only thing he could think of that would prevent this was the difficulty of getting Wana alone away from her relatives. He could think of a few occasions during his courtship with Hyuna when the two of them might have seduced one another, but circumstances had never allowed it. He did not regret this. Things were better the way they had turned out.

But for Sha, there was one more wrinkle.

"Will it be a problem for Klee? Your wife coming from – *that* family?"

Sha looked a little worried, but then he shrugged. "I don't think so, brother. Wana dislikes her brothers just as much as Klee does."

Meanwhile, Endu was having his own reaction. It was important to his pride that his sons should be able to marry any woman they wanted. He did not like the idea of any of them settling for an "interesting choice." His face had registered disappointment at the same moment that Ikash's had become thoughtful.

But now he only said gently, "Is she really the best you can do?"

"She's the one I want," said Sha, meeting his father's eye steadily.

And that was how they ended up having a double wedding.

Endu's two youngest children by Sari were getting married. And in a day or two, what remained of the family he had had with Sari would be split down the middle. Three of the members would stay; three would go. It was the final step in a process that had begun long ago.

Weddings among the People were light on ceremony, heavy on celebration. The wedding basically consisted of the chief declaring the couple married, binding their wrists together, and then they sat on a blanket, and everyone ate for several days. There was little for the shaman to do. This was lucky for Ikash, because if he had needed to sing or recite anything, he doubted that he could get through it. He sprinkled on a small ceremonial fire (not the large central cookfire) the sweet sage that had now become required. He blessed them silently by putting a hand on their bowed heads: his brother and his brother's wife, and then his sister and his sister's husband. Normally at this moment he would be praying in his heart, but he found he could not form any words, not even mentally, during this particular wedding. His only prayer was a feeling of desperate longing, more like the cry of a baby than like a covenant spoken by a grown man.

He returned to his seat, unable to eat, and later in the celebration he made up for his lack of a voice by playing the lute so others could dance.

Zillah, however, had something to say, and on the first evening of the feast she said it.

"Sixteen years ago I delivered two babies not three months apart from each other."

She stood in front of the seated couples, and as she spoke she reached a hand back toward the blanket that enthroned Klee and Setiq. The gesture was not like that of a chief who presents something to a crowd, but more like the tender gesture of a mother who reaches after her baby as it toddles off into the world. Nevertheless, Zillah did not look pitiful. She had enormous dignity. Standing there, tall, slim and straight, her silver hair flowing down her back, draped shoulder to foot in fine beaded buckskin, she looked as if she were not only older but better than anyone else present.

"Both births were risky in their various ways," Zillah went on. She was not speaking in a dramatic manner, but the whole feast had fallen silent to hear her. "Both babies were nearly lost. It was a dreadful, dark time, and out of that time has come … this. Goodness, life.

"I am grateful," she said, and then took a long pause. It was not easy to make Zillah cry; not everyone had even seen her do it. She mastered herself and went on. "I am grateful that my efforts were not in vain. That is no credit to me, for my efforts frequently *are* in vain. But not this time. I would like to thank God – I have never seen God, but the shamans and the ancestors have told us that there is such a thing, and I believe it. I would like to say thank you to God for these young people."

At this point she turned her body and made a gesture that indicated not only Klee and Setiq, but Sha and Wana as well. "I thank God for these young people, and I thank their fathers and mothers."

There should have been three mothers present, but there were only two. Tiny, golden, cat-faced Lien sat proudly not far from her firstborn son Setiq; and near Wana, square-faced, mountainlike Kini sat looking immovable, older and calmer.

Zillah turned and bowed her head deeply to each of the mothers. Then, still stooping, she looked at Klee and Sha, and said to them in a low voice, "I knew your mother. I will stand in for her."

Both of them nodded thanks to her. Zillah withdrew and the feast went on, but for Sari's children, Zillah's speech had stirred up confusing emotions. Sha bowed his head and shed a few tears, but in another moment he was again making jokes and setting Wana giggling.

Klee stared straight ahead, brow creased, not sure what she ought to be feeling nor indeed what she was feeling. She knew only that a great many important things were happening, all at once and jumbled together. After moving along for years in excruciating boredom, her life had begun with a bang. It was not restful, but then, she had not been looking for rest. What she hadn't expected was this bittersweetness.

"I wish she had not done that," said Setiq out of the corner of his mouth.

"Not done what? Saved us when were babies?"

"Oh no, of course, that. I mean, brought up all these things at this moment and – upset you."

"I suppose," said Klee, "She thought it ought to be done. To honor the dead."

Goodbyes.

Some were demonstrative and others were quiet. Some of the ones leaving were mobbed as if their very touch brought healing; others, like Endu, were certainly not touched and were in fact virtually ignored.

Zillah was nearly invisible behind a crowd of adoring women, children, grandchildren. Sha was mobbed by his nieces and nephews; Klee, by her ten-year-old brother and two younger sisters (who she now knew were her cousins). Doon, Mala, and Lana could not understand why Klee was going away. They had been told it was because she had gotten married; Mala and Lana believed it, but Doon clearly realized there was more going on. Klee wanted to say something that would comfort them, but she couldn't think of anything. So she just patted their heads, all of which were smooth, black, and straight, and smelled like roast meat from the feast the night before.

Kai edged up and stood silently, for a long time, near his sister. But she refused to look at him.

At last he said, sharply, "*Klee!*"

She could not help it; she had to turn her head. And then she blazed at him with her eyes.

"*What!*"

"I've let you down," he said, his chin thrust forward and his lips trembling. "I have said I am sorry through Aki, and now I'll say it again. I am sorry. Please give me your pardon before you go. Please don't be like this, sister."

"I am not your sister, I am your father's sister, and you know it."

"But that's not why things went wrong between us. It was because you and Mother were always fighting, and I … I was selfish. I was wrong to be so harsh with you. I've seen since that one person cannot always stop a fight."

"So, having used your teammates to punish me, you are now ready to forgive me for standing up to your mother's harsh tongue?"

He looked thrown, then taken aback. At last he stammered, "That's – that's not what I said. I said *I* am sorry …"

"It may not be what you said, but it is in fact what you *did*."

"I would never have let them rape you."

"Yet, you did."

Kai's tears were flowing by now. He glared at her through them and said,

"I will always think of you as my sister."

"You may please yourself."

She turned and started to walk away, resentful of the guilt she felt.

Behind her, she heard him say, "Remember how we used to play …"

Klee walked faster. She was definitely not going to remember.

She went and called Guide, who was running about madly with the other dogs as dogs will do whenever people have a large event. She sank down beside a travois where she thought no one would see her and put her arms around the dog's middle. He wanted to run, and began scrabbling with his back toenails, but Klee said, "I just want you for a moment, Guide," and he quieted, and she buried her face in his skinny, mangy side. She was not crying exactly, but she was feeling shaky.

Guide gave up and plopped his haunches down onto her lap.

A moment later, a tall thin shadow fell across her. She looked, and there was Jai, towering over her.

"You have not said goodbye to your mother," he said, and frowned.

Klee let go of Guide and gave his rump a light smack. As he bounded off, she stood and brushed off her skirt, collecting her dignity.

"No, you are right, brother," she said coolly. "My mother died when I was a baby. I never got to say goodbye."

He waved a hand in frustration. "You know what I mean. You have been avoiding my wife. You may not like the way she did it, but she worked hard to raise you. She cared for you when you were a baby. You have a duty to go and bid her goodbye."

Jai was perhaps not aware of it, but his face, like his son's, was wet. Seeing all these crying people made Klee all the more eager to get away from this settlement and its stifling, confusing displays of emotion.

"Yes, brother," she said.

She stalked off and found Amal and stood stiffly, nearly shaking with disgust, while her stepmother wept and embraced her.

Meanwhile, Setiq was having a much less awkward farewell with the woman who had raised him. Lien reached up and put her slim, dark-gold hands on her son's shoulders.

"We were afraid you would leave the womb too early." Her surprisingly rich voice was gravelly with emotion. "Grandmother Zillah made me stay in bed … she cared for me … and at last we persuaded you to stay put. For a little while. But now, here you go, slipping away again."

Setiq grinned the triangular grin that he had inherited from her.

"I stayed around a long while, Mother."

"Yes, and I am so grateful. We got to see you grow into a young man. And now you are doing what young men do: they don't stay put. They go off into the world."

She embraced him, resting her head on his chest. He was wearing on his golden torso a vest made of hide that had been cured to exactly the same color.

"Perhaps we will come and visit all of you," he said. "After we have built a city."

"Perhaps," said Lien.

And then there was Sha.

Wana, who like Klee could hardly wait to leave the People, sat patiently on the edge of a small, loaded travois watching with a fond smile while her husband went bounding back and forth around the chaotic, bright, windy scene of farewells that surrounded the now-dead central fire. He had carved small amulets for a great number of people, and he was handing them out to each personally. Sha was one of those people who got to know everyone.

At last he came to Ikash. His brother only stared at him, which was typical, but Sha sensed that this time, the reason wasn't that the shaman wished to think before he spoke, but rather that he was actually unable to speak. To distract him, Sha gave him his amulet. It was a human figure hanging by the head from a leather thong.

"It's me. So you can remember me," said Sha.

His brother looked at the amulet. It had a straight, skinny body topped by a pair of large, wide-set eyes in a huge blocky head. The ears were slightly protruding.

Ikash started to laugh. "This isn't what you look like, brother!"

"It's how I see myself," said Sha. "Besides, this way you can feel for the eyes whenever it's dark and you want to talk to me. See?"

He guided the pad of his brother's thumb to the figure's face and, sure enough, the eyes were detectable.

"What's this?" said Ikash. He was stroking, and then peering at, an incised image on the front of the figure. One arm was folded across the chest, the fist grasping a winding shape. "It looks like you are holding a snake."

"I am meant to be holding it out at arm's length," said Sha, "But the arm would have broken off if I'd tried to carve it that way. You have to use your imagination."

Ikash put the necklace over his head, blinking rapidly.

Sha reached back into his carving pouch and pulled out a nearly identical necklace.

"And *I*," he said, "Will carry *you*."

He dangled the companion necklace before the shaman's face. It was a carving of Ikash. Like the one of Sha, it was exaggerated: it had a small round head on a smoothly sloping body, sitting cross-legged, palms open on the knees, meditating. But the eyes were open and staring. A bumpy line, representing a braid, ran down the middle of the back.

Ikash laughed again. "You've certainly captured my likeness, brother!"

"I couldn't get him to look quite stupid enough," said Sha. He put it over his own head.

"I notice you haven't given us any weapons."

"Our weapons are not of that kind."

"I notice – "

"*I* notice that *you* haven't thanked me."

"Thank you," said the shaman in a very tight voice.

Then he tried to speak again:

"Brother – "

Then he bowed his head and couldn't speak at all. And Sha could not speak either.

It was a terrible moment. The worst.

Finally Sha, who was slightly taller than Ikash, threw his right arm around his brother's neck, almost as if to put him in a headlock. He leaned his cheekbone against his brother's forehead. He stood there for a time like that, feeling the hand that was dangling in front of Ikash's face getting wetter and wetter.

CHAPTER EIGHT
THOSE THAT STAYED

Those that stayed stood and watched those who were departing. They needed, for some reason, to keep looking until the departing party became invisible in the yellow distance.

Twenty-eight people were leaving: nineteen adults and nine children. All ages were represented from one-year-old babies to Grandmother Zillah, who at 105 had been the eldest in the village by far. The party leaving was a large enough slice of the People that everyone watching them go was in the process of losing someone.

The unflappable elder Dusun was losing his daughter Dira and the four grandchildren she had given him by Endu. He was also losing Zedho and Tiwik, two of his teenaged sons. They were going along ostensibly to look after their older sister, but actually for the adventure. That was betrayed in every line of their bodies as they bounded gleefully off into the late-summer day along with the other young men who had agreed to lend their strength to Endu's party: Apik, Kor and Yanab, three of Melek's sons;

twenty-year-old Eyli, who was Magya's son by her first husband Ki-Ki; and Hyuna's little brother, all grown up now, eighteen-year-old Dani, son of Ninna and Hur.

There were a few young families going: Peres, his wife Ispet, and their three children; and Megal, his wife Rini, and their two. Both the husbands were sons of Enmer, the former chief who had died, and both the wives were daughters of Rumi, and thus were sisters. According to the tribe's kinship system, Endu, as Enmer's younger brother, was a "father" to Peres and Megal, and so they felt an obligation to follow him as their father, though the relationship was not particularly good.

Ikash was going to miss Megal. He was a dark, quiet, intense young man who had lost his father around age fourteen, about the same age that Ikash had lost his mother. And he was a close cousin: the son of a father's brother and therefore counted as a brother. Ikash had trained him in some basic rituals, and though Megal had never particularly opened up to the shaman (rightly blaming him and his family for Enmer's death), the shaman felt as if Megal's very standoffishness formed a sort of connection between them.

And, of course, there were the two young couples. Sha and Wana; Setiq and Klee.

The People had been through tragic losses before. Hur and Endu's generation had lost an entire world and with it a world's worth of people. But that had been forty-four years ago, and though by the nature of the world there had necessarily been plenty of tragedies in the meantime, no one of Ikash's generation had ever experienced loss on this scale.

But this was not really a loss exactly. Those who departed were not dead. Those who stayed supposed they would still be able to talk about them without the danger of invoking a ghost. They did not know how to handle this. They did not know how to behave. At least, the adults did not; they stood there and listened to their children crying.

By the time the party that had left was well out of sight, heading south and west, the light was ripening. Those that had stayed felt really at a loss. All of a sudden they had nothing to look at, and it seemed there was nothing to do. They removed their eyes from the horizon and began wandering around aimlessly. They supposed it was nearly time for a meal, but no one felt hungry.

Rumi said, "I suppose we cannot call ourselves the People anymore," and his wife Cara began crying and Hur said, "We will call ourselves the Deer People, perhaps, because that is my family's totem. And they will be the Snake People. We'll know one another again if we meet. There cannot be two groups calling themselves the Snake People, surely."

Eventually they bestirred themselves, because the children were hungry. They reheated food from last night's feast. It was subdued group of families that went to bed that night.

Beginning the next day, Hur and the elders initiated a series of complex projects to keep the grievers busy. This was exactly what the (remaining) People needed: rather than moping off to their usual, now strangely empty chores, they needed someone to say, "Come on, everybody, let's do this!"

One project involved building. Several entire families had vanished into the blue. Hur wanted their houses remodeled, repurposed, and in some cases disassembled rather than standing as reminders that would become sad and, in time, spooky. He led parties into the forest to cut timber. Autumn was a good time to cut it; the sap had stopped running and the trunks were lighter and easier to handle. It would be stacked in the main hall of Endu's house, which had been left intact, and kept warm and dry over the winter, ready to be used as needed come spring. There would be time during the winter months for craftsmen to work on the baking wood: take the bark off it, carve it if they got an idea for a memorial pole. Sha was no longer with them, but he had trained a few other carvers who were eager to try their skill.

Hur also led a series of hunts. Hunting had always been the way he healed his own heart (this dated back to before the long-ago exile). And these people, your people, who worked outdoors all day and had trained their bodies to eat game, could put away a *lot* of meat. They did not feel satisfied by a meal unless it had featured some animal as the main course. Even when grieving, it took plenty of meat to keep them going.

Predators were off limits for the Peoples' consumption. So was anything that looked too human, like the Older Brothers. Everything else was fair game. They liked turtle, river fish, any one of that country's variety of large birds except the bird that resembled a dragon. But they liked elephant most of all, having developed a taste for it during their years on the mammoth plain. It was now too early for snow and thus too early to hunt mammoth, but Hur led some hunts southward into the forest in search of the smaller, more solitary mammoth-like creatures, the mastodon.

Ikash went along on some of these hunts. He had good memories of months-long scouting trips taken in his youth, trips when he could get away from his usual surroundings, spend some time with other boys his age, and be taught history by the elders and meditation by Ki-Ki. Now he was one of the older hunters and was in a position to teach the young teens who came along, however ill-equipped he might feel for it. He did not know who else might want to become a shaman, since they had lost Klee (who had seemed a little interested) and Megal. There was no particular reason to start training someone else right away. Still, he had a feeling that he ought to.

If ever their hunt took them near the possible path of the party that had left, they all found themselves scanning the horizon more than usual and filtering the sounds they heard not just for hints of predators but for human voices. But they saw and heard no human being.

It was strange knowing that they were not the only People any more. It made the world seem bigger, as if it had more than one center.

Hur noticed on the hunts that Ikash was not eating much. He had vowed to fast, but he did not even need to make himself fast. He just couldn't get much down. Hur started setting choice cuts in front of his son-in-law, quietly, so as not to show favoritism. He would place a hand upon his shoulder, saying, "Eat, son."

But instead of causing the younger man's face to bloom like a flower, this produced only a slight flinch as the hand made contact. Otherwise, whether he was working or resting, the shaman would continue with his silent, inward stare. Ikash had always been the type to get lost in his thoughts, but Hur could tell the difference between different kinds of thoughtfulness. He could tell that his son-in-law was not happy.

He tried talking to him. He told him how it had been when his own daughters got married, particularly when it was to men about whom he had doubts.

Ikash agreed. "Now I know a bit of what it feels like to be a father who marries off his daughter. A bit, mind,

Father," he added humbly. "I'm not claiming to have your knowledge."

"You have told us that God is a father," the chief reminded him. "You must ask God to take care of her."

"I have. But what if she has stepped outside of God?"

"Can we even do that?" said Hur.

But then he immediately realized that people could and that he had seen them do it. Enmer, one of Hur's best friends, had removed himself from God for a long time and then eventually come back. Endu had stepped outside of God long ago.

"Grandmother Zillah is with them," he pointed out lamely.

Again, Ikash agreed.

"I know, father, and that's a good thing. It's the not knowing that is hard, isn't it?"

"It is," said Hur, who had had his own grave doubts about the departure of his son Dani. "But be careful you don't stare so hard into the distance that you miss what is right beneath your nose."

Winter came. Winter was not nearly so harsh down here in the land God had given them as it had been up on the mammoth plain, but it was still an uncomfortable and dangerous time, a time when the risk was greater for everything from sickness to insanity. The people, no longer the People now, hunkered down in their homes, burning the wood they had collected. Many activities that were routine during the rest of the year, such as bathing and washing clothes, stopped or slowed. The objective, with winter, was to get the children through it warm and alive. Nearly everything else could wait.

Ikash spent a lot of time playing his lute and singing in a smoke-scratchy voice for Dumish and Sira. The baby, whom they had named Ashar in honor of Sha, grew bigger and started sleeping longer at night. Whenever the weather did not prohibit it, Hyuna brought the children to visit Hur and Ninna. If Ikash ever accompanied them on these excursions, Ninna always commented on how skinny he was.

Indeed, he had continued to lose weight. He was becoming chiseled, and this was not a good thing. Ikash had always been rounded: never fat, for the people's lifestyle did not allow that, but smooth and sleek. Like Jabed, he was not the sort of man whose bones and muscles you were meant to see. Now, on those rare occasions when he was not swathed in furs, his structure stood out, a visible sign of his grief.

Not that he monitored his own body. He was not particularly aware of changing in any way; or, indeed, of doing anything at all. Sadness pressed down on him gently, making things like breathing and thinking seem like too much effort. He was in some ways still trapped in that sense of paralysis that came at the very beginning of a disaster. It had been too much at once, losing Megal, Dani, Zillah, Klee, and above all Sha.

He was barely aware of time passing. Only the people around him, and particularly Hyuna, noticed and worried through their own grief.

Solstice came, and the people had their usual ceremony. Ikash stood before the fire as he had planned to do, with Hyuna beside him, to show the baby to his mother. Hyuna handed him little Ashar, who was now five months old. Ikash felt his arms trembling as he held the child securely and raised him over his head. Before he could say anything, his legs began slowly to buckle. Hyuna realized what was happening and caught Ashar just before he tumbled from his father's hands. Hur rushed forward and pulled Ikash back from the fire. The young man was awake, but he couldn't respond when the chief spoke to him. He was sweaty and shaking with chills and fever.

He collapsed on that night and afterward was sick for a long time.

Ninna had taken on the role of tribal healer when Zillah left, after having worked side by side with her mother for many years. She was not the only woman who knew how to practice medicine. Nearly every woman had some experience in midwifery, and several others had helped Zillah gather and prepare her herbs. The way things had developed, it was generally the women who took care of the physical side of illness: bathing the patients, setting bones, making teas. The men took care of the spiritual side. Ninna was old enough to remember when this had involved animal sacrifice, but these days the shaman's main method was to pray for the sick person and blow smoke on them. Of course, in this case it was the shaman who was ill.

Zillah had always seemed able to keep a clear head and do what was needful, however emotionally involved she might be with her patient. Many times it had been her own child or grandchild for whom she kept vigil or even did surgery. This was natural, since Zillah was matriarch to nearly all the tribe. Yet the more poignant the situation, the cooler Zillah seemed to become. Perhaps she fell apart afterward, but Ninna had never witnessed it.

Ninna was not as good at hardening her heart. She found she felt really frantic about Ikash. She had felt motherly towards the boy ever since he became interested in her daughter Hyuna. In the early days of the couple's marriage she had gone out of her way to spoil him, and she had seen the fruits of her labor. The shaman had flourished. But now, now that he and Hyuna had children together and the stakes were even higher, Ninna felt helpless in the face of his decline.

A fever always made a healer feel powerless. It seemed so arbitrary whether the fever would eventually dissipate and allow the victim to live, or whether it would stay, and kill. Normally the sufferer had to be watched day and night, given water, given willow bark to chew or tincture of goldenrod to drink for the fever. The fire had to be maintained in the patient's house; they had to be covered when chilled, and, when they became dangerously hot, they must have their chest and forehead bathed with snow.

Ninna did not have time to do all this, much as she wanted to. She and Hur were dealing with another crisis.

The departure of Klee had finally put unbearable strain on the marriage of Jai and Amal. Jai grieved wildly for his sister and blamed his wife for driving her away. Amal, who had hoped that with Klee's departure she would finally get her husband back, reacted predictably. Their fights had turned explosive, then unendurable, and then Jai had removed himself and was now living in one of the smaller rooms of the empty house formerly occupied by his father.

Hur and Ninna, as the in-laws, were the ones who bore the weight of all this. Hur tried to talk to his son-in-law, and he got an earful. But he couldn't talk him out of his bitterness. Jai just needed time, Hur thought, but he was not sure how much. Maybe he would need forever. Meanwhile, Jai continued to go on hunts, and he would wordlessly leave meat before the door for his wife and children. He enjoyed being outside with the other men, but he would not hear any of the advice they tried to give him.

Ninna, meanwhile, was living temporarily with her daughter and grandchildren, trying to calm the little ones and to help Amal manage the daily tasks of which she barely felt capable. Amal, too, seemed to have an inexhaustible well of bitterness that could not be cured by listening to her speak. With all this, Ninna had nothing left to give the ones who needed her but who were not bitter, namely Hyuna and her husband. They needed someone who was not already run ragged, who had a cooler head and heart than Ninna's.

Ninna asked for help from the widow of the former chief: her sister-in-law Ninshi.

Ninshi was yet another member of the tribe who had once spent several years unable to function. After her husband Enmer was killed by the same bear that mauled Endu, Ninshi had simply collapsed. She had always keenly felt the tasks and tragedies of daily life, but with Enmer's death, she stopped doing anything at all. She'd been pregnant at the time – a late, surprise baby – and as Ninna recalled, that child had virtually been raised by his older sister Koret. In the years since, Ninshi had begun to stir again, a little at a time, in such a way that most people still did not expect much contribution from her. To this day, she had plenty of time on her hands. She also had medicinal skills picked up from years of shadowing Zillah.

She was also a chronic worrier, which Ninna thought made her the perfect person to take care of Ikash's fever. Ninshi was certain to worry just as much as Ninna herself.

So Ninshi began spending her days and nights in the shaman's hut. The children tiptoed around her and their sick father. "Aunt Ninshi" was a fearsome presence to them, and she did nothing to soften this impression. She had a thin, hooked nose and a naturally severe face, and she was too tired and grieved to bother with soothing any children. And she was too focused on caring for their father.

Ninshi did not know Ikash well at all. She had never particularly cared for him, especially after her husband was killed by a bear that had been attacking him and his stupid father. She began caring for him as a favor to Ninna. But as often happens with nursing, she began to feel invested in the well-being of her patient. She felt dismayed when he was too delirious to speak to her, excited and relieved whenever he rallied. And in these clear moments, she began to find that he reminded her of her dead son Ki-Ki. They looked nothing alike, and their personalities were different too, yet there was a certain resemblance, perhaps because they had both been shamans. She sensed something of Ki-Ki's sweet spirit in this young man.

The fonder she grew of her patient, the more sharply she tended to keep his children away from him. Hyuna did her best to keep them out of the way of the old woman, but finally the children ended up spending their days – and many nights too – in the home of their grandfather Hur.

For Ikash, the two months that he was sick seemed like an extended, unpleasant version of a walk in the spirit world. He had vivid fever-dreams in which the air always seemed too harsh, the sun too bright. These dreams seemed ominous and significant at the time, but afterward they dissolved into pieces, and he could remember nothing coherent except that they had featured his sister and snakes.

Whenever he woke, he tossed uncomfortably, too weak to get up but unable to lie for long in any position because all his bones seemed to have grown sharp, knobbly edges beneath the skin.

Eventually he began to have entire days with no fever. During this time he realized that the person caring for him had not been Grandmother Zillah. He began to recognize Ninshi. He asked about Hyuna, and she came and hung over him but looked so sad that he told her to go away again. He was so lonely; he wished for Sha to keep him company. Sha was gone, Sha was going away.

Sha, he suddenly remembered, ought to be hanging around his neck.

The necklace was gone, and he began to panic and yell for it.

Ninshi came shuffling over, dark hair pulled back in a bun, face severe in the dim indoor light. Ikash tried to calm himself and state simply what he wanted, but Ninshi couldn't understand what he was trying to tell her. She thought he was raving.

He slept, and woke crying, saying, "I've lost Sha, I've lost him."

At length his wife appeared and, bless her, understood immediately. She remembered that the necklace existed and what had been done with it. It seemed they had taken it off him very early on so that he wouldn't strangle himself with his tossing.

Hyuna hung the necklace from the bunk frame where Ikash could see it outlined against the light. It spun slowly. He tried to watch it so as to determine when the eyes were facing him and when they were looking away. But following the movement made him feel dizzy, and he had to close his eyes. He remembered that his own eyes were open, far away, on Sha's companion necklace.

The fever came back at night, so it was not safe for anyone to come near him.

Then the fever stopped coming back at night and then he was *really* lonely. He was too weak to get up and see anyone. Mut and Jabed came to visit. It turned out they had been there before, back when he was unable to recognize them, and had blown smoke on him for his recovery.

Sha might be gone, but Mut and Jabed were there, and they were his good friends.

Ikash asked if he could have his dog with him at least. Frost had whined through the days and slept by his bed-platform at night, but Ninshi hadn't allowed the old, white-faced female up onto the platform for fear that she might bring sickness to the rest of the camp. Now that Ikash's fever had broken, his aunt helped him up and bathed him. He stood throughout the process, goosebumps rising on his skin from the lukewarm water, legs shaking madly with weakness, gripping with one hand the pole that ran right to the roof and was part of the bedframe. That was his exertion for the day.

She burned the bedding from the platform where he had lain ill and made a new bed, a nest, near the family's central fire. Then Frost was able to come and snuggle up to him, and Ikash began the long process of regaining his strength, resting his head on the dog for comfort just as he had done when he was little.

"Ki-Ki gave her to me," he said gratefully to Ninshi.

His aunt looked surprised and pleased. "I didn't know that."

The tiny figure of Sha was back to hanging around Ikash's neck. He examined it minutely during the middle of the day when sunlight came directly down through the smoke hole. He was almost certain that the snake in his brother's hands had been facing the other way before. He hoped it was just an effect of the fever, or of faulty memory, but something told him it wasn't. The snake carving had turned during the winter months. He hoped this didn't mean anything bad for Sha.

CHAPTER NINE
THE STRONG ONE

Endu caught a glimpse of his son's back as he stood silhouetted by the vast glow spread out across the southern part of the sky. He looked fine as far as Endu could see. He was standing very still. Endu figured he must have gone into one of his trances.

After the relief, he felt anger rise in him. It was for this, then, that the whole tribe had been set astir, that Endu had been practically accused of murder in front everyone.

He called out sharply, "Hey!"

Ikash shook himself and turned around.

He was unaware that his face was glowing.

The glow shocked and panicked Endu. He continued walking toward his son, but it was as if the world was tipping under him.

"Stop that!" he said. He put his hands up in front of his face to shield himself from the light.

Ikash looked confused. Meanwhile, his face shone brighter than ever. Endu could hardly see his son's features. He could hardly stand to look at it.

"Stop that, now!" he said again. "What the hell do you think you're doing? Who do you think you are?"

He grabbed Ikash's shoulders. He raised a hand to wipe the glow from the boy's face. The wipe became a slap.

Ikash thought his father was trying to kill him. His first reaction was defensive – thrusting outward with his arms to free himself from his father's hands – but when Endu slapped him again, a giant wave of rage rose up within him. He flew at his father, no rules at all, ready to punch, kick, bite, do whatever it took to stop him, to get a bit of his own back.

They punched and grappled. They head-butted one another in the stomach and dodged at the last moment. They threw one another like wrestlers and got back up again. Inevitably, someone threw someone else from the brow of the hill (each was later sure that he had thrown the other), and they ended up locked together, scratching and gouging, rolling down to the stream and the saplings at the bottom, where it was now almost completely dark.

Physical reality won in the end. Ikash had not got his full man's strength yet, despite that he had the advantage of being momentarily crazy. Endu was taller, long-armed, and had been a warrior since his youth. He finally subdued the boy, sitting on top of him, forearm across his neck in the old familiar way.

He didn't think he was pushing that hard, but suddenly Ikash went limp and to his horror, Endu saw the boy's eyes roll back in his head. That was when he realized that it was his own son he was pinning, possibly killing, and that the light in the boy's face had gone out.

Hyuna woke from a bad dream. It was the same dream as usual: her father-in-law trying to harm Ikash, or Hyuna herself, or their children, in some way. This had never actually happened, in waking life, since Hyuna married Ikash. It wasn't until they had married that she had discovered the extent of Endu's bouts of brutality when his children were at home. Then she had come to hate Endu. But she was unable to do anything about him. Her father-in-law had tried hard, for a season, to charm her, but when he saw that she would not be swayed, he gave up and left her alone, though she had always felt a vague sense of threat.

Her husband's recent illness had taken a toll on her. In her mind, it was yet another curse brought down upon them by his father.

It had long been Hyuna's fantasy that Endu would simply vanish from the life of his son. And now he had … but he had done so in such as a way as to cause heartbreak, taking with him several other people whom Ikash loved. She felt that she should have had the sense to foresee this. It was yet another example of Endu's special genius at doing everything in the most destructive way possible.

All of this finally came to a head in one of those dreams so vivid that even after waking, they make you doubt yourself. She dreamt that she and Ikash were somewhere – she did not know where – somewhere rocky – and something rather confused happened, but it was obvious throughout that Endu intended to kill Ikash. He struck him down with a rock. Hyuna was pregnant, by the way, in the dream, more pregnant than she ever had been, barely able to balance even with her feet planted. But she stood over her husband's body and had not a doubt that she would be able to defend him from her father-in-law, for she was filled with a rage purer and stronger than anything she had ever felt in waking life. But then both men had vanished, and the all-consuming rage was replaced by an equally all-consuming grief. And then she was awake, confused, partly realizing that it had only been a dream and partly feeling that she could easily spend the next ten years crying.

She rose to her hands and knees, crawled, and checked on the children, asleep farther along the platform only a few feet from her. The two older children were fine. The baby slumbered in a sling suspended from the rafters.

Ikash was gone.

She remembered then that he had never come to bed in the first place. She had retired early, worn out and annoyed, and left him sitting up beside the stone basin of coals which they kept burning to keep the chill away. In the past few weeks, spring had begun to come and Ikash had continued to recover. Ninshi was no longer needed in their house day and night, and began making just one or two daily visits. The children had moved back into their family home, though Hyuna still tried to keep them from tiring their father.

She crept down to the center of the house. He had fallen asleep on the floor beside the basin, bare-chested, on his back as usual. He didn't look as smooth and sweet and innocent as he used to do. He looked haggard. His ribs were clearly visible.

She had only meant to check, but his eyes popped open and he levered himself to a sitting position, and then she was caught out. She was forced to explain about her dream and how she hadn't meant to wake him.

Ikash assured her that he was fine, and then predictably said, "It was only a dream."

"It was *not!*" she hissed. "*He* is the one who has caused all of this."

"It was many things – "

"*No!*" she cried. She tried to keep her voice down, but couldn't stifle the passion. "It was *not!* It was all started by him. Klee is angry because she was raised by Jai. Well, that would not have been necessary if your mother had not died. *His fault.* Sha has gone. That is because he had to go with Klee. That is because nobody trusts your father around her. And that is also why we have lost Grandmother Zillah. Everyone else has made their choices to accommodate – *him!* And now, even though he is gone, because of him *you are dying*! You are dying, husband! And he does not realize that he has killed you! All he has ever done is torment you and take from you."

Even as she said all this, she knew that she was breaking her own rule. Usually, complaining about Endu was no more than a selfish move on her part. It vented her feelings but brought no benefit to her husband. It put him in the impossible position of either having to defend Endu, or to face the fact that his father was little better than a murderer. Furthermore, she was aware that not everything she said was even strictly true. Ikash's father had never actually tried to kill him. There was that one time, just before the bear attack, but that had been (he would no doubt say) a case of panic, not of murder. And no parent gives their child *nothing*. Endu had given his sons life, basic food and shelter, and so forth. If he had really been a killer, Ikash would never have grown big enough to catch Hyuna's attention.

She knew all this, but she couldn't stop. She felt as if she had been forced to wear a gag for a long time, not allowed to say even the most obvious things about her father-in-law. And now she had said them and however unreasonable they might be, she knew that they were true, they were true.

Her husband had been looking at her steadily. Now he propped his elbows on his knees, and proceeded to say the worst possible thing he could have said: "Wife, I do not want you to be consumed by hate."

This comment – horribly insightful – destroyed the tiny amount of self-control that Hyuna had managed to scrape together. She found herself weeping.

"Yet, I *am!*" she spat. "I *hate* him! I hate him! You see, he has ruined me too."

While she wept, Ikash made a little sound of dismay.

He said, "Do you really think he has *ruined* me?"

Now it was Hyuna's turn for dismay. "Oh, no, I didn't mean that, husband …"

"I think you did. Tell me, now. Have you always thought of me as some sort of cripple?"

"*You?* Oh God, no, no … that is *not* what I meant."

"What then did you mean, 'He has ruined me *too*?'"

"He ruins every *situation*. He keeps causing us grief. You are good, husband, you are not a cripple in that way, but it's your goodness that allows him to keep hurting you. I thought things would be different if he was gone, but yet, here you are, because of a city he wants to build, you began by refusing to eat …"

She could not stop her mouth from running at all. It was really ridiculous.

"All right," said Ikash as she began crying again. "All right. I understand."

He scooted forward, moved his legs out of the way, and took her in his arms.

Hyuna gave up. She melted. For months she had pretended to be the strong one, because she had to, because he was barely hanging on to life. Now he was acting as if, at least for the moment, he was ready to be strong again. She wasn't sure this would last, but oh …! If only it would!

And, at least for the moment, she was going to let him be strong.

Ikash's little Sha-amulet was hanging down over his bony breastbone. He pushed it aside, over one shoulder, and Hyuna rested her head on him. He threaded his hand, as he had always liked to do, through her hair.

"So," he said after a while, "You think I am dying?"

I did, she thought. *Now I am not sure.*

"Because I am not eating well? Because I have been ill?"

Again, there was nothing she could say.

"You are afraid to ask me for anything, because you believe me fragile? You are afraid to speak of it?"

I have been the strong one, she thought, but she would not say it. She must have hurt his pride already. There was no need to offer it a direct challenge.

"Listen," he said. "I'm going to eat, all right? I'm going to get better."

Hyuna could tell from this brisker tone that he was not going to dwell on any implied insult. And this emboldened her to ask an even harder question:

"Are you sure you really want to?"

He released her and sat back.

"What? What do you mean? Of course. Of course I do, Hyuna."

"You are not going to … you have not … given up?"

He started to answer, then stopped and winced. Closed his eyes. She had hurt him, but this time she wasn't sure how. Then he opened his eyes and said, "This isn't like that. It is only a fever. It is only grief."

It is only grief.

That could have been the story of the People.

She said, "Do you promise?"

"I promise."

To her huge relief, when she climbed back up to the sleeping platform, Ikash followed. It was almost as if the last few months had never happened.

"I've missed you so much," she said. "Oh, God … look at your ribs."

Then, almost immediately, she slept.

And almost immediately after that, he was waking her. No, wait. It was much later. The moon had gone down. It must have been a few hours. She was still exhausted, though. She snorted and rolled her eyes in disbelief at being waked.

Hyuna was tired and sad and thus not particularly eager to make love, but she went along with it gamely because this was obviously something he needed. When a sick man is feeling better again you don't deny him if you can help it. And Ikash was apparently feeling better.

As often happened, when things had moved along a bit she wondered why she had been so reluctant.

Once he got in place on top of her, he whispered, "Am I squishing you?" and she said, "No. Well … a little," and he sought to move into a more comfortable position, but by then it was too late.

Things ended with both of them laughing, and then Ikash said,

"I've missed you, too."

He got stronger.

Dumish, who had been waiting all winter to play in the snow with his father, coaxed Ikash outside and plastered him with melting slush, laughing hysterically.

Dumish seemed unable merely to throw a snowball. He led up to it with a series of complicated moves, and then, having hit the target, did a victory dance. The boy was a natural dancer; Ikash had noticed this before now. Dumish was up and moving in time whenever there was music, and often when there was not as well. He was built exactly like his father, but had the opposite instincts. Whenever there was beauty, Ikash liked to sit still and let it sink in. Dumish would be up and celebrating it.

Was I like this at his age? the shaman wondered. He thought not. He had done a lot of wrestling with his brothers. That was finished now, but he had something just as good: this wiggling, dancing little boy.

Then another slushball hit his face and reflection was over.

As soon as he was strong enough to walk around and visit relatives, Ikash went to see his brother.

This required going to his father's old house, because that was where Jai was staying. Ikash had been inside

Endu's house plenty of times during the four years since the founding of the village, but it had by no means become a second home to him. He had never felt he understood the inner workings of the family his father had built with young Dira, who was only a year older than Ikash himself. All he knew about their family was that it felt different. Different from the one he had grown up in. And so the house had never been exactly homelike.

But now, it was completely alien.

Endu's house was a cavernous rectangle. The door, set in the middle, gave on to a great central hall. On either end of this were smaller rooms where the family slept. This time, when Ikash entered the central hall, he found it completely filled with the dark, fragrant bulk of drying wood planks. The planks were stacked in hollow boxes with aisles in between. They rose nearly to the ceiling and gave the place a completely different feel. One's view was blocked, making the place seem even bigger.

Frost was at his side. She scrabbled her toenails on the wooden floor and then began to sniff around, cautiously, as if in a new place. Ikash put a calming hand on her back and muttered a command to stay with him.

He called out for his brother.

Instead of echoing, the words seemed to be eaten by the stacked wood.

It was evening and Ikash had it on good authority that Jai was here, bedding down for the night. He must be in one of the side rooms. Ikash picked an aisle at random and began advancing towards the side of the house where Endu had usually slept. He almost felt as if he ought to have a weapon with him, as if he was stepping into an ambush. That, of course, was ridiculous.

He came into sight of the end of the aisle. There he could see the wall, and the door to Endu's old bedroom. Jai was sitting with his back against the doorframe. He had a stone fire-basin on the floor in front of him, and he was warming his feet at the fire. His big skinny brown dog lay at his side. The fire cast a long shadow from Jai's sharp nose and lit up a section of the wall around him.

A few steps from the end of the aisle, the firelight fell on Ikash and Frost. Jai squinted, said sharply, "Father? Is that you?" and scrambled to his feet.

"It's me, brother."

"Oh, God," said Jai, visibly relieved. "Of course. It's Ikash." He invited his brother to sit down. Then he apologized for his mistake. "I thought for a second you were his ghost. You looked so much like him."

"I don't look like Father."

"You do, though, now that you've gotten so skinny. I thought you might be his spirit."

"I'm not, but thanks for the compliment."

"I'm sorry I don't have anything to offer you," said Jai. "I don't keep food in this house generally. I had supper at the central fire."

"I thought that might be the case, and I brought something."

Ikash had with him a small satchel containing cakes that his wife had made using cornmeal, cattail-root starch, and last year's dried berries. He brought them out and shared them with his brother, his brother's dog, and his own dog.

He noted with surprise that this brought tears to Jai's eyes, but he didn't say anything. He too had been brought to tears, once upon a time, by the simple fact of someone cooking something special for him.

They sat in silence for a long time. Ikash kept waiting for Jai to speak, but he didn't. He seemed too preoccupied to wish his younger brother a good recovery, if indeed he was even aware that his brother had been sick.

At last the shaman said, "How do you like this house, brother?"

Jai had a small, narrow face topped with his father's long almond-shaped eyes. He now turned the face toward his brother and those eyes gave out their trademark flat stare that might have been hostile or incredulous.

"No, of *course* I don't like this house. This isn't a house at all. It's a goddam warehouse. I am living here because I can't live in my own house any more. I am homeless. *That's* how I like it."

He snorted.

Ikash drew a breath, but his brother wasn't finished.

"And I am living here because, as I think you know, I was kicked out of my *own* house by your wife's sister and her goddam family. I've been replaced by my mother-in-law. *That's* how things are going. And you know what the chief is like, you know the way he is about his daughters. I doubt he'd let me back into that house if I wanted to."

"Do you want to?"

"Yes." The syllable was bitter, but it nearly broke at the end.

"Tell me more," said the shaman.

Jai spoke for several minutes about his wife. He was clearly angry with her, mostly for being so angry with him. He was also very lonely. Endu's house was spooky and unhappy, a far worse place to sleep than sleeping outdoors during a hunt.

Ikash nodded. He had felt the menace as he was walking through the drying wood stacks. He did not wonder that his brother had expected to see a ghost. Jai had the dog with him, that was the saving grace, but even he didn't want to live here forever.

Ikash said, "What if you were to reconcile with my wife's older sister?"

Jai stopped dead in his ranting and his long dark eyes looked sideways.

"Is that even possible?"

"Perhaps," said the shaman. He had not spoken with Amal and knew little about her mental state.

"She insists that I not blame her for our sister leaving. But I have to. She mistreated Klee horribly. I didn't think it meant so much at the time – she never beat her – but I was wrong. Girls are more sensitive, brother. All it takes to drive them away is words. Now I can't believe that I let

Amal turn her against me. I wish I had put a stop to it at once."

"How would you have done that, brother?"

"I … don't know."

Silence descended as both brothers slowly realized that if Jai *had* tried to put a stop to it, it would only have brought on this very situation several years earlier.

"I've been a terrible father," said Jai.

"You are not finished being a father."

"To Klee."

"You gave her a home, kept her fed and clothed, kept her alive as she grew. Now she is grown and gone. Married. As she would have done in any case."

"That is true, brother."

"Do you remember when we were young and we wanted to get out and explore?"

Jai got a fierce, faraway look and said nothing. After a moment he said, "Are you saying that I haven't failed her?"

"Perhaps not as completely as she thinks."

"But she hates Amal and me."

"But she is alive and whole."

"You are right," said Jai. "Let her hate us if it makes her happy. I am still her brother."

"She hates me, too," said Ikash helpfully.

"And you hate our father."

"No, brother, I don't."

"Well, you think he is dangerous, and a bad man."

"In many ways, he is."

"He was a great father," said Jai. "I still don't know how his house got so sad and ghosty. I can't understand it." He shook his head silently for a few moments, and then said, "Brother … I feel as if …" And then with a very fierce look, "Do not mock me."

"I won't."

"I feel as if," said Jai, stroking the dog and not meeting his brother's eye, "As if, were I to … truly let Klee go … I'd be failing our mother. Again."

And Ikash took a sharp breath as if he had been stabbed, but did not reply.

This was too big a matter for words, so the two of them sat in silence a time.

"But she is grown," said Jai then. "Not dead, but grown. Do you really think I can reconcile with my wife?"

"Maybe it is possible," said the shaman carefully. "I think ... I think it might be necessary that the two of you stop talking about Klee. I know that ... I realize what that ... means to you. But you may need to do it if you want to reconcile with your wife. Perhaps you can sort of ... start over."

Jai's face softened. "Start over," he murmured. "If she agrees to start over ..., would you do some sort of ceremony for us?"

"I'd be honored."

His intercession did not make all come right immediately. But Jai began to make overtures towards reconciling with Amal. He did not tell her that this had been anyone's idea but his own, but he must have said something to Hur, for the chief, who cared a great deal about his children's happiness, came to visit the shaman and said a heartfelt *thank you.*

In the early summer, Ikash did a reconciliation ceremony for his brother and sister-in-law that involved smoke and sacrifices. Everyone was as happy as if it were a wedding. At that time, it had been exactly a year since Klee found out the truth about her parentage.

Not long after this, the tribe performed on Endu's house what might be described as an extreme form of spring cleaning. The seasoned wood was removed and re-stacked in a dry outdoor location, with a temporary cattail roof overhead to protect it from rains. The house itself was then dismantled. Some of the timber was salvaged, but most of it, the "ghosty" part, was burned. Ikash performed a purifying ceremony over the land where the house had been. The newly seasoned timber was then used to make a tribal meeting hall. The remnants of Endu's house were used in a remodeling project that Jai and Amal were undertaking.

Ikash would never again be as young, sleek and seal-like as he once was, but he continued to build back up to a healthy weight. And late that summer, at almost the same week, Hyuna and Amal both fell pregnant.

CHAPTER TEN
BEGINNINGS

The little snake stirred in its woven pouch slung around Endu's waist. It was such a small snake that he could barely detect its movement. Had he not known, it would have felt like a mere twitch of the muscles in his side.

The snake had come to him almost as soon as the expedition set out. It had been only the second night they'd camped. Endu had gone down to the river for an evening bathe. He was lowering himself stiffly into the water (this was always an awkward undertaking, because of his maimed legs), and he put his hand on a patch of grass and there was the tiny white snake, with its dark eyes and elegantly sculpted head, no thicker than a finger and no longer than his forearm.

When he put his hand near it, it did not flee or strike. That was not normal behavior for a snake, and Endu thought with a thrill that perhaps it had come to him.

He picked it up, and still it did not strike. It wrapped itself loosely about his wrist. His breath quickened with excitement as he saw and felt it there. It made a captivating picture with its white spirals wreathing slowly about his dark skin.

He needed to bathe, so he set it down, telling it to stay.

And it did. That was when he knew it had truly come to him. It was a confirmation of everything he and his people were trying to do. They were not merely, idly calling themselves the Snake People. They had been adopted by the snake.

The trees had become bigger and bigger. The Snake People traveled through a forest that had clearly never known ice. There was little undergrowth, and the humans went quickly over the loam, the long, sparse party slithering along the forest floor. They found streams to camp by, but while traveling they kept well away from the great river, which was often lined with impassable mud flats. The mud flats were a good place to hunt tapirs, but there were also large aquatic rodents; huge, cumbersome armored turtles bigger than a bear; and, flying, swimming, and slithering, a variety of ugly and menacing types of dragon.

Endu had seven single young men in his entourage, besides the young men Sha and Setiq, who were newly married. He employed these young men in rotation to scout

out a route and to flush out any animals. As a rule they tried to stay ahead of the rest of the party by no more than half a day. Any farther, and their information would be useless by the time they got back. They made a point to go noisily, for that was the best way to avoid unexpected encounters with most creatures that might be dangerous, such as Great Lions, bears, and most kinds of dragons. The strategy, Endu remembered, was exactly the opposite of the one they would have used to avoid a human enemy. Very long ago, when he himself was a young single man, he had scouted out human enemies in the rolling hills on a distant continent. He had been following the lead of Hur, their tribal tracker. This was before he and Hur had realized that they hated each other.

For the first few weeks on the road, Endu slept well at night. Physically, he was worn out from walking all day. His legs hurt, but even that aching helped him. As for his mind, he was flushed with triumph. He had succeeded at last in putting his plans into action. He had managed to win over nearly all of the people whom he had hoped to take with him, and even a few for whom he had had little hope. He would lie down, and his mind would begin spinning pleasantly with plans for the city he was going to build, until the whole bright pattern was dragged under by the tiredness of his body.

He had said goodbye, before leaving, to his three oldest sons. They were happy to see him go, of course. His removal would give them more play for power and advancement; or, if they were not interested in power, for putting forward whatever their own plans might be. He was happy to get out of their way. That was the way of things. More space for them, and for him too. And now he could rule his own family as he saw fit, without over-the-shoulder peering from his father-in-law or from the elders or the chief.

Sometimes as he was walking, during the long, dreary middle hours of the day, a face would rise unbidden to his mind. It was an image that he must have seen during the goodbyes, though he didn't remember marking it much at the time. It was the face of his third son, and it bothered him.

There was something about Ikash's face that was difficult for Endu. It was not a face that he could look at for very long. And he had seldom needed to, especially in his son's younger days, when the boy had usually had his eyes lowered respectfully. Before he was shaman.

He is not my shaman now, thought Endu. *I will find my own, less difficult holy man.*

But he must have looked at the boy's face for a little while on the morning they all left. Probably it had been in the process of saying goodbye. For he had this image in his mind – a recent image – of the boy looking at him with a look that was …

Well.

The face itself was frustratingly closed, a look of dumb, still, brutish … almost masklike stupidity, thought Endu. Really, that still, round face might as well have been a mask. But the eyes …! Those eyes, in Endu's mind, were giving him a look as if they knew him. They seemed to say, "We are not finished, you and I."

That was what was difficult to endure.

That look had reminded him of something, and now he knew exactly what it was. The boy looked just like his mother. Sari used to give him that look in her later years, long after things had gone sour. Endu hadn't at first recognized it when he saw it on the shaman's face, but he had found it familiar and hateful. That was why he had not gazed for very long.

Dira, his second wife, never looked at him that way.

Endu had once seen God peeking out of the shining face of his son. He had tried to wipe the shining away. He remembered the satisfaction of the fight that followed. He found himself, even now, breathing heavily, flexing his fists, eager for the feeling of breaking his son's ribs again. Or the face. He would break the face rather than look on the light.

He had wiped it. He had wiped the shining out. And he had avoided it ever since. But it hadn't gone away.

It was not fair, he thought, that God should show himself through the one face that Endu could not look at. That made it *two* faces he could not look at. Double torture. If the Creator had wanted to reveal Himself, why should it be through the one person that Endu absolutely could not endure?

The snake was more courteous. It was a *normal* god, the kind of god a man could relate to. Less uncomfortable to be known by; or so Endu hoped. He himself had never had a vision of the snake, but he had overhead the shaman describing his own visions. Ikash hadn't talked about that being's face, only its voice, and about being crushed to the ground by the light that came from it, by its power. Or, if you were not its friend, being crushed by its punishing, persuasive pain. He had also mentioned its body, a hypnotic pattern. But never the face. No doubt the being had a face, but it never made you look on it.

Endu was certain he would be able to make contact with the snake. Indirect contact would be fine. Leaving it offerings, receiving whatever signs it offered. He would wear its skin; he would give it blood if need be. All of that was fine. It might be a little frightening, but Endu was brave. He was willing to do anything except look at a dumb, knowing face.

His mother often came to him these days. She always wanted to know what was going on. Hers had once been another gaze that Endu found it difficult to meet, but all that was now past. He was no longer uncomfortable before his mother. She would like to control him, he knew, but she had given up on that. Now she was content to monitor and ask a host of questions. Endu did not mind this. As long as he was clearly the leader, he found his mother helpful and her advice usually good.

And the information flowed both ways. He let her know his plans for the journey and for the city, and she kept him aware of what the weaker members of the tribe, the women, were up to. This was important because, as Endu now knew, if a woman was having a problem (even if it was spurious), she could rise up suddenly, out of nowhere, and do some crazy thing that would bring the entire tribe to a halt. He didn't want that to happen, so it was better to let his mother keep her ear to the ground and then to take potential problems seriously, no matter how trivial they might seem.

Endu even used his mother as a go-between for himself and Dira. He would rather hear about his wife's problems from a third party than risk going to her himself and seeing a look on her face.

Speaking of problems, in the mid-afternoon Sha came loping up from the back of the caravan. He gave his father to understand that something was very wrong.

"It's my wife," he said. "She's *crying*."

The boy looked comically distressed, as distressed as Endu had ever seen him. It was as if he'd never seen a woman cry before.

"Surely," said Endu, "You know how to comfort her?" *And that's your business, not mine*, he added with his tone.

"It's not that, father. She's crying because she can't go on walking. She's too tired. She can't bring herself to take another step."

This was not normal. Endu ran over it in his mind. Unusual fatigue, tears …

"You got her pregnant, didn't you? Already?"

Sha's face flinched. "We think so."

"That was stupid," said Endu.

"Yes, sir," said Sha, who nevertheless couldn't keep himself from a pleased grin.

Endu cursed softly to himself as he thought about what to do. He had asked the couples to refrain from pregnancy until the expedition settled down for the winter. That would only have been another month at most. Surely it had not been too much to ask. Sha and Wana's failure to follow some simple instructions were going to bring the party to an inglorious halt. Now that Wana was pregnant and was feeling the fatigue that came with that, they would have to accommodate her. You couldn't simply expect your women to tough it out through these critical stages, or they tended to sicken and miscarry and that sort of thing. And children were exactly what a new people like theirs needed. A chief who was unfriendly to mothers and babies was a chief who was cutting off his own feet.

Pregnancy was sacred. A people could not fail to honor it.

Endu was frustrated with his son's timing, but also moderately proud of him. He told him so. "Good wishes to both of you, but I wish you had waited another month. Now we will have to seek a place to winter earlier than we otherwise would."

"What about today?" said Sha, who was eager to bring back a report to his wife.

"We can stop for the day," said Endu. It would in any case not have been that long until the beginning of twilight.

"Thank you, father," said Sha with feeling.

One second later he had vanished.

Endu found himself struck in the eye by something sharp. At the same moment, a thin flat surface whipped across his cheek and the daylight was swallowed up in shadow.

He staggered back, eye streaming. The shadow was gone, the light returned. People were running and shouting.

What had taken Sha was a huge bird. The tip of its wing had whipped Endu's eye. Now it was trying to fly away with the young man, but because of its burden it was having difficulty attaining height.

Endu recovered quickly. He ran forward, as many people were doing, and retrieved his bow from the travois.

Sha was now about fifteen feet up, high enough to break bones if he landed wrong. He squirmed mightily, tearing his shoulders from the talons, and began to drop. But the bird, with shocking quickness, dove again and snatched him, this time by the legs. Sha's body swung around in an arc, upside down. Blood flung out in streams from his shoulders.

Endu took his bow and shot the bird: once, twice, in the tail, in the chest. It did not scream, but went into silent death throes. Sha's legs slipped from its grasp and he fell, landing on his head. Then the bird fell, fortunately not on top of him.

All around was the pandemonium of terrified women and children. Endu's adrenaline was pumping and he did not hear any of it. He loped forward, very fast with his sticklike legs and his modified stride, and was the first to arrive at the body of his son.

Sha was on his back, breathing, eyes open but unseeing. He was bleeding from the ears. Endu spoke words to him, but the boy did not reply. Endu slapped his cheeks; the boy's face flinched, but he did not roll his head back and forth. He was very pale, which with his brown skin meant grey.

Endu had seen paralysis twice before. The first was the case of Nirri, a big, handsome foreigner whom Endu's family had found alive and dazed in a state just like this. They had cared for him, and he had recovered his mind, but the lower parts of him had remained paralyzed. Caring for him had occupied Zillah's time and had often slowed the party in their travels.

The other case was that of Enmer. He had been Endu's brother, older and wiser, at that time the chief. A bear had thrown him against a tree, breaking his neck and other large bones. He had died in about an hour. Endu hadn't been the one to care for him (being grievously injured himself at the time), but he remembered everyone saying that before he died, Enmer's skin had become cold.

He thought that his son's case was more like the second one.

If he did not act, death would come swiftly.

Endu's hearing had come back to him as he got his bearings. Now he looked up and saw a gaggle of people clustered round him. Wana, supposedly so tired, had managed to get to her husband's side and was weeping hysterically.

"Someone make that woman be quiet," said Endu. "Or else take her away. I can't think through her wailing." Really, she had the most annoying cry he had ever heard.

Then he looked up and saw his son-in-law.

"Setiq, gather the company. Don't let them spread out and stay in chaos like this. You and the other young men guard them. Tell them all will be well. I am going to save my son."

"Yes, sir," said Setiq, and departed.

Now Endu was left alone with Zillah. She had crouched on the other side of Sha and was feeling his head, palpating his body. Whatever broken bones Sha had, she had probably found them already. She straightened his neck carefully, and by mounding grasses on either side, she steadied it.

"You are going to save him?" she said quietly.

"Yes, Mother. This will not end in death."

"Let me –"

"No, Mother," said Endu. He kept his tone even, but allowed himself to speak the words brutally, without hesitation. "I will do it. You cannot help him. You can never save them when it counts."

She gasped and looked at him, stunned.

"You failed to save Ki-Ki …"

"He had lost half his skin."

"… And my brother Enmer …"

"He was dead when they brought him to me –"

"From an injury just like this one. You cannot do anything with something like this. You can only cure around the edges. My son cannot be helped by your kind of healing. He will die unless we call upon the power."

Endu loosened the top of the pouch at his waist and took out the snake. It came to him, warm and alive in his hand. Zillah's eyes widened as she saw it curve around his wrist, saw him hold it up to his face and murmur to it, praying.

Then he loosened the neck lacings on Sha's shredded and bloody tunic, and placed the little white snake on his son's bare chest.

At first it curled up as if to rest, but only for a moment. After it had paused there, its body beautifully spiraled and its tongue flicking in and out to get its bearings, it unfurled and made its way up to Sha's neck. The black tongue flicked again, for a moment, under his chin. Then it dived to one side, circling his neck, disappearing into the mounded grasses. It emerged on the other side and passed across his neck from left to right, into the grasses again.

Three times it did this, circling with its body the most critically injured part.

After the third pass, it emerged over Sha's bloody right shoulder, leaving a faint brown line of blood as it crawled across the unblemished front of his tunic, and ended up back at the hand of Endu.

Endu whispered to it and put it back into its pouch. The whole operation had taken only a few moments.

Zillah had been holding her breath the entire time. Now she let it out. Endu, hearing the sigh, looked up and smiled calmly at his mother.

At that moment, just when the two of them were looking at each other and neither was looking at Sha, the injured man gave a sigh and a loud, dramatic groan. He stretched, flexing his legs and raising his arms over his head. Then he sat up. He did this with plenty of groans and winces, for he had a bump on his head, and his legs and shoulders were still torn, but nevertheless he sat up far too gracefully for a man who was concussed or paralyzed.

And he wasn't. His head was clear, his brain undamaged. His neck was no longer broken.

"Oh, my God!" Sha said. "That was a close call! That smelly thing could really have hurt me." His eyes focused on Endu. "Thank you … I think you were the one who shot it, Father?"

"Now," said Endu, "The rest of his injuries are the sort that you can deal with, Mother."

The bird was foul. From the smell, it must have nested daily in its own filth. At first the Snake People had thought to retrieve its body for meat, but after approaching it they had no desire to touch it. After seeing – and smelling – for himself, Endu agreed. They were not so starving that they must eat a disgusting creature like this and risk sickness. In fact, he had them move the camp a little ways away, upwind. The snatching of Sha had happened in an open strip of meadow. They crossed this, forded a stream, and made camp among the trees on the other side. Families pitched tents for the night, and Zillah set up a little, canopied clinic.

Endu was concerned that Sha's wounds would be contaminated. Probably the bird had fouled its own claws. He spoke of this to Zillah, and she assured him she would be careful. She had washed the slashes on her grandson's shoulders in potable water and swabbed them with an antiseptic salve she had made from juniper berries. She also had on hand cattail ashes, which could keep the slashes clean as they healed after she had stitched them.

Sha was sitting up as his grandmother worked on him, bright-eyed and seemingly happy. He sat wincing and joking with Zillah, trying through gritted teeth to make her laugh as she sewed up his muscles. Wana had been unable to stand watching this and was off being calmed by Klee.

Sha had some deep lacerations on his shoulders, ankles and calves, and he said these stung but that the pain did not go deep, as it would with a broken bone. In fact, he seemed to be experiencing that surge of well-being that comes after a shock of pain has been and gone. Or perhaps there was another reason for his almost manic energy.

Zillah was good at staying focused when she was helping a patient, but when Endu first approached, she gave him a single, significant glance as if she had something to ask him later. Then she went back, without saying anything, to doing stitches. Endu's flesh cringed as he watched this. When his mother had fixed him up, after his own mauling, she had had to cut and clean and sew, and it had taken hours. It had been the longest – indeed, the only – session of torture that he had ever experienced. Endu had a pretty strong stomach, but ever since then, he found surgery hard to watch.

And all the while Zillah was stitching Endu's scalp, she had been crying over his dead brother Enmer. Now here she was, performing stitches on Sha, and because of the young man's courage she was having to stifle laughter.

She was laughing and working on a live man instead of crying and mourning a dead one, and all because of the little white snake. Endu knew it had happened, but he still almost couldn't believe it.

"Father," said Sha, "I am happy to be alive, but I'm missing something."

"What is it, my son?"

"It's my little amulet. It's shaped like Ikash." Sha paused, gritted his teeth, and then resumed speaking again. "I made him one of me, and myself one of him. I meant to wear it for years and years, and here it's been only a few weeks and it's gone. Shit on by a bird." He laughed, and then he wiped the corners of his eyes. Endu was surprised and a little disgusted. Sha could stand pain like it was nothing, but here he was, crying over an amulet.

"It must have fallen off my neck," he said, "when I flipped upside down."

"Of course," said Endu.

"Will you go and look for it, Father? Will you ask everyone to keep an eye out?"

"I will," said Endu.

He left the medical site. As he walked away, the tiny wooden amulet rubbed against his body where it hung down on the inside of his skirt.

Endu found Dira and his daughters.

"What are we eating tonight?" he asked them, and they said it would be barley and fried fish. Both were almost ready.

Endu was happy. He went off to take a bath.

He had found the amulet – nearly stepped on it – as he hobbled up to Sha right after his son's fall. It had taken only a moment to scoop the thing up. He'd intended to return it, but as soon as it nestled in his hand, he'd seen it: that *look*. The thing was looking at him with those wise, knowing eyes. He had covered it with his fingers and quickly tucked it in his belt, down on the inside where it wouldn't show.

Later that night, as soon as he could do so unobserved, he drew the wood-and-leather necklace out and quietly disposed of it in a campfire.

CHAPTER ELEVEN
WILLINGLY GIVEN

"What did you say to it?" said Zillah.

"I said that I would feed it later."

The Snake People had not traveled many more days. Just far enough to get out of the unlucky valley, away from the foul bird. Just far enough that Endu could select the site of their winter camp, instead of having fate pick it for him.

Sha had been well, though sore, for about a day. Then he had, indeed, developed a fever. Besides this, there was the weakness of Wana. Endu had made the party stop and had gone on ahead himself, with scouts, to find a good place. And they had found one: a wide hilltop, reasonably flat, overlooking a broad east-flowing river. Endu believed the hilltop could be cleared before winter and an earth lodge thrown up by employing the labor of the young men that he had. All of them had experience building such things for storehouses or men's lodges. This time, it would be a large lodge that would house the whole community.

After that there was one more day of travel, nursing the sick along, and then it was a halt, tents up, and to work felling, clearing, digging.

Zillah had brought her son a drink where he stood on an earth berm that was already going up. Now she waited for him to elaborate on what he had said to the snake.

Endu let her wonder.

"What did you feed it?" she said finally, unable to resist.

Endu looked over at his mother and smiled. "Why do you ask?"

He knew why she was asking. It was the same reason that it was she, and not Dira, who had climbed this hill to give him a cup of tea. She wanted to know how he had gotten the snake to heal the injured man so that she could decide whether this healing had been a good thing according to her lights, and if so, how often it could be employed. She wanted to know whether she should use it again.

"I ask because I want to save Sha," said his mother humbly. "There are red streaks coming from his shoulders. I fear if they reach his heart. He may die, my son. I would like you to save him again … if you can do it without defiling him."

Endu turned his body and studied his mother's face soberly. He thought he had better tell her the truth. The two of them were founding a new people. It would not do to found a nation on chaos. He was the priest of his new people, and she was the healer. The priest and the healer of a people need to be in agreement … or at least know where they stand.

"I will tell you the price," he said, "And then you can decide, Mother, whether you want to risk paying it again. I fed it in blood."

Endu had known, without knowing, that this was what the snake required. After dark on the day that Sha was healed, he had approached the now low, redly glowing coals of the cookfire. He had scooped up one in a shell, taken it a little way into the woods, and there he had built a little sacred fire of his own. He needed warmth to wake the snake and light to see what he was doing.

He had set the snake down on last season's oak leaves. The animal knew exactly what was happening, and it had waited patiently.

Endu had secured an old wadded-up scrap of felt. This went on to a leaf in front of the snake. The leaf was dry and crinkled like a cup.

He had taken his flint knife and opened a vein in his right arm, drizzling blood onto the felt scrap until it was soaked. The felt absorbed it. Then the snake swallowed the bloody felt-ball just as it would swallow a mouse.

That was all there was to it. Endu bound up his arm, put out the fire, and retrieved his pet. He had given his blood for the life of his son.

His clay cup was not quite drained of tea. He took another sip from it, watching for his mother's reaction.

She was staring at him, white and horrified. "It wants blood? It wants – blood for healing?"

"Yes. Not the blood of the patient. It wants someone else's blood."

"H – how …" She started to speak, her voice faded out, and she tried again. "How do you know?"

"I know."

And then, while she continued to stare horrified, Endu added, "Well, it worked, didn't it?"

Zillah was silent. She could not deny it. She – and only she, besides Endu – had been a witness to the miracle.

Endu knocked back the rest of his drink. He couldn't hide a grin. It wasn't often that he surprised his mother. She could have figured it out, he thought, if she'd wanted to. All the information was there. You just had to want to understand the snake.

The snake had healed Ikash, Endu's third son, all those years ago when he was on his vision quest, and he had gotten a broken collarbone. It had healed him, seemingly, for free. But it hadn't been for free. The boy himself had told them that the thing had then tried to claim his loyalty. If Ikash had smartened up and given the thing what it wanted, it no doubt later would have asked him for some kind of blood.

He hadn't, in the end. He had wavered – he had not been as stoically silent as he had first lied and claimed to be – but, in the end, he had not pledged to the thing. So it had taken its due in a much messier way. It had caused Sari to go crazy and throw herself into a steaming lake that was, essentially, a cooking pot. It had taken Ikash's mother's blood ... all of it. As far as Endu was concerned, that was entirely the boy's fault.

Endu had concluded from all this that in order to effect healing, the snake preferred blood taken from a relative of the one being healed. And it preferred blood willingly given.

Zillah could have seen all this if she'd wanted to, but she only saw the snake as something terrifying and mysterious, something to be avoided, because she was of the party that had set themselves against the snake.

Endu patiently explained the rules to her. He did not mention Sari. He added that, now that she was a member of the Snake People, it might be well if she learned to operate on the Snake's terms. Sha could instantly be healed of his fever if someone who was related to Sha by blood was willing to open a vein. Or, they could wait and see how well the young man's body did fighting the sickness on its own.

Endu was feeling very pleased with himself that he, at last, had figured out something before his mother. Her face was so transparent. It had gone from confused, to dismayed, to ever more horrified as confusion evaporated before understanding. It was a pleasure to watch her mind work.

But then she ruined everything, as she always did, by saying something that surprised him. "My son. I have *never* known you to sacrifice *any*thing of yourself for another person."

Endu was taken aback, but he recovered quickly. "I do it because I know it will work, Mother."

"And how much of your own blood are you willing to give?"

"Obviously it can't be done very often."

She nodded slowly and took the cup from him. He noticed she was careful not to touch his fingers.

"Well," she said. She was trying to sound brisk but was obviously still shaky. "You have given me much to think about, my son. Thank you for … opening my eyes." She began to walk away.

Endu said, "I take it you don't want to do a healing ceremony?"

"I think … the chances are good that Sha will recover."

She went off, swaying, down the steep hillside toward their temporary camp at the base of it.

Endu called after her, "Let me know if you change your mind!"

Zillah had been caring for Sha in an open-sided tent. She did not immediately return to this place, however. Instead, she directed her steps toward the side of the river. The river was low, running flat and still, with many exposed gravel bars. She watched it mindlessly for a while. It was a sight that she normally would have found soothing.

Then, slowly, she crumpled forward, curving in on herself with her arms tucked over her belly. The clay cup fell from her hand. She put her hands on her knees and stood stooped over like that, breathing shallowly. She felt as if she might vomit.

She reminded herself why she had come here. It was to protect the young ones. It was to protect them, supposedly, from Endu.

She was no protection at all.

Suddenly, just when she thought the sickness had passed, she vomited. She staggered forward and heaved again and again until she was completely empty. Then she backed away from the foulness and sat weakly, for a time, on the large embracing roots of a tree where they were exposed on the bank.

Eventually she got up, retrieved the cup, and used it to dump a little river water on the mess she had made. It had mostly soaked in to the ground, rather than running into the river to defile it. Not that it mattered. The place she had come to was downstream from where the women drew water. And Zillah knew she had not vomited because she had any bodily sickness. Or at least, not any sickness that was *merely* of the body.

She waded a little farther out to where the main flow was strong enough to clean impurities from the water, and there she splashed her face and took a drink. Then she trudged back to her grandson.

Sha was awake, eyes a little too bright, very thirsty, glowing with fever. He tried teasing his grandmother, but she was unable to raise a smile at his jokes and only sat staring at him strangely until he gave up on making them.

The red fingers of infection were getting longer and angrier. It was obvious to Zillah that they were going to reach his heart. Then they would clench about it.

Endu was right. When it counted, she never could save them.

It now seemed like a foolish scruple to refrain from using the snake and its sacrifice of blood. What right had she to let Sha die? He was a young husband and father, a pillar of their tiny tribe. Perhaps the method of curing would defile him. But Sha, unknowing, had already been defiled. Why should he be subjected to the touch of that *thing* and saved from death by shock, only to die of infection a few days later?

What did it matter, anyway?

What did anything matter.

"Grandmother, don't look at me like that," said Sha. His voice still sounded merry, as if he were joking. "I have been to the place before. It is a good place."

Zillah was filled with a surreal feeling.

"Do you *want* to go?" she said.

"Well, not really. There is Wana to think of. I guess perhaps I shouldn't have gotten married after all, eh, Grandmother? But," he said, "I know I will find my mother there."

Then he said, "Hey, Grandmother! Where are you going?"

"I am calling you back," said Zillah.

She went directly to Endu. She told him that this time, *she* would give the blood.

The snake wound itself about Sha's swollen and weeping shoulders and over his chest. He said it tickled, and then he stopped groaning, the discomfort of the fever left him, and he fell, for the first time in days, into an easy sleep.

And later that night Zillah, full of revulsion but also of grim determination, gave the little god what it required. And the next morning Sha was well.

Endu had inducted her into his mysteries. And still they had managed to keep the whole thing secret.

That autumn, the Snake People finished their lodge. This was about the time that the Reindeer People were rebuilding their village and their shaman was refusing to eat.

The lodge was oval in shape, running East and West. Its front door faced west, back (as nearly as they could tell) toward where the original People had come from, generations ago. Its back door faced east, toward the river. The lodge was built of earth berm up to about shoulder height, and above this they laid mid-sized saplings in the shape of an A-frame, reaching right down into the earth on the outside of the berm, to shed water, for in those days that was a very rainy country. This they insulated with grass and woven cattail mats, adding more here and there as the rainstorms blew more and more aggressively. Endu admitted this was temporary and not an ideal lodge, but he did not mind because the floor plan was exactly how he wanted it. Importantly, the doors.

The west door was not a simple entryway. Passing through the gap in the berm, whoever entered encountered a maze of basketwork walls and had to pass through several twists and turns to get in to the main living area. The east door had to be simpler because that was the way that people went to throw out garbage and to go down to the water. But it, too, featured a basketwork tunnel that took whoever wished to exit around a leftward curve before a sharp right showed the outdoors and the view down to the river.

These mazes were put in place to confuse bad things that might try to enter, everything from winds to bad spiritual forces, to two- or four-legged enemies. The curving tunnels also imitated the curves at the head and tail of a serpent. Endu had his people living inside a snake.

These mazes, with their multitude of places to hang things, became convenient storage areas. People took to hanging in the branches gifts for one another, items they wanted to drop off, and spare weapons that could be grabbed on the way out by whoever needed them. The last curve of the east door became a convenient place to drop contaminated items, to be carried out by the next person out that door who was feeling well enough. This became important later when the sickness began to spread.

A plague came to them in the clammy dampness of winter. Victims developed chills and fever, a sickening headache, a feeling as if all their bones were being broken. No one knew how long this would have lasted, or how it would have ended, for they never did let the fever run its course. The sick were so miserable that they were convinced they would die. The Snake People were not willing to let this happen when they had a means of cure at their disposal. As the sickness moved through the makeshift lodge, one family after another was inducted into the snake's mysteries. By the end of the winter, every single family had at least one person who had sickened and been saved, and at least one – often, more than one – who had given blood.

About a week in advance of the Spring Equinox, Endu told his mother that the evening of that important day would be the date for his healing.

"For what healing?" she said.

"Why, of me," said he. "Of my injuries."

She stared at him. Endu kept surprising her. Every time she thought he could not say something that would frighten her more, he did.

Endu, who still cared a little what his mother thought of him, sensed her horror and became defensive. "I am in pain *all the time*, mother. I am tired of it. I would like it to end. Besides, think how good it would be for the people if I were strong and whole."

Zillah thought to herself that in her experience, it was the wounded leaders who had always been the better ones. But all she said out loud was, "Are you certain it will work, my son? After all these years?"

She saw in his eyes that he was certain. The great snake had been giving him more and more, through its little proxy, even as he gave it ever more of himself and his people. And now it had occurred to him to wonder if it could give him his heart's desire. He was so excited by the possibility that he had no room for doubts. It was as if the thing were already happening.

"I mean to try," he said.

"It will take a great deal of blood."

"There will be no shortage of volunteers."

Endu was correct. When he announced his plan, there were several volunteers to bring him healing, all of them women. Not all of them were related to him by blood, and of those that were, not all could be allowed to do it. His daughters with Dira, for example, were still children, and the snake people had not yet begun asking their children to bleed.

Klee would, by the logic of the snake, have been the best candidate. She made it known that she would be willing to give the blood, though she sensed that Setiq had a huge problem with this. But the need for her to volunteer was obviated by Endu's wife, Dira, who literally begged to be given the chance.

"Oh, please, let me do it," she insisted, thin voice straining. "I think the god may accept me. I am not related to Endu, but my blood is mingled with his in our children."

Klee noticed her grandmother looking very hard, during this speech, at Dira. Klee did the same. She seldom interacted directly with her father's wife. There was something about the woman that repelled her. But now she forced herself to look, and what she saw was a long, thin face, somehow distorted by the earnestness with which it begged to be made into a sacrifice.

She is very ugly, thought Klee, and even with his injuries my father is very beautiful. Surely it was an act of mercy that he married her. Perhaps that is why she adores him. Klee had the thought that she couldn't imagine adoring someone that much, so much that you yourself became deformed. Then immediately afterward, she had the thought that perhaps she could imagine it after all.

So they tried it.

They did it indoors, with the rain pouring down outside. They cleared an area in the center of their lodge, in sight of all the different families' booths. On the head end of their central fire-pit, they seated Endu on a wicker chair with a blanket draped over it. It had something of the feel of a sick bed, and something of the altar about it.

Endu sat facing west. He was flanked by his closest family: his wife and mother on the North side of him; and on the South, his children and their spouses. Klee stood with Setiq resting his hands on her shoulders, and Sha was backed by a clearly frightened Wana. Endu's younger children were in the lodge but not gathered around him. Although many of the children had already been healed by the snake during the winter, this was a big, risky ceremony and it was not felt to be suitable for them to witness.

The only exception was Endu's daughter Gupet, who had just turned fourteen. She stood between her mother and grandmother, looking thin, silent and intense, like a copy of Dira.

Something was bothering Setiq, Klee could tell. His hands were restless and kept squeezing and repositioning on her shoulders.

Despite all the blood it had consumed, the little snake had not grown very much bigger during the past winter. Endu removed it from his pouch and held it up, nestled in his hand, to Dira. She whispered to it, took it gently, with a wooden face, from her husband's hand, and set it on his bare chest.

Endu did not like fitted clothes. As soon as the weather was no longer bitter, he would take to wearing only a belt at his waist, and hanging from it, a patterned, woven skirt. After Dira set the snake on Endu, for a moment it simply curled on his smooth dark chest. Then it crawled up to his collarbone and raised its upper body. For a moment, man and serpent regarded each other.

Then, with horrible suddenness, it dived into his exposed nostril.

Klee screamed.

Setiq clutched her shoulders.

They watched, horrified, as the snaked vanished into the chief's face.

A moment later Endu opened his mouth, and out came the neat little white head, covered in saliva. More and more of it emerged, sticking out horizontally and swaying stiffly like an obscenely long and animate tongue.

The animal swished back and forth – Endu gagged – the snake freed itself, and dropped to his chest. He took a ragged breath, and everyone breathed a sigh of relief.

But the snake was still moving. It crawled headfirst down his belly and, almost before any of them realized it, disappeared under his skirt.

Klee screamed again.

A second later it came out the bottom of the skirt and began wreathing itself about his skinny, scarred legs, which had been stripped of muscle by the bear so many years ago. It wound itself around and around them as if around a pole. Endu lifted each leg in turn to facilitate this. When the snake had finished, it crawled back up to his chest – over, not under the skirt, this time – and curled up there. And then everyone who had been watching it work on the chief's legs, looked again at his face. And this time, several people screamed.

Endu had a nose.

And not only a nose. His eyes were again perfect and almond-shaped. The seamed white scars were gone, the hairline low and straight. Even his left ear was a small, neat ear and no longer a pink nub. This must have been what he looked like as a young man. And he was beautiful.

The miracle had a strong effect on everyone in the radius of it. Sha gave a gasp and an involuntary sob. Klee thought she heard him say, "Daddy!" Setiq's hands on her shoulders grew suddenly very still and cold.

Wana, Gupet, Dira, and even Zillah looked badly frightened. Dira was crying. Klee thought she was thinking of all the blood she was going to have to give to pay for this.

Endu saw from their faces that the healing had worked. He stowed the snake in his waist pouch, his hands moving capably while his eyes never left his family's faces. Then he scrambled to his feet. As he did so, he found what he had expected: that his legs also had been healed. They had normal musculature and, for the first time in a long time, he felt no pain.

Endu ran his hands lightly over his face. He traced his nose and tugged on his newly perfect ear. He shut his eyes and opened them, pleased that he could close his left eye just as tightly as the right, that it was no longer torn, itchy, and watery.

Except that it was watery at the moment, for he was now crying happy tears.

Next he crossed to Dira and took her in his arms. And he did this, he felt – and everyone noted that he looked – taller than before. Perhaps it was only the change in gait, or perhaps it was the intensity of what had just happened, but he seemed to tower and fill up the space near the fire-pit.

"Thank you," he said to his wife, "Thank you." And, "It's all right, don't be frightened. Don't be frightened. We will get you through this."

Though he had no plan for how this might be done.

He turned around and there was Sha, and Sha suddenly hugged him with a hug that was almost a tackle. His son was openly weeping. Endu would normally have despised him for this, but at this moment it seemed appropriate. He put one arm around his son and kept the other around his second wife, and at that moment he felt complete.

Setiq and Zillah, though, had already faded away. Out of all those present, only they were not worshippers.

CHAPTER TWELVE
SOAKING IN WORRY

Everything was different afterward. It was as if they had all lost their innocence.

Endu, by his healing, had become a very god. Now, whenever they looked at him, they almost doubted their eyes because of the way he seemed to shine with beauty, confidence, and power. He was at last comfortable with himself, as if he had brought the whole world about to conform to things as he had always seen them. As the Snake People disassembled their lodge, prepared to leave, and went through various ceremonies of cutting-off to unbind themselves from this place where they had wintered, Endu moved about, and kept everyone else moving, with a manic energy.

The others, those who were not Endu, moved about in a daze. For some it was the daze of possibilities. They were dazzled by the thought of the powers that might now be available to them collectively through him. But a few were merely numb, uncomfortable, afraid to look themselves in the eye.

Not everything was bad about the fact that they were all now different. One effect of that strange winter and spring was to smash up all the Snake People's previous relationships. None of them were the same people, Klee felt, and this allowed them to get to know one another afresh. Previously they had merely been a gang pulled, as it were, at random from a number of disparate families among the People, inheriting the assumptions and the tensions that came with that. Now, though, they might truly be called the Snake People because they felt – or, at least, Klee felt – as if none of those old things mattered any more. Together they had suffered, fallen, and been reborn.

In particular, Klee began getting to know Sha as her brother for the first time. He felt more natural as a brother than as a father. He was only twelve years older than she, and he often seemed younger even than that.

Sha had had a hard winter. Besides nearly dying, being the first person to be snake-healed, and then suffering from a fever, he and Wana had had to deal with the loss of their baby when Wana caught the sickness that winter. Sha had given blood for his wife, and the snake's touch had healed her of the plague, but the fever itself had apparently killed the child within her. And for whatever reason, this death was something that the snake's healing did not undo. The baby, which had started moving shortly before Wana first became ill, stopped moving and left the young couple to soak in their hopeless worry. And then Wana had begun bleeding and Zillah had given her a tincture of comfrey to hasten the miscarriage so that they might not lose the mother as well.

Yes, Sha had had a hard winter. This spring he was subdued.

He engaged Klee in conversation one day when they were both down at the river drawing water. Klee was there because normally each woman drew water for her own household. Sha was there because he was helping Wana.

Even in his sad state, Sha was easy to talk to, and by the time they had swung the water-baskets up on to their shoulders, he had got Klee warmed up enough that he was able to ask her,

"Did I do wrong, sister?"

"Do wrong in what?" she said.

He flinched as if this were a cutting rebuke, though she hadn't meant it to be. Then he stepped up to the top of the bank – with his long legs it was just one stride – set down his heavy basket, and reached down a hand and helped her up. Then he swung the basket back onto his shoulder, grunting. He wasn't as graceful with it as a woman would be, but his man's strength made the thing less of a burden.

He said, "I mean was I wrong to tell you that you were my sister."

"No," said Klee as they began walking back towards the camp, which was once again at the base of the now skeletal lodge. Lately, everything that had happened last summer seemed far away. But she felt a curious heaviness flooding back as he asked about it, and a flash of remembered anger. "No, you weren't wrong to tell me. You were wrong to delay telling me for so long."

"I know," he muttered, sounding ashamed, and if he hadn't been carrying the basket, she would have expected him, like a little boy, to drill his toe into the loam. "I wanted to be your brother. But I didn't know how to do it. I guess I thought I was taking good enough care of you as your younger father."

"You weren't," she said, "but it doesn't matter now."

She felt tired. She did not want to help him justify himself. He had left her to the mercies of Amal. Surely he must have seen that. Perhaps he could not be blamed, because he hadn't known what to do. But the fact remained, and remained damning as far as Klee was concerned, that none of them *had* known what to do, that all of them had been content to remain paralyzed rather than bestir themselves on her behalf.

"It does, though," said Sha miserably. He was not normally one to dig about in his heart like this, but he had been weakened by the events of the winter. Klee hoped he was not going to cry. "Can we be brother and sister *now?*" he said.

"Of course, brother," said Klee. Though she felt she ought to be angry, she couldn't help liking him. Despite herself, she smiled. But then she blurted out, "But why did you leave me with her?"

He stopped walking – they were drawing near the camp now – and looked at her.

"We were protecting you from something worse."

"Why, what?"

"*Him,*" said Sha. As he said this, he unconsciously gestured northward ... but then his eyes traveled back towards the camp.

"*Him?* "

"Yes."

"Was he really that bad?"

"Yes. That house was no place for a baby girl."

"But he has girls now …"

"Things were different then. He was different. Not like now."

"So, it's all true, everything the shaman told me?"

"Sure, it's true. I remember it all. He remembers it too."

"I didn't believe him," said Klee.

"I know," said Sha. "He was frustrated as hell. But don't worry, he'll be all right. He'll go and meditate or whatever he does. And he's got Hyuna."

Then for one second, an expression of extreme pain passed over his face.

Klee said, "You miss him."

"I miss him a lot. But at the same time … I don't know. Everything feels different. I lost that amulet, so I lost my connection with him. And Dad is different now, and I am different too. If he saw me now … I don't think he'd approve of me."

He muttered this last line. Klee wanted to encourage him, but all she could think of was, "I don't think he approves of me either."

"Oh, no. He loves you. He loves everybody. Even me. Even Dad, I suppose. But all this with the snake …"

He shook his head, clucking his tongue, and resumed walking.

The water was starting to feel very heavy. Klee kept pace with him.

"So, I wasn't wrong, though," she said. "Our father really is different now. Not like all … the stories … from before."

His brow was furrowed. "Well, he must be. He looks just like he looked when I was little. But he doesn't seem like the same person. Or like a person at all."

Sha shrugged with the shoulder not bearing the water.

"He seems like a god."

"I don't see how he can be as he is now," said Klee, "and at the same time really have been as you say. I wonder if I'll ever really find out what happened in the past."

"I was *there*," said Sha, irritated. "I just told you."

"Everyone tells a different story, and things keep changing. Do you think it's even possible to know?"

Sha cut his eyes toward his sister. He wasn't sure how to take Klee. Speaking of things changing, she seemed constantly to be changing herself. One minute angry, the next friendly. Shifting back and forth. He never knew how she would react to any given thing.

She was beautiful, it was true. He'd always loved her as his beautiful little sister. Today she was wearing her hair in a great knot on top of her head, which was a style that all the Snake People – male and female – had begun adopting in this warm and rainy climate.

And she was brave. There was no doubt about that. He remembered just weeks ago, when she'd saved the life of Dira.

His father's wife had been giving blood, draining it into a basin, first from one arm, then the other, growing paler and paler. Giving blood to pay for Endu's healing. Already it was more than the snake would ever eat. They all knew that most of it was going to end up dried out in the basin. And Endu had been standing over her, saying, "Give more, give more. If we don't give enough it will take one of our children." And he hadn't even looked human, nor as if he had blood at all in his body. And Dira had apparently been too overwhelmed by him, or too tired, to fight back.

And everyone present had been watching with ashen faces, wondering where this was going.

And then Klee had stepped forward and said, "Stepmother, enough," and the chief's wife had shaken her head. But Klee took a knife and cut one of her own arms and contributed her own drizzle.

Sha still remembered the way she had drawn the flint across her flesh, with only the slightest hesitation. It was the first time Klee had given blood. That was brave. There was a massive hesitation the first time you went to cut yourself. You learned to hurry with it after a few times. Sha knew that now. Yes, his sister was brave.

He wasn't sure why she had saved Dira, though. Perhaps she just didn't want to watch someone die. Klee certainly didn't act, in daily life, as if she loved Dira. She didn't act as if she loved anybody.

He looked, covertly, at her arm. The bandage was off, and she seemed able to sling water without favoring the arm much. It must be a good healing.

Sha wished he could make friends with her. He missed having a sibling to talk to. He could talk to Wana – sort of – but not about just anything, because Wana frightened easily. She wanted him to be strong. Sha couldn't talk to Wana about much of anything at all, in fact, in this environment where there was so much to worry about and be frightened of.

When Wana lost her baby, it was the most helpless he had ever been. As a kid, whenever something bad happened, he had always been able to provide a lightening, a distraction or a joke, to his mother or brothers. Or failing that, he would just get away. None of that would work here. A joke would not be fitting. There was nothing encouraging he could say, because at that moment they weren't even sure if she'd be able to conceive ever again. He couldn't get away, because she needed him there. (Needed someone, anyway.) And it was the middle of the winter and people were sick and the whole lodge was filled with distressed moans. So, as she lay on her side, curled around the cramps, he had kind of draped himself over her and not said anything and just stayed like that, feeling like the biggest failure ever.

Was I wrong? Was I wrong to marry her? Was I wrong to drag her off on this little jaunt where everything, even the good things, *everything* is turning into hell?

Later, he had gone outside, bare-chested as he was, even though it was the middle of the winter and rather cold and there were alligators and dragons and things about. He had gone down to the river, which was pretty high even though it was winter, and just stood there dumbly, thinking, *I will never be able to cheer her up. I will never be able to fix any of this. I don't want to be married to her. I don't want to be with any of these people.*

I am trapped.

That had been the worst moment of his adult life.

Then, for no reason at all, right in the middle of the worst moment, he started to feel better. He took a deep breath and straightened his back. Raising his eyes to look across the river, he saw some large humanlike things crashing around over there. He was pretty sure they were Older Brothers, which made him smile. He had first seen Older Brothers on his manhood ceremony, years ago. They were his totem animal.

He raised a hand and waved.

Sha thought someone must have been praying for him at that moment. Even though his amulet was gone, someone was praying for him.

He wished he could tell Klee about this and then maybe it would happen to her, too. But they didn't have that kind of relationship yet. And besides, here they were, back at camp.

In the days ahead, the Snake People began making boats with which to brave the river. This was of course an insane thing to do. It was spring; the river was flooding, and from time to time, despite the warm temperature, large chunks of ice would come bobbing downstream, as if the river were hurling rocks at them. Ordinarily, taking to the river would be suicide.

But nothing was impossible with Endu. He had a well-laid, gleaming plan in his mind, and he carried everyone else along on the strength of it. He wanted to build a city, a *large* city, and that meant finding a good place near a large river. And this river, he knew, would be larger if they followed it farther down. And the quickest way to do that was on the surface of the water. Furthermore, he was convinced that the river itself, being snakelike, would help them and carry them there, though perhaps not without sacrifice. The river itself was a version of their god. They had three gods, now: man, snake, and river. And they had an anti-god: the giant bird.

The boats they made were of large, tough reeds, which grew in endless stretches to the south and east of their hilltop. The men would go out for days in a row, cut these with jarring knife-strokes, and at the end of the day carry them back in long bundles draped over several men's shoulders. Klee, because she was young and strong, often helped with the carrying back. There was a method for binding these reeds tightly together that, it was said, had actually been used in Sinar, that unimaginably distant place, and that had perhaps been developed before the Flood ended the last age of the world but one … at an unimaginably distant time. Endu remembered this method, and so, surprisingly, did Zillah. This increased, for Klee, the spooky impression that the two of them were creatures from another world.

The Snake People lost several test boats on their way to recovering the construction method. Endu, far from being angered by the lost labor, only laughed serenely at this.

"I remember a time when I thought my brother was crazy to put our whole party on boats," he said. "Now here I am doing the same thing. Those were not reed boats, though. We had cattle and horses to transport."

No one, except Zillah, had any idea what he was talking about.

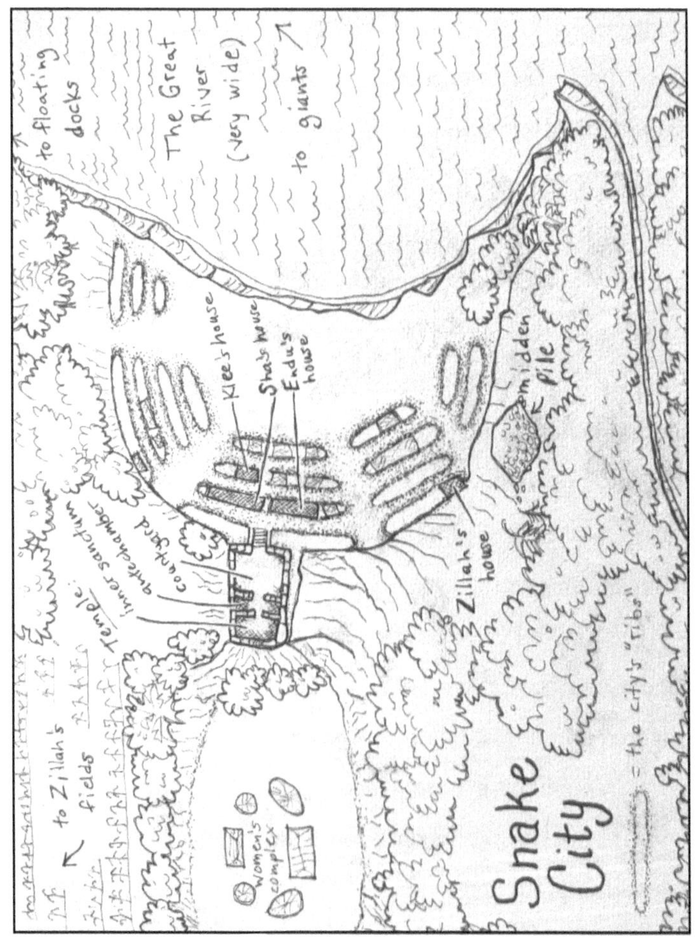

to floating docks
The Great River
(very wide)
to giants
to Zillah's fields
Temple
inner sanctum
antechamber
courtyard
Klee's house
Shala's house
Endu's house
midden pile
Zillah's house
Women's complex
Snake City
= the city's "ribs"

CHAPTER THIRTEEN
TIME FOR ALL OF THAT

You are not the same when you have come down the river, led by a god. You have seen wonders: water-dragons leading your fleet, men steering the boats, just as a woman threads a needle, so as to keep the line of boats inside their perilous wake. You have seen a turtle the size of a family hut rise gleaming before you, nearly capsizing your craft, sending it spinning. You've seen children lost overboard and then rescued, young men risking their lives to wrestle the great toothy crocodiles. Heroism and nonsense. You have lived on fish and lilies.

Strangest of all, you were there when the seven young men of your people killed a great, bottom-dwelling catfish with a beard like a dragon's and wrestled its body ashore. You saw how when it was sliced open to be cleaned, there gleamed gold in its belly, worked gold: powerful, royal shapes that could only mean the presence of other people somewhere in this new land. The gold, like so many other things among the Snake People, when you looked at it gave you a cold dread in your own belly, which unlike the fish's, was still intact, at least temporarily.

All this time, your leader, your father, the father of your people, could be seen in the bow of the lead boat, balanced dramatically on it like a carved figurehead, his eyes fixed up and forward on something that, most of the time, only he could discern.

"Behold!" he said. "My son is not the only one who can see things that are unseen."

Occasionally you thought you got a glimpse of it: a snake, yes; shining, yes; tail trailing back over the fleet like a wisp of the vapor that it probably was, but stretched out on either side of it, you got a sense of massive, rose-gold wings.

In your father's mind, this god had literally lifted up his boat, bearing it safely over rapids and waterfalls – and perhaps it did for him, but unfortunately it had dragged the rest of the party chopping and bumping behind.

Your people did not, during that summer, do any more blood healings. They wanted to rest the god for its labors; also, perhaps, to rest their own bodies.

And then the city. In retrospect it seems you saw it bloom like a flower, though at the time there were intermediate steps, and it took several years.

Your people built it much bigger than they needed it to be at that moment. The father had seen how quickly a people could grow, seeming to double and treble before his eyes in the space of a few decades. That is how it was in that early age of the world, when a typical couple might have ten or twenty children, and a healthy woman could be fertile well into her sixties.

Before they could build the city, they had to build its foundations. They had many synonyms for these: "rocks," "mounts," "turtle shells," or sometimes they just called them the city's bones. But what they were was man-made hills.

Endu wanted to build near the river so that there was not a long walk for water, but he also knew enough to know that a city ought to be built on a high place. They ended up on high place from which, to the east, the land dropped away to the river. Streams cut cliffs on the north and south sides of their plateau.

They built the city's bones with sheer, back-breaking labor, the men and boys carrying and carefully layering the rock and clay and dirt. There was a formula, a special mix of the grit with the fine that would be less likely to erode. Every layer was laid with prayers and sacrifices. Endu began letting blood again, though it was mostly his own blood. He would not pressure them; he would accept only willing sacrifices for his city, and nearly every young man involved in the building did voluntarily give his own blood whenever he was worried about how the project was going, or whenever he was the one responsible for laying a new rib.

It was in a rib formation that they built them, parallel rows of hills bending toward the riverbank in a semicircle, like a giant man lying with his feet toward the river and his head toward the setting sun. Among the ribs there ought to be a heart or a breastbone, and there was: the temple mount, perched to the west of the city on even higher ground. From its summit you could look due east, over the city, and watch the sun rise over the wide gleaming river beyond. The city itself would serve as an observatory. Lines of sight ran through it, four aisles breaking up the ribs, and down these the Snake People would be able to sight to the sun at the solstices, whereas the temple mount stood opposite the sunrise at the equinox. From the temple, you would be able to stand and watch light flow down the aisles, through the city, like blood in a man's veins.

Endu was able to see all these things in his head, and he could draw them in detail for others to see. And he could get impatient with the others when they didn't immediately know how to interpret his diagrams or apply them to the ground before them. The whole layout had come to him, as if in a vision, the moment they got the ground cleared and he was able to stand in the wide space they had created, overlooking the river. (The cleared wood they saved and seasoned, and Sha was already itching to carve it into lintels and idols, bowls and house-posts.)

Of course, the suddenness of Endu's ability to envision the city was not actually sudden. He had been planning out cities in his head for many years. Whenever the People (even before they were the Snake People) had come in to a new landscape, Endu would begin observing it, noting the natural lines of sight, imagining what sort of a city one would build on that particular ground. It had been a massive frustration to him that these plans were never realized. The People (the *old* People, that is) had always just built their settlements out of sheer convenience, like a glorified hunting camp. All they cared about was that their huts should be in a sheltered place, near their relatives, with access to wood and water. They never thought of using them as observatories.

In fact, not only were Endu's plans in the past never realized, but they were also often only half-made. All sorts of things were always coming along during those years to interrupt him. Those had been the years that he and Sari were growing their family, and nothing can soak up all a man's attention like the needs of a newborn baby, especially when there were no servants about.

Also, Endu reminded himself, he had been younger then, less developed in his powers of focus and attention. He had been learning during those years, but oh …! How slow his learning had been! He would try to build his new hut on some kind of logical principle – door facing due east, for example, sleeping benches in a perfect circle – but inevitably Sari or one of the children would ruin the thing, and then he would lose his temper. He had been quicker to anger in those days, less in control of himself and less in control of the goings-on around him. Not like now. Now, at last, it seemed as if all his latent abilities were gathering momentum, rolling together into one luscious ball of light.

He still had some difficulty in getting others to implement his ideas, but it was at least possible. A few of the young men understood what he was about. Melek's sons seemed able to visualize as Endu could, or at least had the potential to do so. And Endu had found an unexpected ally in his nephew Megal.

As for building materials, for the time being they were forced to use wood. Stone would have been better, but there was not at this moment a convenient way to get stone. Here beside the river – and even on this ridge overlooking it – there was a great deal of very fertile soil. In fact there was a black layer of ash just below the surface, as if the gods had put it there on purpose to help people as they came to settle. But there was no stone. The group found themselves farther south, now, than the ice had ever come, so there was no longer a ready supply of boulders, sitting conveniently on the surface, that had been rolled there by the ice. To find and quarry and transport bedrock would take too many of the young men whom Endu needed for other things.

If only they had had giants, now.

Giants, he had learned from his ancestors, had always had a special way with stone. They were stronger, for one thing, able to handle larger blocks than the children of Noah, but there was more to it than that. Not even a team of giants could do the things that had been done before the Flood, perfectly placing huge megaliths. Not by natural means, at least. Everyone knew the giants were related to the gods, and there had been rumors.

They could shape stone with their hands, fitting it like puzzle pieces. They could levitate it when called upon to do so. These were the rumors.

Endu, of course, had never seen any of this with his own eyes. The Flood had wiped out the giants – that had been its purpose – and the men of Si Nar had used not stone, but the materials that were to hand, namely mud-brick. He had been taught, as a young engineer, of the methods that men might use to work stone and produce an approximation of the works of the giants. Heat and cold could be used, and wedges. Stones could be "walked;" greased and slid along; shaped before being transported to the place of their using. (Shaped before being transported to their places, he thought with a rueful grin; much as had happened to the children of Noah!) All of this he might try some day. He could expect to live another hundred years if he did not meet his death by violence. Endu had plans for every year, every month, of his remaining century.

But for now, it would be dirt, clay, and river rocks, and wood. Endu had no love for wood; it reminded him too much of the desperate days of the tribe's wanderings. But Sha seemed to have a feel for it. It responded to his hands as stone had responded to the giants' hands. So the Snake People, Endu was confident, within a year or two, would have a city built of fantastically carved wood, and probably painted, too. The most he could manage, for now, was that the temple itself would be made of fitted rocks from the river.

There would be time for all of that.

While the city's ribs were being built, the Snake People made their camps down in among them. This gave them a cozy feeling. For the adults, it reminded them of the years of travel through the corridor, when there has always been a mountain or cliff or glacier towering over them. It also afforded them some protection from the giant birds, which continued to be a problem. If you were running along the depression between two ribs and you suddenly darted into your hut, to the bird it was as if you had vanished.

As the city's ribs grew in length and number, the birds made fewer passes over it and when they did, they did not linger. The city, said Endu, was laid out not only looking like a man but like a huge snake, half uncoiled, sunning itself. (The temple mount was not yet built at this time, but eventually, it would be the serpent's head.) The bird goddess, said Endu, sees in the snake her counterpart and out of respect she stays away.

Before this happened, however, his warriors managed to fell a number of the birds. The people now had a taboo on eating them, but they would retrieve, pluck, and clean the feathers to use later in decorating their bodies and their temples. (Later, they discovered smaller birds whose feathers were more colorful and not as foul.)

The bodies of the birds would be thrown into the river to be carried away, so that they might not attract scavengers.

The disadvantage of living in the depressions between the city's earthen ribs was that the spaces between the mounds were not designed for this. They were too narrow to accommodate huts and also foot traffic from humans and dogs. The result was that the first depression they settled ended up feeling like a warren. To dispose of waste, you had to step out of your hut (likely being crashed into by a running child), and carry the chamber pot or trash or whatever it might be down the long corridor, until you got to the end where you could dump it on the midden pile at the base of the hill on the south side. Meanwhile four or five dogs would be following you, begging for a bite of whatever it was. No one enjoyed the garbage walk.

There would be a sewer system, said the planners, when the city was finished. Houses would be built on top of the ribs. It would mean lots of climbing up and down stairs, but that was a small price to pay for living in a light and airy place instead of in a smelly valley, a place where you could look out your front door and see the sun rise, or look to the west and see it setting behind the (planned) roof comb of the temple. Waste would go down from the houses in channels made of well-fitted rocks – (which would be lined and sealed with something. Perhaps dried mud, but Endu hoped to find something better) – into an underground channel, and out the side of the hill, *directly* onto the midden pile, without befouling the streets. No more "going down to the river" for the Snake People. They would live like kings.

What to do with sewage was not a problem in a group consisting of thirty people. But it would become one when their population reached ten, one hundred, or one thousand times that number. When it came to disposing of waste, even a broad river was not infinite. Endu remembered this from his days in Si Nar. At that time he had been mostly occupied with chasing girls, but he had been ambitious enough that he had also put some effort toward his training, and this had included city planning. It was best to train the people *now* to think of sewage as something taboo, so that they would have good habits in place before the population grew enough for their waste to be a real problem.

Those were the growing years. The city was shooting skyward, the people expanding outward. Sha and Wana hit their stride at last and began cranking out babies. Megal and his wife, and Peres and his wife, also continued to have children. As soon as a house was built of a suitable size for a young couple, young Eyli (son of the old shaman Ki-Ki was who dead) married a woman with whom he'd had an understanding for several years: Rumi's daughter Kit. The other young men were going to have to wait for their brides until someone was widowed, or the little girls in the settlement were grown, or until – a distant but intriguing possibility – the Snake People encountered others.

In the meantime, Endu did his best to keep them busy. He was forming a fighting force.

Endu had not forgotten the gold in the belly of the catfish. There were people out there somewhere, perhaps many months' walk away, perhaps very nearby. These were sophisticated people, able to mine and extract ore and to make things in molds. And so perhaps they would have sophisticated weapons and armor. Endu would try to make friends with the strangers if he could find them. He was a cosmopolitan man by nature, eager to trade goods and ideas on the way to expanding his empire. You could learn nothing from people if you killed them. Still, it seemed best to be prepared for all contingencies.

He sent the young men out to kill the dragon-like creatures that lived in the river. Not the great water-dragon of course; it was snakelike and therefore sacred to the People. Endu would feel loss if they managed to rid the river of such a magnificent creature. But there were a smaller type, a type that had small, fat, ridiculous legs and evil-looking faces with the eyes set on top of a long, flat head. These loved to lie in still water, and then when a person or an animal came down to get a drink, up the dragon would rise and grab its victim in its great toothy jaws like the very incarnation of terror. Endu had seen it happen to a deer, and even to the large, sheep-faced rodents who loved to swim. He did not want it to happen to any of his people. These squat river-dragons were also surprisingly fast on land, and like many of the megafauna in those days they never seemed in all their lives to stop growing. By the time the Snake People arrived at the site of their city, some of the four-legged dragons had gotten three times as long as a man. Perhaps this had taken them decades.

So the river-dragons had to go. This was a perfect project for the young men. Endu set them a task to clear the area. You could shoot a river-dragon in the eye (if you could spot it), or you could – and this was what they were usually forced to do – lure it onto land and then climb on its back and cut its throat. You did not want to be forced to wrestle it in the water. The dragon loved to drag you into his realm and then roll over and over until you were disoriented and drowned.

Their meat was delicious – greasy and gamey – and their skins were even better: a workable leather set with interesting patterns of large and – when not decorating the river-dragon's blobby body – beautiful scales. This dragon-skin could be used to make armor. In a single summer, Endu had outfitted himself and every man of his people with dragon-skin chest plate, arm guards, greaves, and codpiece, and with helmets which they decked out with waving feathers that grew larger and more glorious according to the rank of the bearer. His army might be tiny, but he would make it as well-equipped and impressive-looking as he could. He had the young men drill against each other. When wearing the armor they were braver and more obedient than before.

CHAPTER FOURTEEN
BEYOND THE DOOR

It was during these growing years that Klee had her first baby. It happened in a strange way.

Her father called her to him. This was during the second autumn the people spent at the site of the city, when they had been building it for only a year. It was shortly after Klee had turned eighteen.

Klee's audience with her father took place among the foundations of his temple. The temple mount had been built, the floor plan laid out, and the temple itself begun, with squarish stones set and mortared in the places where the walls would be. The foundations were knee high most of the way around, but already waist high on the west wall, which would be the deepest and most sacred part of the temple. Endu liked to stand here, looking down over the city, with his oracle wrapped around his shoulders, resting comfortably. The snake had grown astonishingly larger and thicker. It curved around the back of his neck like a heavy, collar-style necklace, the white head and tail contrasting with his blue-brown collarbones.

But he was not, on that day, wearing his headdress or his armor. He was three-fourths father and only one fourth king.

He welcomed Klee kindly, asked about her health and about Setiq's, and then, coming immediately to the point, commanded her that it was time she and Setiq began having babies.

Klee submitted to this command. She told herself that it was because she had also been thinking the same thing, that he had commanded her something she was already eager to do. But even as she bowed her head, she felt a little stirring of anger like a worm in her chest. Some things, she felt, were sacred. Some things were private. Endu should not have the authority to direct the intimate lives of the married couples who were his subjects, even if he was their king and priest. Even if he was her father.

She hated herself for failing to speak up. But it wasn't worth it.

Her father then backed off slightly, as if he sensed her resistance. It was up to her, of course, he said. Though he had never heard of a woman who didn't want to become a mother. Also, hadn't Klee been talking for years about wanting to build a women's lodge and direct the women's mysteries? It was more appropriate that a woman in that position should have womanly experience.

Endu glanced over his shoulder, over the waist-high western wall, out to the west across the jungle. There, where the land began to fall away, a space had been cleared and a mound built up. This was the planned women's lodge. Endu could look down on it from his temple.

Klee, instinctually, followed his gaze. She knew this mound, but she did not feel that it was hers. Ceremonies had already begun on that western mound, but they were not the wholesome, singing-and-storytelling ceremonies that the child Klee had once imagined. They were private, ad hoc, compulsive. They were carried out by her father's wife, Dira.

Dira had grown more anxious with every year the people traveled, with every new loss or danger they faced. She had been somewhat relieved when they settled, but the building process brought on a whole new set of worries. Dira wanted some way she could control what happened to her people, and she had settled on the letting of blood.

While most people gave blood only rarely – once a year at most, depending upon the needs of the tribe – the queen had begun to bleed herself more and more often. She explained that she was the mother of the tribe just as Endu was the father. Thus her blood should be good, not only for the healing of those immediately related to her, but for the protection of all the people. She had, perversely, become an expert on the letting of blood. It was foolish, she explained, when blood was needed, to cut one's arm or hand. These were parts that people used daily, and moreover a cut on the hand took a long time to heal. Dira had discovered that earlobes bled profusely even with very little damage, and she had experimented with working a hole in her lobe, then drawing a twig with thorns through it. Even better was the tongue, because it healed faster.

Now the women's mound had a hastily constructed brush hut upon it, looking, in proportion to the mound, about the size and shape of a nipple. In this hut, Dira could be found daily – even several times a day – drawing thorns through her lobes or tongue.

Klee had visited the hut a few times, but the atmosphere was repulsive to her: the smell of the dried blood, the crazed, glazed look upon her stepmother, the darkness.

Yet bleeding was the only thing that kept Dira calm from day to day. She had said that when in pain she would have visions. "Did you see my mother?" Klee had blurted, and Dira had looked at her in simple confusion. Then Klee had realized that, wherever her stepmother went during her visions, it was not to a normal place where she would see anything or anyone that Klee would recognize.

And now Dira was pregnant, which must mean that Klee's father still found the woman attractive, even though she now always appeared with fresh, weeping scabs on her earlobes and sometimes with blood showing between her teeth.

Have a baby, Klee's father had told her. Very well, she *would* have a baby, but it would be because *she* wanted to, not because he had told her to. She would do it for Setiq, not because her father wanted a multitude of people for his stupid city.

Klee was not certain how she felt about babies – or, specifically, about becoming a mother. She admitted this to herself as she descended the steps from the skeleton temple. There had been something wrong with every mother she had known. They had been unkind, like Amal, or dead, like her birth mother, or … off, like Dira. She was not certain about motherhood … but she *was* certain about Setiq.

Setiq was the most normal thing in Klee's world, a world in which she had a desperate need for normality. He was the only one who had not been thrown, three summers ago, by her drama. He had not been intimidated by her decision to run away from the tribe, but instead had come after her. He was easy to talk to, because he was comfortable with silence; but this did not mean he was shy. Setiq, in fact, liked people. He did not feel the need to show off or talk, but he gravitated towards groups. He preferred to be around them quietly, observing, absorbing in a way that somehow also gave back, just as Endu (she suddenly realized) gave off energy in a way that somehow also took.

As a result of his quiet, social habits, Setiq was a walking directory of what each person in the tribe was good at. If Klee needed help with anything, he could usually point her to the right person.

She and Setiq had been using a series of work-arounds to avoid becoming pregnant. Now they would need to reverse that. Telling Setiq about this was fun. When she told him, he looked at her with disbelief and then began to glow.

It was more difficult than expected to fall pregnant, but Klee managed it thirteen months later, in the autumn she was nineteen. By this time the city had considerable progress made on it. There was a sewage system, everyone had houses, the temple was built with a plain wooden roof-comb that Sha would climb up every day to carve upon. There was a dock on the river. The river flooded violently and somewhat unpredictably, so the Snake People built light floating docks that could be re-made as needed. The river, when flooded, was so wide that the Snake People could see no details upon the other bank. It looked like a line of darkness.

The women's lodge was now no longer a stinky brush hut, but a complex surrounding the mound like a crown. It included, on the south side, a birthing room. Pregnant women could live there for their last month or so before delivery, when their condition made impossible the main city's many steps. Around this complex, and stretching to the west of it, were Zillah's fields and gardens. Zillah in recent years had all but sworn off the healing arts, not liking the direction the Snake People's doctoring was headed. She had turned her attention to maize, beans, and squash.

There were a number of bad omens during the month that Klee was due to deliver. All of them looked like good omens at the time, but in retrospect, Klee felt differently.

The great water-snake had been seen that spring, for the first time since the Snake People founded the city. He came gliding down the river in the midst of the full, swollen flood, which had risen up almost to the height of the city, looking like a partly submerged city himself, merely a hint of something unimaginably large and cohesive beneath the water, with a fin on his head to draw the eye and mark his passing.

He was seen by the six unmarried young men: Dani; the three sons of Melek; and Dira's younger brothers Zedho and Tiwik; as they were out on the easternmost rib of the city, practicing running in their armor. Oddly, a few of the married young men were with them too: Sha, Eyli, and Setiq, but for some reason not a single one of these saw the snake. Those that did see it, however, confirmed each other, and everyone who saw it, also saw his status go up considerably in the days following. It was encouraging that the People had been visited by their god. It was a good sign for the crop, a good sign for women's fertility, a good sign for everything.

The spring wore on, summer began to come, and the maize was knee-high in Zillah's gardens. The weather became unseasonably hot and humid. This was another good omen, but suspicious as well, as if the land was trying to rush its maturity, or to convince itself of something.

Then Klee went in to labor, and this also was exactly right, exactly as expected, and yet it turned out wrong.

She labored for a day and a night – long, but not unheard-of for a first baby – and then she pushed for several hours. And then she was at the end of her strength.

Zillah had been in the hut with her, for she had requested Zillah, the woman with the soil on her hands, rather than the blood-soaked Dira. And others had been coming in and out to help. The men were not directly involved, but they followed her progress anxiously through messengers. They were not allowed to climb on the women's mount.

Setiq stood in the yard just outside the temple (the temple was now complete, and he would not have been able to see, from within it), staring down at the birthing hut and pacing and praying. When Wana came waddling up from the women's complex on the second morning, she found him collapsed into sort of a leggy squat, having fallen, right where he was, into an uneasy doze. His golden face was drawn and there were deep, chocolate-colored circles under his eyes.

But Wana hardly noticed this, having just come from the hut of horrors.

"Grandmother," she pronounced, "says there is very bad news. The baby is not coming."

Setiq looked up at her with a thin, haggard face, instantly awake. He had heard her words in his dream, and they had seemed of piece with it.

He struggled to his feet and, stammering, made her repeat them.

While she was repeating them, Endu came around the corner from the entrance of the temple.

"What does it mean?" asked Setiq in confusion, though he had a feeling he knew what it meant.

And Endu said, very businesslike, "Can my daughter be saved?"

Wana did not want to speak out clearly about what it would take to save her. She mumbled into her chest, but Endu understood.

"Do it, then," he cried. "Have my mother take a knife and cut her open. We can save *her* life at least. We have the ability to heal her –"

"No," said Setiq harshly.

They both looked at him and asked him to repeat it. So he did.

"No. I refuse to heal her *that* way."

"If you are afraid," said Endu, "I can give the blood –"

"It's not the blood, my lord," said Setiq. "It's that – thing. It's gotten so big. I won't have it going inside my wife's body."

Endu was mortally offended. He raised his eyebrows and backed away.

Then he remembered that he was the king.

"What, pup?" he snapped, striding again towards Setiq. By this time there was a crowd around them. Everyone was looking at Setiq, and many people had heard his words. "You would defy me, and defy your god? I won't allow it. She is my daughter. I won't allow *you* to close down *any* road to life."

Setiq's mouth twisted.

"*Life*," he repeated contemptuously.

That was when they came to blows. Endu charged him, intending to put him down on his back with a shove to the shoulders. But Setiq lowered his head and then the two of them were grappling, shoulder braced against shoulder, like wrestlers. Setiq was as tall as Endu now, but he was lighter, not yet having got his full man's muscle.

Sha came up and began to pry them apart, and Peres was saying to Endu gently,

"My lord … we are near the brow of the hill."

Endu stepped back. His pulse was thundering in his ears. He hated his son-in-law, his stupid yellow face, his stupid wavering scruples. But he didn't want to *murder* him. He was still stronger, Endu realized. He could make this son of slaves obey him. And, he knew from experience, if Klee developed an infection, Setiq would agree to snake-healing eventually. People always did. Endu would show his authority and the authority of his god, but he would not leave his girl without a husband.

"Thank you," he said to Peres. And he nodded at Sha.

Wana was terrified, but she wanted to save Klee's life. So she spoke up, and though she meant to speak to Setiq she could look only at the king. "Whether, whether, or not w—we use the god later," she blundered, "we must do the cutting now."

So the two men gave their consent.

Everyone who had witnessed the scene on the temple mount was shaken. Endu withdrew into the temple, presumably to commune with his god. Children and young women were crying with worry for Klee, and comforting one another. The older women made their way quickly toward the birthing hut to help out in any way they could.

Setiq sat down, right where he was, and rested his arms on his knees. His legs were shaking. His head was heavy; he couldn't raise his gaze from the ground for a long time. His body had turned to water.

Zillah had done a number of C-sections in the years before the tribe split in two. She was a competent surgeon and she had knowledge of the necessity for clean hands, how to suture the wound, how to pack it with antiseptic herbs. So she gave Klee a draught to knock her out, and then she saved her life.

The baby, a boy, was born dead. His head was squeezed almost into a cone shape and after Zillah pulled him out, they were not able to start him breathing.

When Klee woke, the first thing she saw was that her husband and brother had both broken the taboo on coming into the women's complex and were crouching beside her pallet.

She was dizzy and nauseous and in a great deal of pain, but she had always prided herself on her toughness. She gritted her teeth and spoke to them.

Setiq was apparently unable to speak, but his face told her everything she needed to know. He brought her water. Sha brought her a doll that his two-year-old had made for her, fashioned out of cattail leaves and flowers.

Later Zillah brought them the baby. Klee was not certain she wanted to hold him, but Zillah said, "You must go through this thing and realize that it has happened. You must treasure it."

So Klee accepted her firstborn. His golden skin was badly discolored around the head, but he was tiny and soft and his weight was perfect, and he had the face of Setiq. Her heart melted as soon as she held him, and a great wave of love hit her and knocked her down and then flowed over her head, like the current in the river. She wept – which she did not usually do, except in anger – and then she knew that despite everything, she had indeed become a mother.

And she realized that there had been one good mother, Grandmother Zillah, before her eyes all this time.

She and Setiq held their child for a few hours, and then they named him a secret name and buried him with Sha's grass doll and with a handful of last year's dried corn.

And then that horrible summer went on.

Klee recovered without the use of the snake. It took a long time. For a month she stayed in the women's complex, because with her severed belly muscles there was no way to get her up the steps to her and Setiq's empty little house, or even, in the early days, up the hill to the city. Wana, who had become stronger with each child she bore, hauled basket after basket of water for Klee to be bathed in, and Zillah insisted that all this water be boiled before it was used. They could see the steam curling up from the surface and the evil of the water leaving with it.

Ispet and Rini, two older married women who were sisters, cooked their hearts out for Klee as she recovered. She ate a lot of cornmeal mush, a lot of catfish, a lot of eggs of quail and turtles … and, as the summer wore on, squash. She loved the sweetness of its orange flesh. In those days, small physical pleasures seemed the only vivid things in her world. She was no longer certain who she was or what she valued. She had always had a warrior's heart; then her heart had changed, softened, with anticipation as she prepared to become a mother; then that, too, had been snatched away. Now she had nothing. She knew only that a good night was one in which the pain would let her sleep. A good day was one in which she could eat the soft, golden squash and feel its strength go into her. All that was real were the sensations of pain and relief, and the occasional flash of beauty. All other moments faded into vagueness and confusion.

Grandmother Zillah was with her constantly. Especially in the early days, when Klee had to be lifted and turned and bathed by someone else, Zillah did these things expertly and even, it seemed, with pleasure. Then she would sit with her granddaughter, not speaking unless Klee spoke, drinking her ever-present clay cup of tea.

Klee was surprised by how much she missed her baby, considering that they had never really met. Apparently she had gotten to know him while she was carrying him. Apparently she had invested quite a bit of thought and hope into him.

One day she said to her grandmother, "Does it ever stop?"

And Zillah said, "No."

Setiq was in the hut at the time, and he looked at the old woman with curses in his eyes. He could not be induced to stay away during Klee's recovery, so Endu, high priest of his own religion, had invented a workaround. Men could visit the birthing hut, but they must be covered in cornmeal first. Maize, like beans and squash, was a female thing, and a crust of cornmeal could serve to blunt the masculine energy they brought, to spiritually disguise them as women.

"Why must you tell her that?" he cried, and then with an effort added, "Grandmother?"

"Her body will recover," said Zillah, "And she will not always feel so confused. But she was talking about the grief."

She glanced at Klee, who nodded, then lowered her eyes as they filled with tears.

Setiq understood. He was in grief as well. But he wanted his wife to live, and he knew how important hope would be to her recovery.

Zillah had told them that Klee had very narrow hips. They should be careful, she said. Any future baby might have to be delivered in the same manner.

She was implying that they should perhaps not have children, but she wouldn't say this out loud. Everyone wanted children. Not to bear them was the greatest possible personal loss. Whether the young couple wished to risk Klee's life for another chance to participate in the Great Dance, was something the two of them would have to decide. Zillah would not push them in either direction.

Zillah was familiar with grief. In her 107 years, she had lost an awful lot of people. And what she had told Klee was true: it did not get better, not really. Zillah was better than most people at putting things to the back of her mind and continuing to function, but this did not mean that grief went away. When she let her guard down, when she opened that part of her mind (and also other times, at odd moments), she could feel how she was surrounded by a great cloud of witnesses.

There was Golgal, her first husband, a very good man; and Nirri, her second: a rogue but she had loved him. She had lost a son, Sut, who had had something about him that reminded her of the way that Setiq looked today. And there were others, all equally loved: her extended family from before the fall of the Tower, and Ki-Ki and Enmer and Klee's mother Sari. And all the dead babies besides.

Actually she had been relatively lucky, she supposed, to have lost so few in 100 years of living. But these things were cumulative; they weighed on one. Her body was still healthy and strong, but with all the grief, her mind was tired.

She wondered whether she wanted to go on through another century of this. She wondered whether she would be called upon to do so.

When she looked at these two, sitting before her, looking stunned from their – well, not their *very* first, but an early loss – to her they looked like beautiful little children. Sending them into this world full of tears and tragedy, she felt, was as irresponsible as if one of the mothers were to let her baby toddle out the door and down the long flight of steps from one of the houses in the city. Grab the child's hand, pull it back, let it practice walking in safety a little longer! But what could she do? They were already in this world, already being battered by it. There was no place else she could put them. There was nothing that corresponded to closing the door.

Her one surviving son thought he had found a way, of course. The snake could heal anything, if you were willing to pay the cost. Keep on healing, and in theory, you could put off death forever. It was the cost, though, that Zillah was unsure about. She was not certain that a toddler would really be protected if there was huge snake waiting to devour it, rather than a steep flight of stairs, beyond the door.

CHAPTER FIFTEEN
THE POWER

Summer ripened into autumn. Klee healed. She was able to climb the hill to the city. She was able to go up the stairs to her house. The stairs took longer than they once did, but she took them at least once a day and could feel herself getting stronger.

On her first night back in their little stone eyrie, Setiq came to where she was reclining and propped himself near the head of the bed. He rested his chin on the top of her head and wrapped his long golden arms around her shoulders.

Klee found the point of his chin uncomfortable. She could not move her head freely. She hoped he would not hold the pose for very long.

Just as she had this thought, Setiq was apparently tickled by her curly hair. He lifted his chin from her head and raised one hand to rub his nose, and then he laid his head back on her hair, resting on a cheek this time.

She could feel the strength flowing from her body into his. She could feel his sorrow.

She said, "In a year or two I will be healthy again. Then I'll give you another baby."

She had meant this statement as a comfort, and was not prepared for his gasp of horror.

"What? Oh no, no, no, my love, you mustn't *do* that!"

He was kneeling in front of her. He was grasping her shoulders.

"But … of *course* I must," she said, confused. "We know now that we can conceive. I want another baby. I want to get him back."

And now she was weeping. That hadn't been the plan.

"But it won't be him," said Setiq.

"I want a baby that lives, then."

"But do you want to go through all of this *again*?"

"I want a baby more than I want to live," said Klee.

"But I want you to live."

Klee shrugged. She was so tired; not living seemed like an attractive option.

She was not thinking clearly, of course. One could not die in childbirth and at the same time go on to enjoy and take care of a living baby. Dimly she realized this. Then, dimmer still, she apprehended that here on the edge of sleep she was trembling on the edge of sanity. Thinking two contradictory things at the same time; thinking that somehow she could make both of them happen. Going mad.

So it was possible, then, to be sane and mad at the same time. When one was on the edge of sleep. When injured and exhausted, or in the surreal days after a birth.

So it was possible, then, that the same person could have been both crazy, as her father had said, and also be as her brother had said: completely sane and pushed past the limits of her endurance, and taking the best, the rational option.

And then she knew that she was asleep. She watched in fascination as, with beautiful clarity, a dream unspooled before her.

A woman walked among blood-red bushes, trudging slowly up a hill. Before her was the most attractive lake Klee had ever seen. It was laid out like an agate in concentric rings of unbelievably vivid blues, the surface glassy, glossy, and steaming.

The woman set her baby among the shrubs. She made as if to sprint. Her movements showed the traces of what had once been athleticism. She was as tall and strong as Klee, but older, stooped, and carrying more weight.

Klee wished herself under the beautiful water. It was hot down there: far hotter, she realized, than a living person could survive outside of a dream. At the bottom, it was the darkest and the hottest. She stretched her toes down towards it. It felt so good, after the weeks she had spent in recovery, fighting shock and blood loss and often feeling cold.

Above her, a large object struck the water. The leather skirt blossomed out. The leather-clad feet were broad and flat and rounded. The falling object brought with it wedges of light and a sudden cloud of tiny, prickling bubbles.

Klee reached out and grabbed one smooth sturdy ankle. She pulled the object downward. It came easy: everything that was happening was dreaming, and easy, and smooth and slow.

The woman's face appeared before her. It was an attractive, round, chubby face, the eyes squeezed shut and the white teeth gritted against the pain.

Klee waited until the dark eyes opened.

"Hello, Mother," she said.

She wrapped her arms around the object, smooth and easy, warm and comfortable. The two of them soared upwards.

She woke.

She was back in the cold stone hut, but she was warm because Setiq had pulled a fur blanket over her. He had stretched out beside her and his arms were wrapped about her waist. He had just dozed off.

She was weeping, but not with sorrow.

She looked down at his arm stretched across her belly. The narrow cut of it, the prominent veins and ropey muscles, the scars from sparring.

She traced it with a finger. He woke.

"I'll stay alive … for you," she said.

There were ways it could be done, Grandmother Zillah had said. She could try to deliver the baby early (though that was risky). She could do a cut again, sooner this time, before mother and child ran out of strength. That, of course, was risky too. In fact there was no method that was not risky, but that was the way life was. Women as well as men, to do the things they were made to do, were constantly taking their lives in their hands. Living by dying.

Klee mentioned a few of these thoughts to Setiq. "In a few years."

He nodded. His forehead brushed her shoulder. He did not seem to notice that she had been crying; or, if he noticed it, he would have no way of knowing that it was because of a dream, or for any reasons other than the usual ones.

Then he said, "The scouts have found something horrible."

The horrible thing the scouts had found was goats' skulls. They had found a grove of them. A large area had been cleared, the vegetation trampled, and on the trees that ringed it were hung the skulls, facing inwards, as if to look on the slaughter of their brothers. And in the middle were more skulls, great piles of them, some bleached and brittle and – frankly – bone splinters; a few on top fresh, with bits of flesh still clinging.

And the smell!

Not all of the skulls in the pile were goats' skulls. There were wild horses, antelope, deer. But on the trees, it was all goats.

There were a great variety of goats in that land in those days. The scouts noted mountain goat skulls, with their outsized, curling horns; and the heavier skulls of the wild goats of the plains, their horns simple and angling back. They saw horns that twisted and others that hung low over the forehead. All of these were mounted higgledy-piggledy on the trees. Whoever had hung them knew their way around knots, and cord-making, but there had been no hints of anything ceremonial: no writing, no diagrams, no smears of ash. There was no smell of smoke, even. And the skulls were not hung all at one height, or all in the same manner. It was almost as if they had been hung playfully, as if a game had gotten out of control.

All around the city, other men were telling their wives the same news. The tale was only moderately disturbing at first, but it got more so, the longer the Snake People thought about it.

"What are dealing with?" said Megal, earnestly, in council.

The meeting was being held in the city street, at the intersection of the ribs and the main artery, around a low-burning bonfire. It was an autumn twilight. Besides the grown men, there were quite a few women present.

Peres, the oldest and most senior man after Endu, summed it up gravely: "We have something strong enough to clear the trees, dexterous enough to tie the knots.

Something that eats a lot of meat. It tears the heads from its prey and puts them in one place –"

"After eating the meat off them," said Sha.

"Perhaps," said Peres.

"So are you saying," said Endu, "we have found their midden pile?"

"A being that would sort heads from bodies," said Peres. "A being that would decorate its midden pile with skulls."

There was an uncomfortable silence.

"Other people, do you think?" said Zillah.

"Strong ones," said Eyli, doubtfully, who had been on the expedition.

"And either very numerous or very ravenous, to eat all that meat," said Megal.

Endu looked at Sha. "Do you think they might be Older Brothers, son?"

Sha shrugged. He did not know a great deal about Older Brothers, for all that he was considered the expert. Older Brothers were elusive. He had never seen them in large groups, and certainly he had never seen them hunt. Of course, that didn't mean they didn't do it.

Endu and Zillah were looking at one another, and it was a look fraught with meaning. They were thinking the same thought, but they would not speak it in front of the younger ones.

The meeting ended inconclusively. The younger men wanted to know whether they ought to go out and try to find the cache of animals' bodies, and at length Endu instructed them to do so. His first instinct was that looking for the bodies could only cause trouble, but then he changed his mind because more knowledge was always better. He instructed them not to take or even disturb anything, whatever they found.

A few days later, after casting many pregnant glances at each other, Endu and Zillah at last got to have their talk.

Zillah's house perched on the southwest side of the city, partway down the tip of the southwestern-most rib. Her flight of stairs was shorter than most. Her house was a short walk from the women's complex to her north, and, to her east, the town midden pile. A south-facing window let her look out over the yet-unexplored countryside. It was the only house, as yet, in this part of town. She had wanted her dwelling place to be this way, had insisted on it over

Endu's objections. He hadn't wanted her to be off by herself. He had wanted her closer to the temple.

Once it was built, though, and she was settled in it, he had to admit that it made a sort of sanctuary. He found himself coming here often, seeking her wisdom, though he should not need to, living as he did at the center of power.

Endu barely lived in his own house any more. Nor did Dira. All her time was spent in the bleeding-hut, and all his in the temple. Their household was run, effectively, by their daughter Gupet, who was now sixteen years old. What Endu did not know was how heavily Gupet relied on her grandmother.

Zillah's bones were old, and she had asked Sha to carve her some comfortable chairs. Wana had provided the cushions, weaving them and stuffing them with wool from a particular long-necked wild goat. The chairs were wide, sturdy, generous, and low to the floor, so that it was almost as if the old woman were still sitting on the floor, but with the additional comfort of a seat below her and a back to lean against, behind. Zillah had been sitting on, and ministering to people who sat on, floors, all of her life. It would never occur to her to do otherwise. But the floors in the old days had been dirt covered in hide; these new floors were of river-rock, and having something between her and that cold, hard surface made a huge difference to the matriarch.

She settled Endu in his chair and gave him his tea (the carved wooden arms had built-in niches for the clay cups). He scooted far back in the chair, rested his body against its throne-like back, drew his ankles up on the edge of the seat and sat there hugging his knees like a little boy. This was not his usual self-assured sprawl. Zillah had concluded, in recent years, that Endu had exhausted his capacity for being horrified. He had even come, she suspected, to *crave* horror. (Witness his eagerness to be violated by a snake.) But now, he seemed genuinely shaken by the thought that was in both their minds.

That thought was *blood-eaters*.

The pile of goats' skulls could perhaps have been caused by a large, and not very reflective, tribe of human beings. It could, at an outside chance, have been Older Brothers, though from what the Snake People had observed so far, Older Brothers were more omnivores than true predators, preferring fruit, pine nuts, and fish. Still, of Older Brothers she thought there was a slight, slight chance.

But there was a much more likely explanation.

Once before, many years ago, Zillah's family had encountered a race of beings that pulled apart live sheep and ate them raw. Twelve to fourteen feet tall, humanoid and with more than human intelligence but without man's sense of right and wrong, they had posed such a threat that the entire party had risked building boats and taking *horses* on them, though they were not seafarers by nature, and sailing a long way out of their way to avoid them. They had, in fact, given up the chance to live in a very pleasant land because it was already taken by the blood-eaters.

It was these creatures that best fit the puzzle posed by the bone-pile. What else had an obsession with removing heads, but no desire to bury them decently? What else had such a love for mutton?

Neither mother nor son was going to say the name, which would make it too real of a possibility.

But Endu said, and she heard in his voice that he was shaken, "How on earth did they get here ahead of us?"

For their last sighting of the blood-eaters had been a generation of travel behind them, a world away.

And Zillah said, "Anything we can do, they could do, could they not, my son?"

His mouth twisted and he spat, "You are saying they are faster and stronger than we are. And more clever."

"As clever, at least. I fear we must face that fact."

"Anything they take it into their heads to do, they can do, and no one can stop them."

Zillah was silent. It certainly looked that way. *God* had stopped them, once, but that had taken the overwhelming power of water and the destruction of an entire world. Was it really true, she wondered, that destroying the world was what it took in order to stop the blood-eaters? In her heart she cursed the foolish people who had made shift to bring these giants back again. Probably they had wanted power, sovereignty over the world just as her son wanted sovereignty. Probably it had not crossed their minds that there could be a down side to creating a power that nothing could stop.

And now here sat Endu. He was scared at this moment, sitting in her house and acting like her little boy. But once he left this house, she knew, he would begin seething, unable to stand the fact that there was, loose in his territory, something stronger than himself. He would begin thinking of a way to make the power his own. It would probably not occur to him to flee from it. She should bring the thought, at least, before his mind.

"We could move," she said, "before they find us. We have done it before. That way, we would have time to plan. We would not be forced to flee."

Her son waved a hand dismissively. "That's a last resort. Look at how much time and effort we have put into this city. You have your fields, don't you? I have my temple. Why should we have to leave all this at their pleasure?"

"I agree it would be unjust," said Zillah slowly, "but that is not really the question."

"I don't mean to fight them immediately, Mother. They have minds, don't they? Minds like men. Remember the way those others were able to build fortresses? Perhaps we can speak with them. Perhaps learn something of their lore."

"Perhaps become their slaves."

"Not necessarily," said Endu. He had put his feet on the floor was now sitting forward, hands braced on his knees as he prepared to rise. "Do not forget that we too have a power."

Zillah waved as he descended the steps from her house. Then she went to her bed and pulled a fur blanket around herself. The Snake People had come into a subtropical zone where snow was rare even in the winter, but they had built these rock-floored houses that retained the cool of the nights, and now, Zillah sensed an icy shadow from the past or the future completing its slow stretch over them. Her body felt very cold.

All that winter, Klee healed and grew stronger; Dira bled out her life but did not die; children grew; young women took over from their mothers as the leaders of households. Endu, meanwhile, kept hunting for the giants.

The skull-pile had been found on the other side of the river, which during the winter was lower and easier to cross. No matter how many scouting parties Endu sent out (and they always hunted while scouting, so that their efforts were not wasted), none had found any evidence of blood-eaters on the river's west side, where the city was. So Endu kept making them go farther and farther east. Sometimes he went along; sometimes he didn't. Eventually, he had to go himself, because the men were overcome with a feeling of foreboding the farther they traveled into the territory on the east side of the river, and at long last only Endu's personal presence, insisting and driving them, would induce them to continue their searches.

Despite the almost physical revulsion they felt on these expeditions, they did continue to find evidence of blood-eaters. They found clearings, traces of bonfires, and once a great sheep-pen made by laying unshaped logs whole across the mouth of a cave.

Then they began to find roads.

The road was made of large stones, split but not finely dressed, perfectly fitted like a puzzle, stretching off level through the forest, heading due east. Like the skulls in the clearing, it gave the impression that it had been built by a being that was intelligent and powerful, but fundamentally lazy. The builders, whoever they were, had been able to sling about stones that weighed easily as a much as a man. They had found stones that would fit together with almost no need for mortar. They had split them to make a flat surface. But they hadn't taken the final steps. They hadn't chiseled them into regular shapes, they hadn't used mortar on the road. They hadn't built up the road bed very much so as to allow water to run off. Even the humans could see that in a few years, the rainfall would cause the stones to slide out of place, lumping up like mountains, so that before long, that stone road would be the most difficult place to walk in the whole forest.

It was as if the builders had thrown down this great project almost as an amusement.

Suddenly the whole party – Endu, Setiq, Zedho and Tiwik; and Sha – took fright at the same moment and bolted off the road like a warren of rabbits. All had sensed something coming up the road. They made their way back into the bush, flattened themselves, and peered back the way they had come. As they watched, a giant furry turtle-beast made its way slowly west along the road. The creature was enjoying the smooth dry surface, moving faster than it was usually seen to move, gripping and scritching with its claws.

Sha let out a breath and made a comically relieved face. Looking at Setiq and the sons of Dusun, he saw that they were relieved as well, and that, like him, they had been frightened by the road itself. Sha's father, as usual, looked bright-eyed and excited. To him, the road said, *Great engineers.* To the younger men, it said, *We are drawing near their city.*

Sha said under his breath, "Father, I think that if we get any prey in this place we should leave its head on the road as a thank-you."

And Endu replied, "Good idea. They like heads."

CHAPTER SIXTEEN
MORE POWER

By spring, through a series of increasingly elaborate gifts and signs left on the east side of the river, contact had been made.

The first signs had been left on the road. Endu and company left an elk's head with antlers of ten points, and when they returned they found a head made of gold … small, the size of a man's palm, flat and about a knuckle-joint thick. It seemed to represent the head of an Older Brother, or perhaps that of a blood-eater, it was difficult to tell.

No gift could have been better calculated to bring Endu's interest in the strangers to a fever pitch. He was mad to meet these people, to dress in his best and follow the road to their city. But the younger men talked him out of it. They felt strongly that such an expedition might be seen as an attack, or at best as very impudent.

So the next head was left in one of the mysterious clearings closer to the river, and the blood-eaters seamlessly adapted to this change, leaving a copper item in the same place in exchange. The gifts and counter-gifts, signs and counter-signs, continued until a meeting was arranged for the spring equinox in the clearing where the exchange of signs had taken place. By this time, most of the Snake People were hardly afraid of the blood-eaters, whom Endu was now calling "the engineers."

In the midst of preparations for this exciting day, Endu called Setiq to him at the temple. Setiq climbed the tiny steps, his calves burning. He entered the courtyard and stood for a moment enjoying the way the brick walls and paved floor cradled the heat and held it, like a water bath, around the visitor. Then he stepped across the threshold, ducking his head, into the enclosed part of the temple.

For a split second, as his feet crossed the threshold, he thought he saw something enormous. It was big enough to send his pulse racing. There was Endu, on the simple stone throne; there, behind him, rose the white folds of a giant body, mounded up as if to support his reclining form, curving around the sides as if to enfold him, meandering into a tapering tail that reached out of the inner sanctum, through the anteroom, and almost to Setiq's feet where he stood just inside the door.

Then he blinked, and it was gone. Endu was sitting upright on the throne as usual, and as usual, the snake, now thick as a bicep but nowhere nearly as large as Setiq had seen, was draped across his lap. Endu was running his fingers over it affectionately, as if it were his pet rather than the other way round.

Reality, at times, seemed to bend itself around Endu. Setiq was not really certain what he had seen. He said nothing.

His father-in-law beckoned, and he crossed the anteroom, stooped under the second door, and stood before the throne.

"I want you," said the king as if he were doing his son-in-law a great favor, "To lead the party when we cross the river tomorrow."

"Very good, my lord."

"And," the king added, "I want you and my daughter to have another child."

Setiq had already begun to bow his head, but his neck snapped upward as if of its own accord. "My lord, what happens in our household is surely our own business."

"Nonsense!" barked Endu. "I am the king. I am in control of my people. If I say they are married, they are married, and for only as long as I say. If I say they are to have children, they shall have them. Do not try to take this power to yourself. I have already allowed you much leeway, son of Hur-kar. I have let you, a son of slaves, be the husband of my daughter."

Setiq did not know exactly what the word *slave* meant, but he gathered that it was not a compliment.

"I was not saying, my lord, that I am the one who has this power. Am I God, that I can open and close the womb?" This was still a painful topic, but he moved over it smoothly. It was a familiar, not a brand-new, pain. "I am saying, instead, that the making of families is not something that is in a king's authority. It belongs to a … a different reality."

"Reality?"

Endu slung his pet behind his head so that it draped regally over his shoulders. He lunged to his feet, laughed scoffingly, and spread his arms, taking in the temple, the city, the landscape beyond.

"*None* of this is real!" he said.

And he stood smiling, handsome, with the snake framing his head like a collar of royal armor.

Setiq did not reply. Now he knew what he had to do. He only hoped he had not already shown too much of his mind to Endu. He began to bow out of the room, hoping that the king would take his silence for assent.

And the king appeared to. "Don't forget!" he called cheerfully. "Tomorrow! Wear your finest feathers!"

Klee reacted to Setiq's idea, at first, with dismay and confusion. She sat on their bed, knees draw up in front of her, fingers pleating and unpleating the woven edge of her skirt.

"Go away? Just the two of us?" she whispered. It was night; their chamber was dark; there was no danger of anyone hearing. But Klee reacted as if she thought his words might explode.

"'None of this is real,' he said." Setiq repeated his father-in-law's words for about the fourth time. It was obvious to him how dangerous this attitude was in a leader. He wondered that Klee couldn't see it.

"What does that *mean*?" she murmured. "Are you saying that he's right … that this is all an illusion?"

"It seems real enough to *me*. I helped to build this city, after all. I mean ..." He shrugged his thin shoulders. "... you can smell our midden pile for yourself."

His wife giggled.

"But," continued Setiq, "If he thinks this is all something that he made up, well ..." Words failed him. "He might do *anything*. Anything," he finished lamely.

"I don't know which is more frightening," said Klee. "Someone once told me about a being that could alter reality, and it was the most terrifying thing I'd ever heard. I had forgotten until now. I got distracted by my stepmother. As if that meant anything."

She flopped her glossy dark head forward. It was difficult for Setiq to see what she was doing by the faint starlight, but he gathered that she had rested her head on her knees and was clutching her hair.

"I followed him here because I thought he was the one who would show me the *truth*," she moaned. Her voice was ragged and teary.

Setiq's heart went out to her. He nudged her over, sat beside her, and hugged her playfully around the shoulders. Klee always hated for him to do that for more than a few seconds, but he wasn't going to stop doing it. At a moment like this, she needed that human contact. Sure enough, after a few beats she shoved him away. But when she spoke, he could hear that her voice had lightened.

"'You made a mistake, babe.' Is that what you are telling me?"

It was, but he saw no need to rub it in. "It's not too late. We are young and strong. We can make the journey back to the Reindeer People. Or we can set up on our own."

"We won't be able to start a people. I can't have babies, probably. Not without Grandmother Zillah's help."

Setiq flinched. "That's true. Perhaps we can come back and get her at some point. I don't know. But I have a feeling we need to get out of this city your father has invented. The longer we stay here, the more likely that something bad will happen."

Then he fell silent to let her think about it. She was quiet too, but he could sense her nodding beside him in the dark.

When she finally spoke again, her words set his pulse pounding. "When? Do you mean now? Tonight?"

"I promised him I would go to see the engineers tomorrow," said Setiq. "He wants me to lead the procession. We'll do that, and then, in the next few days, we can go. Whatever happens with the engineers, he'll be so excited about it that it will be all he can think about. It will give us time to get away."

"Agreed," said his wife. She reached and clasped his hand, as if they were men friends, and they made a vow on it. Then both went to sleep with a new calmness, excitement, and resolve.

The party that crossed the river to the fateful clearing consisted of Endu, his wife and children, and the core of Endu's little army: the young men Apik, Kor, Yakab, Zedho, Tiwik, and Dani, with Setiq in the lead. Besides these seven, there were some older officers: Sha, son of Endu, and Megal, son of Enmer, Sha's cousin.

They crossed the river by raft from their home dock. The water was no longer at flood, early spring having passed. They traveled a little way upstream before docking, disembarking across the mud, then filing in between the giant trees as they bent their steps east along the path to the clearing. Klee was walking in the back with the other women: Endu's daughters Gupet and Kari, and his wife Dira. Dira was blood-free today, the usual scabs on her earlobes covered by huge elaborate earrings that Sha had made, which hooked around the entire ear and hung down below in cascades of jade beads. She also had a net of semiprecious stones draped over her head. Dira, usually stooped, stood straight today, but as ever, her skinny form gave off a visible nervousness, like a spear quivering after it has just sunk its point solidly into the target. She strode forward, clasping her daughters' hands on either side, quivering and never becoming still.

All of them had dressed up for the occasion. After several years in the city, their clothes were no longer the same as they had been when they lived with the hunting people. Instead of leather, the women wore plant fiber, dyed and twilled into patterns. Though Klee usually preferred a shorter skirt, today her clothes, and Gupet's and Kari's and Dira's, draped. Instead of being held up in practical buns, their hair hung loose down their backs.

Men's fashion, as it had developed among the Snake People, erupted upward, and the warriors marching ahead of them were adorned with spectacular feather headdresses that nearly doubled their height. Women's fashion was supposed to drape gracefully down to the earth, and the long skirts, which had taken so many hours of work to fashion, slowed their steps and caused them to walk in a dragging way that the Snake People found very feminine. Behind them they dragged disposable trains, which had been woven of river reeds and grasses.

They looked stately, but Klee did not feel festive.

Sha and Megal were walking on either side of the four women. Klee saw her brother glance over at her sympathetically.

She was not sure what she feared. Being eaten was, of course, the biggest concern. But she couldn't help suspecting that, after all this buildup, the party would arrive to find an empty clearing, that the giants would never come.

The giants did come. They were waiting there, in the sunshine, when the human party arrived. There were four of them.

Everyone's heart starting beating as soon as those huge forms came in sight. The giants were not doing anything threatening, but they did not need to. The humans' reaction to their mere size was instant and natural. Klee could feel the blood soughing in her ears.

It seemed like a long, long time that the Snake People stood taking the in the sight of their humanoid neighbors. Perhaps it was only a long moment.

The giants were not, like the great water-snake, so huge that they could not be taken in with one look. They were about twice as tall as the Snake People. They stood in a row, lounging casually against the backdrop of the trees on the other side of the clearing. Their heads came about halfway up the younger, brighter, new-growth trees that edged it, though these were still only a fraction of the height of the old sentinels that loomed beyond, in the virgin forest.

The giants were good-looking, but clearly not human. Three of them had skin that was a shocking milky white, with pink noses, chests, and shoulders. The fourth was a ruddy, orange shade. The white giants had reddish hair, and the red giant had yellowish hair. All of this made it hard for the Snake People to credit what they were seeing.

The creatures were muscular and well-formed, having prominent staring eyes, a visible down of hair on their arms and legs, a triangular line of hair tracing down their pectorals.

Also, they were naked.

This last fact threw the Snake People perhaps more than any other. They had come to meet the engineers. They had expected them to be clothed. It was surprisingly disconcerting to go out to meet an enemy – or even a potential ally – and find that he had not bothered to get dressed.

Dira pulled her daughters to her on either side and covered their eyes with her hands. Klee tried not to stare at the nakedness of the giants, but she couldn't help noticing that some of them were already aroused.

The giants grinned. If they had been people, Klee would have thought that they were enjoying the other party's discomfort. But then they began to hail them and to call out cheerful greetings, though of course the humans couldn't understand what they were saying.

Sha and Megal, after consulting one another with a glance, both dropped back and gently herded Dira and her daughters back down the trail and into the bushes. Klee remained rooted to the spot. The rest of the party advanced, Setiq in the lead, followed by Endu and the other six young warriors.

"*Haa hoo gabbada gabbada!*" said the giants.

Endu spoke a quiet word, and Setiq went forward, the green and gold feathers of his headdress bobbing in the sun.

Then everything exploded.

The ruddy giant stepped forward, grabbed Setiq, wrenched his spear from his hand and threw it into the trees. He bent him over and flipped up the skirt of his armor. It was obvious that he was about to defile him.

Klee, recognizing the position, yelled, "Stop him!" at the same moment that Endu and the six younger warriors released a hail of spears from their spear-throwers.

Some of these hit the giants and stuck in their skin. Some didn't. None were fatal. But they did succeed in deflecting the orange monster from its intended purpose. It did not rape Setiq. Instead, its starting dark eyes glared at the spearmen with a look of rage. Then it grasped Klee's husband, in one big hand, by the ankle. It swung him upside down. It took the other ankle in its other hand.

Klee recognized this gesture too. It was what she did when she went to pull apart a bird's carcass for cooking.

There was a crack.

Setiq screamed.

Klee screamed. It seemed that her whole body was screaming.

The giant completed its operation. The wet pieces – now no longer Setiq – hit the ground with a thump. That thump would stay for a long time with all those who had heard it.

The monster raised the skinny, golden leg still held in its hand and began to strip the meat with its teeth.

Then Klee went out of herself for a while. She did not see or hear the things that happened all around.

But things continued to happen. A number of people vomited. Her father himself retched, but then straightened, grey-faced, and said to the bird-killers, "Prepare for battle."

They arrayed themselves, ready to fling the spears again. If they had actually done so, then probably all of them would have died. But, at the last moment, another enemy intervened. Large shadows fell over the clearing, along with a sudden whiff of unpleasant odor. Squawks were heard.

Several of the great foul birds, the ones the people had previously driven away, descended and began to fight over Setiq's remains. The giants gabbled their booming gabbles and shooed at them. The birds retaliated. The giants received gouges in their hands and arms, but didn't seem ready to give up the meat.

"Fall back," barked Endu.

In order to retreat, the party had to gather up their spears and spear-throwers and carry them in a way that was not battle-ready. Klee was curled in a ball, and no one could rouse her. Sha scooped an arm under her ribs and ran with her, awkward, banging, that way. Her trailing dress was tangling around his arms, and he paused for a second to tear off, and fling frantically to the side, the train made of grasses. Then he was off down the trail. The soles of his feet felt on fire. He lifted his sister to his shoulder when they got to the river.

They crossed the river, desperate, exposed. Dira and her girls hadn't actually witnessed what happened, but they were screaming and keening inconsolably.

Endu kept saying, "Shut up! Shut *up!*"

Klee was still unresponsive, huddled, staring.

The humans found a sheltered position on the other side of the river. The activity of the giants, owing to the distance and the huge trees that intervened, was now harder to see. The warriors stared until their eyes dried out. It seemed that the giants had driven away the birds, gathered up most of the remains, and, munching, began to head in the opposite direction. Sha was certain that he saw one look back over its shoulder with a casual grin, but later he re-interpreted this as a hallucination brought on by the state they were all in. Nobody could really see in such detail across the vast width of that river.

Thus began a time of war for the Snake People. They would find out later that the giants hated water and, even in the summer, would not cross the river. This proved to be the people's salvation. If there had been no river, or if it had been of the type that goes completely dry in the summertime, their city would not have lasted long.

But on that day, they did not know this. They hurried back to the city, gathered everyone up, and put them all inside the temple, because it was highest, made with the most stone, and thus the most defensible. They all lived there for about a month, sneaking, sending out scouts, making quick frightened dashes to go and get water.

Those days were the worst that Sha could remember living through. At the age of thirty-three, he had already seen some horrors. But none of them compared to this. All the women and children were terrified. Some wanted to hear the story again and again; others forbade anyone to tell it. They sat crowded in, side by side. The floor was hard and cold. They dumped their chamber pots down the slope towards the women's complex, and the stench rose up and soon the whole temple smelled like a latrine. The children were constantly crying. Everyone – at least, if Sha could go by his own experience – everyone who had been on the expedition kept reproaching themselves again and again for allowing what had happened to Setiq, which was actually worse than they had previously been able to imagine.

They should have known, they thought. They should not have allowed Endu to reach out to those blood-eaters. They should have known. They should have known.

Sha remembered the guilt after his mother had died. It was just like this. If something happened twice, did it count as a pattern? Someone died a horrible death somewhere in the vicinity of Endu. The death ought to be his fault, but it somehow wasn't. Blame rolled off him like water and adhered, sticky, to everyone else instead.

This imperviousness to blame, was this divine power? It was certainly a power of some kind, but to Sha it was beginning to seem the opposite of divine.

Klee did not speak during this whole month. She ate and drank because Wana made her. She vomited daily. She spent the rest of the time not thinking about anything at all.

But when thoughts did pry their way in, they had a lot to say.

To her father: *Did you know? You knew. You never liked him. You thought of him as a son of slaves. You wanted someone expendable. Was this all part of your plan?*

To Sha: *How could we have let it happen?*

And above all, to Setiq. *I am sorry. I am so sorry I got you into this. I am so sorry.*

And then at night, she would hear a wet *thump* and sit up straight, awake, panting. If the moon was up, she would be able to see the outline of Sha where he lay, one arm around his wife, eyes wide open with the silver light glinting off them. And she would know that he was hearing that thump too.

CHAPTER SEVENTEEN
WHAT THEY DID THEN

Only Zillah refused to imprison herself in the snake temple. She went out daily, working her gardens, bringing back food for everyone. When they pleaded with her, she would only say firmly, "If I perish, I perish."

After a month, she announced that she was going to start sleeping in her own house again. If anyone else wanted to leave their self-imposed prison, they were welcome to join her.

Endu, Sha, Megal, and Peres talked about it, and they agreed. The people could not live in a little rock-and-wood box forever. Soon it would be time to harvest the maize. People needed to eat, they needed to wash, they needed to get out and feel the air. And by this time, there had been a month of daily patrols, prowling the river bank, seeing and hearing mostly nothing. Twice they had ventured onto the east side of the river; once, all the way to the giants' city. They saw no preparations for war (not that these creatures seemed to prepare very far in advance for anything). On the second occasion, they were discovered before getting near the city. Then they ran like children with the most terrifying of demons after them, and the pursuit had stopped as soon as they stepped in the water. That was how they first learned that the blood-eaters were unwilling to cross it.

So, led by Zillah once again, the Snake People began to come back to life.

All except Klee. She no longer wanted to live. The horror of that sunny clearing had got in amongst her and was clinging to her insides.

She did not want to do anything any more. She was tired of trying to contribute to the city, to make herself understand her father, to force herself to like the snake. She was tired of trying to figure it all out. She just wanted to go back to that land that was so far north, so peaceful, so beautiful, that once she had hated so much.

She just wanted to go back there and rest.

The quickest and easiest way to do this, she knew, was death. But she had a compelling reason to go on living. Actually, a couple of compelling reasons.

Zillah and the other women did a maize harvest. As they stood in the fields, they were constantly on the lookout for the enormous birds, which they now considered an early warning of the presence of giants. If they saw one go by, even at the edges of their sight, they would hurry back to the city to wait for news and look out from the heights.

Ordinarily, Klee enjoyed the harvest. But this year, she did not go out with the other women. She had reached that stage of grieving where one cries and sits with a dog.

Guide had been with Klee ever since he was first presented to her by her brother, Jabed. The rangy, wolfish dog had in recent years faded somewhat into the background. The Snake City was not as natural an environment for dogs as the Reindeer camp had been. Not all of the dogs could navigate the steep steps that led up to the people's houses. The dogs still knew, in a loose way, which family they belonged to, and they would still accompany their men on hunts and attend closely when animals were butchered, hoping for scraps. But when at home in the city, they had become half-feral, hanging around the midden pile in order to eat the garbage, moving in packs through the tunnel-like streets.

Now Klee put her arms around Guide's skinny ribs and half dragged him up the steps to the house that had been hers and Setiq's. Guide had become almost more Setiq's dog than hers in recent years, and she did not know how to explain to him that Setiq was gone. But perhaps he got the message when she sat, day after day, on the river-stone floor, crying with her arms wrapped around his shaggy middle and her face buried in his ruff.

Sha came over, shyly, and asked Klee to move in with him and Wana. Surely she didn't want to be alone in her cold, lonely house?

"I do want to be here," said Klee. "*He* is here. I don't want to stay anywhere else."

But then she began to cry and explain how guilty she felt that she had neglected Guide. His fur was matted and dirty, and she thought he had fleas.

Sha was somewhat thrown by what appeared to be a change of subject, but he helped her haul water so that she could bathe the dog, and found a brush so that she could maintain his coat. Sha was glad to have a practical task that would perhaps help his sister.

The next time he visited, she asked for his help with an impossible one.

It was well after dark, because Sha couldn't get away until his children and even Wana were all asleep. Sha himself had been unable to sleep lately, and he was sure the same was probably true of his sister. He had just come up to her house –

Now, whenever the Snake People visited one another, what they always did was "come up." To get from one house to another, you first had to go down the steep steps away from your house of origin, then along the narrow alleys between the ribs of the city. Then you had to climb another narrow staircase, "going up" to your destination. This was true of all visits except in those cases where your house and your friend's were on the same rib, in which case there was often a narrow path you could take, the friendly houses on one side, the steep drop on the other. Thus it was always the guest who "came up," and always the host who waited at the top to welcome him. The house that Klee and Setiq had shared was not on the same rib as Sha's house, but on a "lower" rib, one level farther from the temple.

Sha, then, had come up in the dark to his sister's house, and just as he expected, he found her wakeful. She was sitting in the outer room of the house, building up a fire in the stone fire circle. She had not bothered to do anything with her hair; it cascaded down her back in frizzy firelit waves, and there was a light of determination in her eyes.

The stone circle was situated directly underneath the highest peak of the house's roof. There was no ceiling, and the cone-shaped roof acted as a natural chimney, drawing fumes up towards the square smoke-hole. The bedroom, an inner room, had been made by walling off the back portion of the floor plan. It would have a lower ceiling that sloped down towards the eaves at the back. Sha wondered whether, since the horrible event, Klee had even entered that bedroom.

"We have to warn them," she announced, by way of greeting. She did not even seem surprised that her brother had ventured out after dark. It was as if she had known he would come.

Sha had not, like Klee, become catatonic, but he too had been feeling shocked and disoriented ever since the – event. So, although he was not at that moment sure what was going on with Klee, he had gotten used to tolerating a certain uncomfortable level of confusion. He lowered himself wearily to one of the woven sitting-mats on the floor and prepared to rest there until his sister made her purpose clearer.

There was a scratch of canine toenails at the door. Sha jumped. What dog could this be? Guide was already here, sitting beside Klee.

But Klee said, calmly, "Come in, my daughter," and in came Goldie, smaller, smoother, and less scruffy of fur than Guide, but still with the same rangy look. Goldie had been more Setiq's dog than Klee's, and she still occasionally came to the house that held his smell. She was somehow able to handle the steps.

Now Goldie entered and lay down beside Sha. He automatically began to pet her. It was impossible not to pet a dog that lay down beside you. He was reminded sharply, for a moment, of the old days.

"Who do we have to warn?" he asked.

His sister looked up at him, startled, the yellow light of the fire flaring in her eyes. "The Reindeer People," she said.

"Oh," said Sha, and felt foolish that he hadn't thought of this. Then he said, "How are we meant to do that?"

Klee patted the floor beside her. She had already prepared, Sha noticed, a largish pile of something. It could have been almost any plant material. It was leaves, not a grain like maize.

"I don't *know* that it will work," she began, defensively.

"Well, let's hear it," Sha encouraged her. After all her weeks of silence, it was a relief to him to hear her talking. But the relief he felt was mixed. She was talking, but it remained to be seen whether she was talking sense.

"They need to know about the blood-eaters," said Klee. She said this calmly, dryly, as if the blood-eaters were a fact of life, or as if all the emotion had long ago been wrung out of her, so that she had none left to cause a tremble in her voice. "Obviously, we cannot make the journey and warn them. You have a wife and a passel of children, and I … well, brother, I am not strong."

"You are very strong," said Sha.

"You know what I mean. I couldn't outpace those monsters if they detected me and decided to go for me. And they would."

He stayed silent. Of course, no one could outpace them. Not a full-grown man. Not an army.

"So," she continued, "our only option is to try something stupid and dangerous."

"I'm always up for stupid and dangerous."

"We have to try to walk in the spirit world."

She glanced at him to see whether he was horrified. He wasn't.

"Well, I'm not an expert," he murmured. "I *have* been there, once, on my vision trip, so I know it's possible. And it's in our blood, at least a little. There is our brother, the father of Dumish. He does it all the time. It does," he added doubtfully, "seem to cost him, though, Sister."

"Exactly. I wouldn't ask you to risk yourself. You have a wife and children. At first, I was worried that as soon as we crossed the veil, we would be met by the snake."

Meeting the snake under any circumstances was a terrifying thought, but meeting it during a vision trip, let alone one's first real vision trip, sounded beyond foolish to Sha. It sounded like the sort of thing that would drive a person permanently mad.

"And what is to prevent that?" he ventured.

"We have to do it the old way, not the snake's way," said Klee. "We won't use blood. We'll do it the way the shaman used to do it."

"Which was how?"

"Don't you remember? He used to use sage."

She picked up a handful of the plant matter and poured the leaves gently on the fire. Instantly a pleasant smell began to fill the room. It filtered upward towards the smoke-hole.

Sha was filled with conflicting emotions. The smell brought before his mind, very vividly, many memories of his brother. But the next moment he remembered that he would not be the only one to recognize that smell.

"If that smoke comes to our father, he will know what we're up to."

"He is in the temple," she said, still dryly. "These days he is always in the temple. And the smoke should flow south over the city. Towards the midden pile. The breeze is blowing downstream."

Sha raised one shoulder. "All right. But whatever we are going to do, we'd better hurry, just in case."

"What are we going to do?"

"You tell me."

"I will tell you what *I* am going to do. But I won't ask you to come with me, Brother. You have been so good to me, and I have never appreciated you … just as I have never appreciated anyone. I won't ask you to do something that might destroy your mind. You have other people who need you --"

"We need *you*, too, you know."

"No you don't. I don't contribute anything. I never have. Yet everyone has been throwing themselves away trying to take care of me. If it weren't for me, perhaps you wouldn't even have come to this awful city. You and Wana would be Reindeer People. You'd be hunting all winter, and carving up wood houses and things. Making babies."

"We *are* –"

But Klee was in full flow. She cut him off with a slicing gesture.

"Important thing, you wouldn't be *here*. In hell. We've created our own little hell here. I guess I did it more than anybody. But now, the least I can do is keep that hell from spreading to them. I had an idea that you could sit with me, sort of take care of my body until I get back. And then if I don't get back, you'll know what to do."

"Panic?"

She actually cracked a smile. "Something like that."

"But, Sister, how are you going to actually *do* it? How are you going to avoid the snake, and find them? Surely the sage won't be enough."

Klee nodded, and drooped her head shyly. Her tangled hair hung forward over her bare brown shoulders. "I have an idea," she said, much more softly. "I don't know whether it will work. I am going to try to call on – *his* god."

"His? Setiq's?"

"Ikash's. Don't you remember, he had a god he used to talk about?"

Sha's throat constricted and he whispered, "I remember."

"I think it was the – creator," said Klee, and she too dropped her voice to a whisper as if this were a sacred mystery.

"He called it the Father," said Sha, clearing his throat to get the words out.

"Did he? Well, anyway, brother, I think this god of his is at least as great as our father's snake. I don't expect it will like me very much, given the way I've treated … well, everybody, or almost everybody. But our brother, he loves everyone. You once said so."

"I did."

"So I'm thinking that perhaps this god of his will allow me to pass – at least temporarily – for his sake. Maybe just this once, it will let me through to warn him."

Relying on love, thought Sha. Love was the only way to have a vision quest, really. How was your spirit going to find someone else's, over a long gap of time and a distance of a year's travel? You could never hope to find them, never, not unless you followed the cord of the love you had for them, and they had for you. If you took that in your hands and then just went by feel, hand over hand, paying it through, there was a chance that might lead you home.

If Sha knew anything, he knew that he loved his brother. He could not let Klee go alone to find him.

"I'm going with you," he said.

CHAPTER EIGHTEEN
GOING

They put more sage on the coals, piling it carefully so that there would be air space and the pile of herbs would fall slowly as it smoldered. They lay on their backs on two floor mats, not wanting to collapse and hit their heads if they were to pass out while attempting a vision in a sitting position.

They said a prayer.

They held hands.

Despite this, as soon as the two of them left their bodies they almost immediately became separated.

Klee saw herself and Sha on the floor for an instant. She saw through the wall into her old bedroom, where she glimpsed a reclining, smiling Setiq and then he was gone. She followed the sage smoke through the smoke-hole, and in the harvest moonlight she saw the city and the river and the empty stalks in the fields of maize, waiting to be cut and used as fuel later.

Next, she passed into a smoky, misty, grey place and there became frightened.

And all the time, under her breath as it were, she was chanting a prayer: *I just want to help. I just want to warn them. Please let me warn them. Please let me get there.*

This was indeed stupid and dangerous.

And then she saw the Reindeer village.

Its layout looked different from what she remembered, and she had moment of panic that perhaps she was approaching a different village, one populated by people she had never met. But she was not in control of the path of her flight. Almost no sooner had she had this thought, than she was inside one of the wooden lodges and there, indeed, was someone she *had* met, someone she knew very well.

It was Kai, her brother. Oh, perhaps technically he was her nephew, but they had grown up as siblings and now she knew it.

He was lying in the unfamiliar lodge, covered by a bear blanket, with his arm around a woman. On the other side of the woman lay a toddler. All three were sleeping. Kai's brow was creased and his eyelids flickered as he dreamed.

Klee did not recognize the woman, nor did she stop to study her face and figure out who her brother had married. She was more worried about how she was going to get through to Kai. He had never seen visions that she knew of. How was she supposed to make him hear her?

"Kai!" she called sharply.

The frown and the eye flickering intensified, and then Kai gave a jump and sat up in bed, revealing a chest that was bulkier than when she had known him. His eyes darted here and there around the room. The room was quite dark, and Klee ought not to have been able to see at all, but in her vision state she could see every detail of a person if she focused on them.

"Kai," she called again, "Can you hear me?"

More darting of eyes, and quick breathing.

"I am sorry I was a bad sister," said Klee. "I was so angry with you, but it was no one's fault really. It was a tragedy. A tragedy."

This was not what she had come intending to say, but it seemed to be working. Kai whispered, "Klee?" Although he said it softly, she could hear it as if it were the only sound in the world.

But then things went wrong. Kai began speaking, and his words were not words that Klee could understand. Some of the words sounded a bit familiar, but they went by too fast, and she could not follow one sentence before a new one began.

Klee was dismayed. "Listen," she said more urgently. "Blood-eaters, do you hear me, Kai? They are real. They may be coming. They have killed Setiq. Blood-eaters, do you hear?"

Her brother began listening and staring again, and then his body collapsed on itself and she realized he was weeping. That was all she had accomplished. She had managed to bring the idea of herself before him, and all it had done was to make him weep.

"I am sorry, Brother. I am so sorry." But by the time she said this, she was again back in the grey place, and then she was waking up in her old house – her new house, rather – holding hands with Sha.

Klee was crying. This was stupid. She had never used to cry, and these days it seemed that it was all she did. But the vision had not gone as badly as it might have. She was not trapped on the other side. She still knew who she was. She had seen no snake.

She looked over at Sha. He was crying too. The tears were sliding down from the corners of his eyes as he lay on his back. But his face was smiling.

"Are you back?" he asked. "Oh, God, it was good to see him again."

"See who? Whom did you see?"

It turned out that Sha had indeed gone straight to Ikash, and furthermore had been able to speak to him without any problems.

The shaman had been sitting, perhaps praying, before his own hearth-fire. As soon as Sha called his name, he had jumped up startled and had been able to see and speak to his brother.

Klee suppressed her jealousy. Who knew why Sha had understood his brother, and she had not understood hers? Perhaps it was because Ikash and Sha had parted with their relationship in a good condition, whereas she had parted messily with Kai. If that was so, it was a fair punishment, and she was ready to accept it. She did not deserve to be heard by Kai. She only hoped her visit would not ruin the life he had with his wife and family. Probably it would not. Perhaps he would even ask his shaman about it, and receive reassurance.

Or the difference could be simply that Ikash, and not Kai, was accustomed to listening to the spirit world.

"Were you able to tell him about the blood-eaters?" she asked.

Sha had. He had told him everything.

"There is bad news, though," he added. "Ikash told me that a few years ago, they moved their camp to the east side of the river."

That explained the differing village layout, then. But it was worrisome. Brother and sister sat up, wiped their cheeks with the flats of their hands, and stirred up the fire. They talked through the implications. The giants would not know of the existence of the Reindeer people, unless the giant population and territory were very large indeed. In order to find them, they would have to travel roughly north for many months. Hopefully, the giants' laziness would prevent this. But it was a good thing, Klee and Sha decided, that the two of them had warned their loved ones.

"How did you make out?" asked Sha, wiping his nose with the back of his hand, and then his hand on the back of the dog. "Did you get through safely? Did you see … you know …?"

"I did not see that," said Klee. "I saw my brother."

And then, though she had not intended to say a word about her vision, she found herself pouring out to Sha all her history with Kai, her guilt over the way she had treated him, her worries about the disruption her visit might have caused.

Sha was a good listener. He didn't minimize anything she said, but he did incline to go easier than Klee did on both herself and Kai.

"Oh, come on, you were both kids. Stupid kids," he said soothingly. "I admit, I was not impressed with the way he handled himself when those idiots attacked you. You had a right to be angry. I'd have whipped him, too, if there hadn't been so much else going on."

"Yes, I know that, but by that time he had already blamed me. But then he was sorry … and I wasn't ready … but I should have realized how important it was, because we were going away forever."

"Stupid kids," said Sha again. "You can't expect kids to conduct themselves with any wisdom. Not even when it's a case of life and death. When I think of the things I did – and didn't do – well …" He shook his head as if shooing insects. "The important thing is that we got through and managed to warn them."

"Yes," said Klee.

"And that," he added with emphasis, "we got lucky once, but we might not get lucky the next time. No matter how much we miss them, we should never do this again."

"Yes," agreed Klee. But she knew this was going to be a hard promise to keep.

Winter was coming. Winters were not particularly hard in the Snake City, but Klee found within herself a strong resistance to the idea of spending another season there. During the winter, the Snake People concentrated on long-term projects such as weaving, building up and improving the city, and Sha's sculpture work. And religion. Ordinarily, in the rainy season Klee would be spending a lot of time in the women's complex. She did not now want to spend any more time there.

She did not want to be around her father. She had visited him in his temple, which was now cleared of refugees and consequently seemed larger than ever, to ask him whether he had intentionally offered her husband up to the blood-eaters to be defiled and killed. Endu had said of course not.

Surprisingly, though, after rejecting responsibility for himself, he went on to take responsibility on behalf of his god.

"*He* could have told me about those blood-eaters," he said. The usual gestures accompanied the word "he": an eye roll and a slight head twitch, to indicate that he was talking about the snake. Some things were too holy to speak about normally. These days, when Endu spoke about his god, he appeared to be having a seizure. "But he didn't. I was going in blind. But I don't think *he* was going in blind, my daughter. He knows them from of old. So he must have had his reasons, and I think I can guess what they were. A man can't defy his god and live long after that."

"Defy his god?"

"Oh, yes, your husband defied him. It was when you were having your baby."

And then the whole story came out: how Endu had wanted to use his god's healing powers, how Setiq had resisted because he didn't want "that thing" going inside her body. How they had come to blows.

"I didn't know," said Klee softly, in dismay. "You are certain that he attacked you first?"

"Yes, definitely," said Endu.

Klee knew as soon as he spoke that he was lying. Later, this would cause her to realize that Endu had also lied about his long-ago fight with his son, Ikash. But at the time, her head was filled with another thought.

Setiq died for me, then, if what you say about the snake is true. I was died for. He protected me. Even if what my father says is not true, Setiq still died for me. He came along on this journey to protect me. If it had not been for me, he would not have been here. He would not have gone through – that.

Klee did not like the idea that she had been died for. Before the slaughter of Setiq, she had never wanted to be indebted. She hadn't liked anyone making unsolicited sacrifices on her behalf. But regardless of her wishes, it had happened, and now that it had, she felt differently. Now that it had been made, the sacrifice had changed her. It had transformed the way she looked at everything. And she welcomed the change, even though she would never have looked for it. She could not be angry with Setiq.

Setiq had come to her, long ago in her lonely, bitter camp, though she had not been looking for him. He had presented himself to her as a gift. And that gift, it seemed, was still giving.

She thanked her father, coolly and respectfully, for the information. Then she turned and walked out of the snake temple, stepping over the two thresholds, through the courtyard, down the stairs. It was the last time she would ever set foot there.

CHAPTER NINETEEN
UNSOLICITED SACRIFICE

Klee made her preparations. It was hard to do this secretly; she did not want to be seen taking supplies, so she had to gather the things she needed under the guise of helping others. That meant she had to start coming out of her house, and doing as she used to do: weaving and making garments, processing maize, washing diapers for the mothers. She was surprised and dismayed at how easy it was to slip back into her old routines. She needed to get away quickly, or the routines would swallow her once again.

The only thing that was different than before was that she did almost no cooking. Setiq was not there to cook for, and Klee was not hungry. Nevertheless, she squirreled away dried roasted maize as trail food. Perhaps, if she lived, she would become hungry later.

Zillah had some things that Klee wanted. There were herbs and powders to help with nausea, and various substances to pack onto an injury and stop the bleeding. Klee would use these for her little medical kit. She must get into Zillah's house while the old woman was out. But that should not be difficult, for Zillah normally *was* out for most of the day. Once, she had gone about on her rounds for the purpose of helping people; now it was mostly for the sake of the crops and dogs.

Klee waited until she had to make a trip to dump some things on the midden pile. The midden pile was accessed by a low cliff on the south side of the city, and Zillah's house perched near this cliff. Klee tossed her garbage over the edge, wrinkling her nose at the smell that came up from below and even gagging a little. Then, instead of going back through the town's ribs to her own place, she walked along the edge until she saw Zillah's small house looming over her.

Up the steps, and into the cool darkness.

"Hello, granddaughter."

The old woman had outsmarted her. Zillah was at home after all.

Klee greeted her respectfully. She accepted the chair, the same one her father had sat in a few months previously, and delighted at how comfortable it was compared to sitting on a river stone floor. She tried to make small talk, to pretend she had come only for a visit.

But Zillah was not fooled. "So, granddaughter," she asked briskly after a few moments, "what items from my stock can I give you?"

Klee was startled and shamed, but decided to pretend she was there merely to replenish her personal supply (not that she had ever had one). She asked for item after item, and Zillah gamely filled small pouches, labeling each with a distinctive bead tied into the drawstring, and handed them over. As she did so, she reminded Klee which shape of bead indicated which herb.

Then she said, "You will need some bandages as well, if I am not mistaken."

"Why would I need bandages?"

"You are about to make a long journey. There are all sorts of things that could happen."

Klee turned and stared hard at her grandmother.

Zillah stared calmly back.

After a few seconds of this, it became obvious that the old woman knew exactly what the younger one was planning.

Klee wanted to speak at once. She ought to say something extremely wise and insightful, something that would, at one stroke, save face and also stop Zillah in her tracks if she had any thought of detaining her granddaughter. But Klee couldn't think of a single, non-foolish-sounding thing to say. And she was so tired. She put her elbows on the wooden arms of the chair, drooped her head down low, and stayed stuck that way. She didn't weep, but there came to her eyes tears of frustration and exhaustion.

"How did you know?" she asked finally. Once the words were out, she contemplated, dully, how stupid they made her sound.

But Zillah was also feeling stupid. "My dear," she began, and her voice emerged sounding as trembly and defeated as Klee's. "I am not as observant as I should be. I have missed many things that, if I had noticed them, could have saved lives."

For a moment, Klee wondered if her grandmother was talking about Setiq. And perhaps she was, but there was more than that to her thought.

"And I am a slow learner," continued Zillah, "but I do learn. I do learn. Once, long ago, I failed to notice it when a woman under my care had been driven to desperation and was planning to run. She ran, and she died. I swore then that I would not let such a thing happen …"

"My mother," said Klee.

"I failed to notice," said Zillah, "even that she was with child."

Klee looked up, shocked, and met her grandmother's eyes. Zillah was staring directly at her, with a warm, swimming look.

"But how," said Klee. "How could you possibly … I mean, I am only two months along …"

"I am more observant now," said Zillah.

Klee sat, stunned. Then she rallied and said, "You have to let me go, grandmother. This is different. I am not planning to kill myself."

"No," said Zillah, "if I am not mistaken, I think you are planning to bring Setiq's child back to his people."

"I am," breathed Klee, now very close to wonder.

"But that is nearly as much of a death sentence as the path your mother took. How are you going to find your way, on land, over the route we took by water? How are you going to make a year's journey alone?"

"I'll manage.…"

"And if you don't, you will not really mind, will you?"

"Well …"

"Furthermore," Zillah pressed, "How on earth are you going to get to them before your child is ready to be born? And what if you don't? The last birth nearly killed you. Are you going to face that on the road?"

Frustration rose up in Klee, and she cried out, more sharply than she had intended, "I won't deliver him here!"

"Then you will need someone to go with you, to make the journey go more quickly and – if all else fails – to help you with the delivery."

"Wait." Klee drooped again; thought; shook her head slowly. "Are you saying you are planning to *go with me*?"

"I swore to myself that I would never again let a desperate pregnant woman under my care run off to face death alone."

"But how are you going to help? What chance to do we have? Just two women, traveling through the winter … a pregnant woman and a crone?"

The crone chuckled. "You think you are stronger alone?"

Klee's head jerked backward slightly. "You are right," she murmured after a moment. "I am used to thinking of myself as stronger alone. I am used to rejecting all help. I recently learned my lesson, but I still tend to think in the old ways. Forgive me, Grandmother."

"So, you will accept my assistance? With more than herbs and bandages?"

"I will," Klee whispered.

It seemed like the sort of conversation that should have been taking place at midnight, but instead they were having it in broad daylight, in Zillah's house. They agreed to meet that evening, on the north side of town, which was closer to Klee's house than Zillah's. They would not delay any longer, as Klee had her supplies mostly gathered already, and Zillah was always ready at a moment's notice. More delay could mean they were found out.

Klee said, "Could we persuade Dira to come with us too?" As long as they were saving people, she hated to abandon her father's bloody, broken wife.

Zillah said, "No. If we take her away, then Endu will start seeking wives from among the younger women."

They met at the north side of the city, at twilight. Klee was not overly worried that anyone would notice her departure, or much care about where she was going. She had them trained to leave her alone. The one possible troublemaker was Sha, but luckily, he was being kept occupied by some sort of crisis with one of his children: a tooth that had been knocked out, a fall, or something like that. Klee did not want Sha to know anything about where she had gone. She did not want him to have to lie to their father. *A man can't defy his god and live long.*

This, setting out in secret, felt familiar. Klee felt as if she had done this often in her life, though actually she had never before done it in exactly this way. Her "secret" trips, in the past, had actually been very public. But they had felt private, on the inside, in her heart.

It also felt familiar to be setting out, in secret, of an evening, with her grandmother. There was one instant of shyness when Zillah first approached. Then Klee's grandmother gave her easy smile, and it was just as if they were going out together to the field. Zillah had a heavy string bag on her back, suspended from a tump line that went around her forehead, the tump line making a wide dark band against her silver hair. She had brought her ever-present short stabbing spear, which doubled as a walking stick.

They made to emerge, for the last time, from where the shadows fell between the broken ribs of the city.

Then they were arrested by a noise from above. A step, a voice: "Who goes?"

They had forgotten the guard.

The guard in this case was Megal. He was one of the sons of the long-dead chief Enmer, which made him Klee's cousin. He had been pacing the mostly uninhabited outer ridges of the city, scanning the jungle for birds or giants, and the exits for women who might be foolish enough to venture alone down to the water. Tall, dark, lean, wearing a swingy breechclout and crowned with a small crest of greenish feathers, he looked very much like Endu as he scampered down from the top of the man-made ridge above their heads, clutching a spear that was much longer than Zillah's.

There was no way for the two women to hide the fact that they were not merely going down to the water. Even before Megal's feet had touched the ground level, he had seen their equipment. It was true that Zillah carried her spear with her everywhere, and equally true that women would sometimes bring a bundle of washing down to the river. But they would never do this at dusk. Megal was not fooled. He reached the bottom and stood there in a defensive stance, and in the twilight they saw his eyes move over them.

No one knew what to do for a long, silent moment.

Klee had no pride left. She said, in a very soft voice, "Please, cousin."

Megal did not speak. He planted the butt of his spear on the ground and held it elaborately behind himself. Then he bowed, ushering them with a gesture out into the fading twilight.

There was a moment of golden light as they took the few steps, hearts pounding, between the city and the edge of the late-summer jungle. Then they were in the brush, and all was dry smells, singing insects, and patchy shadows.

Their hearts had not yet had a chance to slow down when they heard Megal's voice from behind them, speaking in a relaxed, conversational tone. "So, you want out too, do you?"

And a moment later, trotting along the path came Klee's old dog Guide, leggy, scruffy, and snuffling. Guide knew exactly where the two women were, and as they emerged from cover he was already loping up to them. He approached Klee and leaned his skinny ribs on her calf, looking up adoringly. His mouth was open, tongue dangling, in an ugly, heartwarming smile.

"Are we going on an adventure?" he seemed to say. "Why didn't you say so? I'm ready!"

They walked all night, cutting far to the west because that seemed the direction least likely to be searched. Then they rested all the next day. Klee was dead on her feet, between the walking and the fatigue that comes with early pregnancy. They hoped, given their recent habits, that it might be a day or more before they were missed from the city. They hoped Megal would keep their secret, and, as things fell out, he apparently did.

They repeated this pattern for a few days, resting and walking with no urgency other than the needs of Klee's body. All the better, they figured, if their stops were unpredictable. They ate the trail food that Zillah had brought. They found birds' eggs and ate those. Guide caught his own food for the most part. Klee even got a rabbit with her sling. She was still not very hungry, but she knew they'd need meat on the journey. She was already starting to miss (at least in theory) those big feasts that the Reindeer People used to have in the days of her childhood, with several wild cows roasted and laid out end to end, everyone full and content, the dogs trotting from blanket to blanket, begging.

After the first seven days or so, it was easy. All they had to do was follow the river north. Granted, there was no trail, and often the rough country would force them far from the edge of the great river. But they were in no hurry. They always found a way through, and they always, sooner or later, found their way back to the river. This being autumn, the water was low, and often they were able to walk over the mud flats on its banks. They could stop whenever they wanted. Sometimes in the middle of the day they would stop, Klee would nap, and Zillah would fish with a line in the water.

They fell into a pattern: a late start in the morning (until Klee's fatigue ended a few months later), a morning walk, a noon break to nap and fish, an afternoon walk, an early night. As long as they gave Klee plenty of rest breaks, they could make good time during their walking hours. Klee slept long at night, more than she could ever remember doing. The fresh air and exercise wore her out, and her body's tiredness overrode any troubling thoughts in her mind. Zillah would often sit up through a good part of the night, guarding her granddaughter. She needed less and less sleep as she aged, and she also seemed able to sleep during the day, stumping along in a sort of trance with her eyes open.

The weather became cooler. Both women found they had more energy after the breaking of the enervating heat. After they had been traveling for about six weeks, Klee entered the middle leg of her pregnancy and suddenly found she had more energy again. They made better time during the days and even began to hope they might find the Reindeer People before Klee's time had come. The baby was beginning to move, dancing around at night when their walking ceased. This was encouraging. All seemed well.

The winter brought rains. The women consulted with each other, but both felt well enough to go on. So they walked on, at their easy comfortable pace, through midwinter and into the early part of the turn of year.

One thing Klee discovered when living closely with her grandmother was that Zillah talked to herself. It wasn't just occasionally, either. It was every day. It was multiple times per day.

"I know," she would say.

Or, "That's a good point. Thank you for that."

Or, "Why indeed?"

Zillah's interlocutor seemed to be clever, and to know more about a variety of things than the old woman herself. Klee tried not to be bothered by all this. She guessed that Zillah had somehow taken her own wisdom and knowledge, and made it into another person in her mind. If that was what she needed to do in order to be able to use it, then so be it. Zillah's knowledge was keeping the two of them alive, and Klee was not going to criticize.

She did try, whenever her grandmother spoke, not to answer immediately until she knew who was being addressed. This extra moment of restraint got easier as Klee's pregnancy progressed and she became more and more uncomfortable. Being expected to speak was so effortful that it could be annoying at times, distracted as she was by indigestion, swollen ankles, hip pain and various other physical complaints.

They had been traveling four months when they came upon the remains of the Snake People's winter lodge from several years ago. Now it was only an oval ridge of earth that ringed the top of a hill. Saplings had sprouted on the berm, which was already fading into the forest.

Zillah did not want to enter or even to look at the ruin. But for Klee this was important. She struggled up the western approach, taking it at her own slow pace, and stood before the gap in the berm, at what had been the lodge's front door. She faced the place where they had all lived that fateful winter. At that moment, she saw everything just as it had looked then. She could see the cozy firelit inside, the sheltered smoke-gap at the pinnacle, the A-line roof coming down to the earth to make a narrow corner. And she could see herself and everyone else … how young they looked! They were all gathered around the ash pit, just where they had gathered when Endu staged the ceremony that left him healed … or at least, turned him into something else that was less weak and injured.

The illusion was helped because two small, straight saplings were growing out of the berm on either side, framing the space that had once been the entrance to the wicker tunnel. For a moment, Klee' stomach growled. She smelled the food they used to eat. For a moment, she felt like that old Klee. Then, her baby shifted its place inside her, and with a disorienting snap, she was back to being her present self again. And that snap left her grateful to be who she was now; fearing, chiding, pitying, and wishing she could warn that younger Klee, who knew so little.

It had begun to drizzle. If only the lodge were still in place, with a roof they could shelter under. But Klee understood why her grandmother had no wish to stay in this place. The Zillah of years ago probably did know as much as the Zillah now, yet that past Zillah hadn't been able to stop events unfolding. It was easy to imagine how present Zillah would be quite frustrated with her.

Zillah had become adept at throwing together a brush hut, often in just an hour or two. She built it tonight a bit farther inland than the ruin; it was positioned, in fact, about where the women's hut was in relation to the Snake City. But on this hut, the entrance faced west, away from the ruin, away from any place where the two women had previously lived. Sleeping on the ground was uncomfortable for Klee, who was now entering her third trimester, but so was bending down to pluck up dry winter grasses. Zillah did this, bending and straightening, her hard, capable hands working with machine-like determination. Before long, she had made a comfortable nest for her granddaughter.

There were no eggs and no fish. They ate leftover beans and cornmeal.

Klee was feeling warm (finally!), lying on her side, her legs tucked over her travel pack, her feet elevated, almost ready to sleep, when Zillah did that disconcerting thing again where she appeared to speak to someone who wasn't there. Only it didn't start out that way.

"You must forgive me, granddaughter," she said.

Klee opened her eyes and looked across at Zillah but did not bother to sit up. The old woman had a distant look in her eye, but she had said "granddaughter," so Klee replied, "Forgive you? What for?"

"For not noticing that you were pregnant."

There was a long pause while Klee tried to make sense of this. At last, she gave up. "I rather think you did notice, grandmother."

Zillah seemed to come to herself.

"I mean," she said, "for not noticing that your mother was pregnant. With you. If I had noticed, I could have saved her."

"You saved me," said Klee.

"I am thinking how to save you again. It is clear to me, granddaughter, that we will not get to the Reindeer People in time. This winter lodge was two months' travel from their old place, and our pace now is slower than it was then. And moreover, the Reindeer People have moved. Even if we reach the old place, we will have to get across the river."

"Which puts us crossing the river just as I am about to go into labor."

The women had done their calculations before now. They expected that Klee would deliver in about another two and a half months.

"Yes, and that is if we aren't delayed at all. Which we will be. And there is no guarantee we will find them as soon as we cross the river. They may not be settled right on its bank."

"And you do not want to be alone if," said Klee, unflinching, "you have to cut me open again."

Now it was Zillah who flinched. "You are a brave woman. You are right, I do not. Even with help, it is dangerous process, but without help …"

"Damn," said Klee. She began to shed tears, which ran down hot into her left ear. "I don't care if I die, Grandmother, I really don't. But I wanted to see Setiq's parents. I wanted to show them their baby."

"There may be a way," said Zillah, "to save at least you, if not the child."

"Better the child than me."

"I doubt I could keep it alive without you. But listen. There is a certain root; I can prepare a tincture. I can give it to you a month or so before the child is to be born."

"What would be the point of that?"

"To induce birth. If he comes sooner, he will be smaller. You may be able to deliver him through – through the usual door."

"But he may die?"

"They often die when they are so small and come so early. But there is a chance he could live. The key is, we must keep him warm, and I must give you herbs to stimulate your milk."

It sounded terrifying. It sounded inevitable.

"That sounds like the sort of thing we would have to stop for many months for."

"It is. It will be. But not here."

"Not here," agreed Klee.

They agreed that they would walk a few more weeks. This would allow them to take their time, and to build something substantial once they found a good hospital spot.

The next morning, Zillah went to the place on the stream bank where she had once stood and mourned her inability to protect the children from the snake. This time, she only stared at the water for a few moments. Then she got out her fishing gear.

CHAPTER TWENTY
THE CALL

Ikash did not always hear from God.

Nor did he always listen.

There had been seasons, though he prayed, when the large, dark presence was silent for months. For years.

But more often, the shaman did not wait for his maker to become silent. Instead, he would simply neglect to seek him. Some years he felt too worn to put forth the energy that it would take to wait patiently, to summon all his attention to a mystic's pitch. When he did have visions, it was exhausting. Usually it was during some crisis period. Almost always, there was pain involved. Knowing that behind it, whatever else there might be, there was pain, he did not always make himself open that door.

Ever since Sha left, and since he had failed to save Klee, Ikash and God had been for the most part in a standoff. The Reindeer shaman had come before the Presence sometimes on behalf of groups of young men who were about to go through initiation, and sometimes on behalf of his children. But he had not come on behalf of himself. And they did not talk about Klee.

This year, there had been no initiation ceremony and so there had been no cohort of young men to pray for. The shaman had gone about his business, hunting, gardening, caring for his family, resting his mind. He had felt no need to open the terrible door.

But all of a sudden, one night in the spring, he heard something.

It worked. Against all the odds, it worked. Klee and Zillah made better time than they had expected. They made it into country they recognized, only a day or two downstream of the People's old habitations.

By this time, the great river had drawn away from them to the east. The country that Klee had grown up in was full of streams flowing east toward that great river. The women would have to walk in that direction, the better to cross it, eventually. But that would only become necessary if they succeeded in the most dangerous step in their plans.

Zillah built them a brush hut. She hummed as she did so, singing some unrecognizable tune that reminded Klee of distant, ancient cities. She gathered her supplies and made her tincture. And Klee, in the single biggest leap of faith she had ever in her life brought herself to take, drank it.

Then she sat sweating and puffing in the hut. She was constantly wrestling with her hair, which had grown out at last and was long enough to sit on. It was the hair of two pregnancies. She would shift her hips off of it, tie it in a bundle high on her head, and during the seemingly immeasurable time of labor that followed, again and again it uncoiled itself, thick and sleek, slithered down her back, and was soon getting in her way again.

The cramps were much stronger with Zillah's tincture. And they achieved their intended purpose: the baby was born while he was still small. Covered in downy hair, he was skinny and golden and looked very much like Setiq in the face, as had his older brother. But he was alive, and Klee could sense that his personality was different.

When Klee went to deliver the afterbirth, what came out instead was another baby. This one was a girl, also alive, darker and redder than her brother, with a pile of wooly curls on top of her head.

Both women started laughing and crying when they saw that the birth was twins.

Klee felt blissful and at peace for the first day or two after the birth. After that came the anxiety.

How was she going to make enough milk to feed the two of them? How was she going to keep them warm? Where was Zillah going to find sufficient food to keep Klee strong enough to care for her babies? How would they ensure that the two, the son and the daughter, did not dehydrate, that they put on weight? What would be done when Zillah, as was almost inevitable, was taken by a predator? (For several days, every time Zillah was gone from the hut for a few hours, Klee was almost certain that this was what had happened.)

They stayed in that place just over a month, but to Klee it seemed like closer to a year, between her tiny snippets of sleep, her painfully swollen breasts, and her constant looming worries that made every moment seem sharp, vivid, and eternal.

At last, at *last*, the babies began to put on weight. At last neither one of them seemed about to die. Klee's fears were as numerous, varied, and all-consuming as ever, but Zillah said they must begin hiking to the old camp, they must try to make it to the river before a proper spring came on. If they left it too long, the ice would begin to melt upstream, and the river would flood and become impassable. They would be cut off from their people.

If they were to make it to the river, she said, and find it flooded, all need not be lost. They could return to their old home, stay there and raise the babies until later in the summer.

She painted these scenarios with as many reassurances as she could muster and still remain honest. Klee's anxiety felt soothed while Zillah was speaking, partly because she knew that her grandmother did not shade the truth. But whenever Zillah was silent, Klee would begin again to fall down the long stone staircase of worry. She could feel herself starting to panic, and then loomed the prospect that if she panicked herself into madness, she would be mentally unfit to care for her children. Thinking that she was doing a good thing, that her actions were entirely reasonable, she might instead without knowing it be doing a mad, destructive thing, as her mother had done. As had her father.

At times like this she would set her teeth and whisper prayers – to whom was unspecified – for strength, for the ability to hang on, for sanity. She would whisper "please let us reach our goal." She felt that things would be all right if they could just get into the presence of other people.

And she would keep walking.

They reached the river. They walked up and down it for a day or two, trying to find a good place to ford. Unbeknownst to Klee, Zillah was also weighing several other things in her mind. She was waiting until the river was at its lowest, when they had had a dry day or two. She was realizing that the flood, when it came, might come in response to events far upriver, unseeable by her; might come without warning. She was wondering whether it might be best to try and make a boat. She was, like her granddaughter, struggling with fears and deep doubts about her own judgment.

On the second night, they were up in the dark, walking the babies. The baby girl usually slept well when left alone to do so, but her brother was thin and intense, restless and colicky. About half the time, his fussing would wake his sister. This was usually just when Klee had got both of them fed and was trying to drift off herself. Sometimes Zillah would get up, a child in each arm, and tirelessly walk around and around their brush hut. Snake City had been large and guarded by teams of men, but the two women's world was small now and it only took one wizened, indefatigable crone to pace their tiny perimeter.

On this occasion, as often happened, both women were up, each with a baby. Klee had her daughter, relaxed and heavy in the sling against her shoulder; Zillah had the boy, who was (mostly) content as long as you kept moving but would protest as soon as you began to stop. The women were plodding in a daze around and around their brush hut, occasionally varying things by padding up and down the little stony path that led to the river.

The night was chilly, but bearable with movement. The moon was up; the tops of the trees were soughing, but at the ground all was still. These details always seemed especially vivid at night. Klee's dog Guide, who had been with them on their entire journey, circled the brush hut too, often brushing against his mistress's leg, making about two circuits to every one the women made.

Klee was thirsty, so on her next lap past the hut's opening, she bent and retrieved a water skin, slinging it over her unoccupied shoulder.

Then, by unspoken agreement, the two women turned away from the tiny circle they had been walking and to the line that branched off from it, the sloping path to the river. Guide's toenails clicked on the occasional stone as he trotted after them.

Zillah walked ahead, muttering to herself.

"Really?" Klee heard her say. "Are you certain?"

"Grandmother," said Klee. She stopped walking. She had been struck by a thought. "Grandmother. Do you see visions?"

Zillah, when her granddaughter halted, had stopped walking as well. She turned around, bouncing on the balls of her feet because her great-grandson was fussing, and approached Klee in the moonlight. Klee saw with relief that Zillah met her eyes. Her look was clear and grounded. This, and the bouncing behavior, was reassuring ... but only somewhat, especially in light of her next words.

"Oh, no," she said with a little laugh. "Oh, no. Not I. I don't see visions."

Klee cleared her throat and spoke softly; her girl-child sighed in her sleep. "The shaman told me you did, once. My uncle. My brother, I mean. When I was very small."

"The shaman was mistaken."

Klee was afraid to ask her next question. She had been trained not to ask about difficult matters, and she didn't want to embarrass her grandmother. But the question, at this moment, seemed a matter of life and death.

"Then … forgive me, Grandmother, but … who were you talking to just now?"

For an instant, Zillah's dark eyes got wide. "Oh, that," she said. "Oh, I am sorry, Klee. I see I have frightened you. But, don't be afraid. I don't see visions, but I … I hear things sometimes. I have a … a friend, who sometimes tells me things and helps me."

It sounded to Klee as though Zillah had auditory visions. At least, she very much hoped that her grandmother did, because the only alternative Klee could think of, was that she was out in the nighttime forest with, that she and her babies were entirely dependent upon, a woman whose mind was not stable.

"Is this .. friend … a spirit, then?" she asked.

Zillah laughed again, and Klee did not find it entirely reassuring.

"Oh, no," she answered, with a fond tone to her voice. "He is human. Purely human. Perfect in his generations. And," she added suddenly, "I don't mean to alarm you, granddaughter, but he is saying that you and I must cross this river. Right now."

"Right now?"

"Now, my dear. Again, I don't mean to alarm you, but I imagine that the reason he tells me this is that a flood is coming."

"Can we …" Klee quavered, "… go back for supplies?"

"No," said Zillah.

Klee was terrified. She did not know whether she trusted her grandmother's "friend" or not. She was too sleep-deprived and rattled to think methodically, but a quick, whirling, disorganized glance at her options seemed to show that refusing to obey Zillah was at least as dangerous as going with her. Perhaps other options existed, but Klee was not in a state of mind to come up with them.

So she followed.

Zillah came out ahead of Klee as they reached the moonlit riverbank. This consisted of smooth round rocks of just the right size to turn an ankle. The ford, which lay spread out before them, was more of the same such rocks with a thin layer of water murmuring over them. There was neither sign nor sound of a flood; the water seemed, at this moment, lower than ever. As Klee emerged from cover she spotted the glistening fur of a huge rodent as it slithered into deeper water downstream. She wasn't sure whether it was a beaver or a water-hog until she heard the slap of the tail.

With a scritch of dog-toenails upon river-rock, Guide emerged from the brush behind her, where he had taken a side trip. He showed no interest in engaging with the beaver.

The soft sling in which Klee was carrying her daughter was generously sized. Zillah took the baby boy and settled him in it next to his sister. The two of them were now slung across Klee's belly. Klee shifted them a bit and adjusted her tender parts as best she could. She was accustomed to bearing discomfort, for their sakes, more or less indefinitely, and she was certain that the river crossing would be so nerve-wracking that she would soon forget about her swollen and tender breasts.

Zillah sought about among the brush at the river's edge and selected a sapling-sized staff. It was straight, broad at the base, as tall as she was. It was too soft for long-term walking, but Zillah did not think she would need it for long. She only needed something to use for a third foot as the two women made their way across the river.

She took the staff in her left hand, and they began the crossing.

Zillah walked half a step ahead, feeling her way with staff and feet as if looking for a path that she had known before. Her right hand was held out like a firm and unwavering guide-rope. Klee grasped on to it with her left, and Zillah's arm did not fall even when Klee put weight on it.

Klee breathed out loud as she walked, whimpering with each exhalation. She needed all her energy to concentrate on placing her feet, carrying her babies, not screaming or crying. She could not spare energy to muffle her breathing or hide her terror. But neither woman stumbled. The river flowed on, very cold, but rising no higher than their ankles. Despite this lack of disaster, Klee's panic did not diminish. So they walked on like this, Zillah saving, Klee moaning, as if they had reached an acceptable compromise. The dog, responding to Klee's anxiety, proceeded whining, with his side pressed against her leg, which sometimes helped and sometimes hindered matters.

Two-thirds of the way across the river, Zillah stopped. Klee gave a squeak of alarm, fell silent, and then stood resting, taking breaths deeper than her whimpers had been but just as noisy.

"Listen," said Zillah. "Can you hear him singing?"

Lacking breath to answer, Klee shook her head.

But just then, she did. She heard it.

The singing was ringing out from behind them, across the river, to the west: a deep male voice singing unintelligible words. A wind had picked up and was rushing downstream, but the voice reverberated, warm and very human, louder and clearer than the wind. It came from behind them, yet it sounded nearby. The tune did not remind Klee of any tune she had heard a person sing before. It gave her the strangest feeling, as of something unutterably ancient, utterly alien, and, at the same time, almost familiar. It seemed to evoke a whole world.

"I hear him!" she cried out. She should have been frightened that something eerie was happening, but instead she was near to tears with relief that Zillah was not in fact crazy. "Oh, Grandmother … is that what you've been hearing all this time? Is that your friend?"

"Yes," said Zillah to Klee, and then to someone apparently ahead of them, she said, "I am coming."

Their canine companion, however, was not coming. He gave a cry of alarm and then suddenly scampered, splashing, back across the ford in the direction they had come.

Klee did not try to call him back because she had gotten used to not yelling while holding her son and daughter. But she blurted in an unnaturally high voice, *"Guide!* What was that? Did he hear the singing too?"

"Perhaps," said Zillah, "or perhaps he was reacting to the wind. Come, let us hurry. It is urgent that we continue."

They struggled on. Just before the eastern bank, the river became deeper than it had yet. It went up to their knees. The water tugged their skirts around their legs, nearly hobbling them, and down at the level of their feet was a bone-chillingly cold current that seemed to be growing stronger by the second.

The moon had gone down. The bank was muddy. The moment of grace in the middle of the river had passed away like a wind-blown cloud, and everything was impossibly difficult once again.

"You go first, my dear," said Zillah. "I will give you my staff. I will boost you. I am coming."

The eastern bank was so steep, the grass so slippery, that Zillah at one point was practically lifting Klee by pushing upward on her rump. Klee grabbed a handful of grass with her right hand, which she thought might buy her perhaps a couple of seconds. She heard Zillah say,

"Here. Take it."

She looked over her left shoulder, and there was her grandmother, standing up to her waist in dark and rushing water. She was thrusting the staff upward and forward toward Klee's left hand.

There was no time to panic about Zillah. If Klee kept looking over her shoulder for one more second she would fall. She took the staff, repositioned her hand, and drove it into the ground, doing this as she did everything these days, with her arms held unnaturally far out from her body so as not to squish the babies. She rocked her weight forward, and for a moment she was not looking backward nor forward nor at anything at all, but only struggling with gravity, hers and the babies', and her face was very close to the earth and all she could see if she had looked was the mud and the grasses.

Then she won the battle, stumbling forward onto her knees for a moment; but her weight was centered, and she was on dry land.

Behind her, she heard Zillah say, "I am coming."

Klee used the staff to get to her feet and climb the last few steps up to the earthen ledge above the bank. A sweet lassitude of weariness washed over, and she was barely able to turn herself around to face the west and lower herself to a sitting position before her legs gave way, dropping her onto the comfortable dry leaves.

What she saw before her was a raging river.

Then the sound hit. It was a terrible, insistent sound, a drowning-out kind of sound.

The water was up past the bank that Klee had just so laboriously climbed. It was almost lapping at her toes. Great rocks of ice were being carried downstream, bumping into the banks and tearing out unlucky bushes.

There was no Grandmother Zillah.

"I am coming," she had said, but she had not been speaking to Klee.

The babies were safe. They were sleeping soundly, their little feet entwined with each other's, warmed by Klee's body weight.

Klee herself was cold. She scooted back a few paces in the dry leaves. Then she groped about the found the staff and used it to struggle weakly to her feet. She stumbled back into the woods, as far back as she dared in what was now the pitch dark, desperate to get away from the fury of the water. She got stronger as she went, as she became more and more aware of the danger. This was a spring river, carrying pieces of the ice. It might not stop at its banks. It was unaware of human boundaries.

When she had climbed gentle slopes several times and seemed to be on a low hill, the babies were hungry. Klee found a grassy hollow to sit in, with an icy boulder to put her back against, and, crying and shivering, she nursed them. Then she refreshed herself with a deep drink. Miraculously, the water skin was still slung over her shoulder.

Klee began to pray while she nursed. Nursing was always a desperate time, but this prayer was surely the most desperate of them all. She never knew, later, whether she had spoken aloud. It felt as if she had leaned back against that rock, and the cry for aid had come tearing directly out of her heart.

Please help me. I don't know what to do. I have crossed the river and I have lost the children's father and I have lost my dog, and I have lost my grandmother. I have nothing left. I have no one to help me keep the babies alive. I cannot go on. Please, come and get me. Please, please, somehow, help.

However unsafe Klee might have felt, her two babies were perfectly content. After eating, they slept again.

Klee could stay awake no longer. She prayed, in the same unfocused, desperate manner, that she might not smother the children in her sleep. Then she rested, just as she was, back to the rock, children suspended in the sling, limbs shaking until they shook into stillness.

Dawn came, and no help had come. Her neck was cricked, her legs asleep, her tailbone in agony, but she was alive and so were her children.

She shifted and stretched painfully and then began the slow, awkward process of getting them out of the sling and the sling off from around her shoulders. The garment was damp; she spread it out on the boulder where it loomed above her head. The sun was starting to strike the hilltop and the day promised to be warm. Klee was ravenous; she and Zillah had left their food in their brush hut in the other world. She would worry about that momentarily.

She had set the babies on the sweet green grass. When she unwrapped them, they flexed their legs and toes in a way that did her heart good to see it. As per their personalities, the girl kicked energetically; the boy stretched but also complained.

Neither one had smiled at Klee yet, but they smiled often at each other.

Klee kissed their sweet soft faces and then proceeded to clean them up, using generous handfuls of dew-drenched grasses. She wiped her hands on the grass, relieved herself nearby, wiped her hands again. She drank the remainder of the water-skin and nursed the babies. Then she set them on the ground again, one on each side of her, and leaned back against the rock where she had spent the night, unsure what to do.

And then she heard voices.

They were coming from the eastern side of the hill.

It was the voices of two or three men. They were calling out to each other as if hunting for something. Occasionally Klee would catch a word that she thought she recognized, but for the most part their talk flowed on, just past the grasp of her understanding.

She did not think these were like the singer's voice. They were real, living people. The question was, Were they ordinary people or giants?

She had just decided to stay very quiet on the west side of the boulder, when her son let out a loud sharp cry. It sounded a bit like a bird's cry, but no one who had been around babies could mistake it for anything but the voice of a very young human.

The voices stopped.

Klee scooped up one baby in each arm and sat rigidly still.

Someone called out something.

Still she sat.

Then the atmosphere changed. The smell came first: a smell of sage and woodsmoke, a smell that Klee remembered from the long ago. Then the sense of a human presence. And then, the human presence itself: a dark bulky figure stepped its way lightly around the south side of the boulder, backlit by the morning sun, casting its shadow on Klee. And with the shadow, the sage smell came on stronger than ever. Among the Snake People, the smell of worship was the smell of blood; but among the Reindeer People, it was the smell of sage that meant a shaman.

And here was the shaman. It was someone she knew. He looked a bit like her father, but shorter, more faded, less handsome. Less glorious and frightening. Quieter and less charismatic, but more real.

He spoke to her, and though later, Klee would prove unable to understand the Reindeer People's speech and would have to re-learn it, for whatever reason this one sentence, at this one moment, she understood.

"We came as soon as you called," he said.

EPILOGUE

So Klee came back to her own people, bearing with her the children she had borne, neither among the snakes nor among the reindeer, but in the in-between place, guarded by a grandmother and by an invisible singer, guided across the perilous river. As she walked back towards the Reindeer Village, surrounded by her brothers and by other men whom she recognized as relatives, this sense of unreality clung to her. It was very, very slow to fade. Even when they made it back to the place where she had ostensibly grown up, nothing was banal. Nothing was really the same. The village itself was different, for one thing: location, vegetation, and smells. It was farther east, among hardwood forests. The families were all different, because some people had gotten married, others had died, and there was a new generation. There was nothing about this place to remind Klee of the village between forest and scrub where she had spent her unhappy childhood.

Speaking of that childhood, there was one thing from the past that she instantly recognized. Kai had insisted upon coming along on the shaman's rescue party. He came around the rock not too long after Ikash, and he came at a run, and the first thing he did was embrace his sister.

He was babbling nonstop, so fast that Klee could not catch a word of it. But it was obvious that he was overflowing with joy, having been offered the same thing she had been offered, the thing that neither of them had ever expected they would receive: reconciliation.

The next thing he did was to fuss over her babies, which further melted Klee's heart. It was at about this time that she realized that her inability to understand him was not just due to the speed of this speech. Apparently the Reindeer language had changed quite a bit in the five and a half years that Klee had been absent. (*Or perhaps it's the Snake language that changed*, she thought.) She was not even greatly disturbed by this. She had been prepared for it by her vision-visit to Kai; and, in a strange way, it did not seem like such a change for her to be around people with whom she could not communicate, but who clearly loved her.

The first thing was to let Kai know that he was forgiven. She had struggled to her feet, and she leaned forward and embraced her stepbrother. His skinny arms tightened around her shoulders, and they stayed that way for a long time, both of them weeping silently. And Klee sensed that she had imparted not only her forgiveness but her regret.

By this time, the rest of the party had come around the rock and were standing about. There were five men: Ikash, Kai, Aki, Dani, and the sixty-two-year-old Rumi. All were heavily armed, as if they had expected to have to fight a monster, which, given the tribe's history, was not an unreasonable thing to anticipate. But the monsters had all either triumphed or been defeated, and the rescue party was faced only with a mother and her children.

Klee wiped her cheeks with her hands and became practical. She fell to communicating what she could by dint of patience and saying only one thing at a time. It would later emerge that they could understand quite a few of her individual words, when spoken in isolation. She indicated the babies and said "Setiq." Then they babbled, and when they fell silent she said "slaughtered" and could not keep from bursting into tears at the memory. They did not know the word she had used, but her tears they understood. And they also recognized, and strongly reacted to, the next word she uttered: *Blood-eaters*.

She brought them to the river, which was still in flood. In fact, she could not bring them all the way; the spot where she had sat on the bank was now underwater. She pointed to it and said again and again the name of Grandmother Zillah. They understood enough. A few months later, when she had re-calibrated her ear, she was able to give them a fuller explanation.

Then they escorted her back, and the way they were treating her was extraordinary. She had thought she was crawling back in weakness and shame, that she would never be able to atone for having been deceived by the snake and her father, for what she had gotten Setiq into, for what she had allowed to happen to him. But the way they walked all around her, guarded her, carried the babies for her, encouraged her to rest, spread out a feast; the way they looked at her as if she were almost divine … it was like the return of a queen.

It was less than a day's walk to the Reindeer village. Going at Klee's slower pace, this got them there around evening. People came running out of the village as soon as the party was spotted, and Klee froze, overwhelmed. But the shaman drew a blanket out of his pack, threw it about her, and under this covering he hustled her into the house he shared with Hyuna and their now seven children. They kept her in that house all night and let no one in to see her.

Hyuna, who was as lively and cheerful as ever, was clearly bursting with questions and with things she wanted to say, but Ikash would barely let her speak to his sister. So she and her ten-year-old daughter Sira contented themselves with caring for the twins, almost as playthings, and bringing them to Klee when she needed to nurse and generally doing all they could to pamper mother and babies.

One month after Klee's return to the new Reindeer Village, Guide came trotting in from the north. He had crossed the river on his own and scented his way back to her.

Everyone wanted Klee, just as everyone had when she first ran away from the village, just as no one had wanted her throughout her childhood … except that, in retrospect, everyone but Amal actually had. Amal now reacted in a positive, though complex, way to seeing her stepdaughter again. She was stunned, obsequious, complimentary. She was full of praise for Klee's babies, her strength, her beauty, and especially her hair. She and Jai invited Klee, if she wished, to live and raise her babies in their extended household. But Klee knew that, even after the momentous changes that had taken place in her and in the Reindeer village, one thing she could never do was go back to live with Amal. She also did not want a lot of attention. Jai was the chief now, his house a busy place.

It transpired that Hur had died the third year after the Snake people departed. The distant, mythical, red-haired Scyths had got him in the end. The spear that all those years ago had taken his eye, apparently had left a tiny part of itself inside his head, unfelt, imprisoned in walls built around it by his body, waiting its moment. He had, the shaman explained to Klee when she could understand, begun having headaches and blackouts, and periods where his vision or hearing suddenly left him. By the end, he was incontinent, palsied, and had smelly fluid leaking out of his one remaining eye. It was a horrible way to die, said Ikash. An undignified way.

"Yet we are lucky that God let him have us for forty-six years after the injury," Ikash told Klee. "He did so much for our people during those years. He was a father to me."

"And who is your father now?" Klee asked him.

The shaman's eyes flickered upward, and a smile played upon his face. But all he answered was, "Now *I* am the father."

Melek had been the chief for Hur's last months and for about six months after that. Then he said that he was old and tired and did not want the responsibility. Neither did Damai, Rumi, or Ikash. A coughing sickness had taken Dusun. Jai was a good hunter and warrior, the most charismatic man left in the tribe, and about a head taller than any of the other men his age. So, by a long, excruciating process, Jai had been selected. Klee thought it was good selection. Her brother was born to be chief. He had some of the gifts of his father Endu, without – she hoped – being as marred by darkness.

But Klee did not want to insert herself into the life of the chief. She wanted to live a quiet life. And she needed to deliver an apology.

She ended up living with Hur-kar and Lien, Setiq's parents, in their housing complex, which was out of sight and hearing of the rest of the Reindeer village. She brought the babies to them, along with her tears and her brokenness over what the giants – what Endu – what she herself – had done to Setiq. And in her broken words she begged their forgiveness.

Her in-laws were both small, quiet people, but they were not weak people. To her surprise, neither of them blamed Klee for what had happened to Setiq. Both Hur-kar and Lien had lost their mothers at a young age. They were familiar with sorrows, acquainted with grief, and Lien's main reaction to the Klee's sad story was the impulse to comfort and restore her daughter-in-law.

Klee lived with them and with their daughter, Shuli, and son, Shin, who were still children. Klee put her babies on Lien's knees and let her raise them almost as her own, though of course they were Klee's as well, and so they ended up having two mothers. She stayed away from the village, resting in her in-laws' quietness and solitude. Sometimes, even a year or two after she'd returned, she would be filled with confusion and find herself wondering what this place was and whether she was really here.

The babies, Tiq and Zinlah, grew, looking exactly like their two parents. The boy was narrow and golden, the girl brown and plump. They were inseparable, and they complemented each other perfectly. Tiq, who had been colicky as an infant, grew up keen and quiet, with a habit of looking a long time at the world and then taking decisive action. Zinlah was more fierce and ready to start things.

In time, Zinlah would overwhelm with a war cry, and Tiq would move in for the final killing stroke, later, when they became warriors together who helped their tribe drive back the giants.

Klee, though a mother, was only twenty-one years old when she returned to the Reindeer People. Most of her age-mates had married, but in the years that followed, she found, to her annoyance, that she was being pursued by several of the younger men. The younger women were jealous of her, and even some of the wives. At one point, things got so bad that Klee considered striking off on her own again. Eventually, however, she married Grinn, a son of Rumi, who was five years her junior, and they lived together happily.

ACKNOWLEDGEMENTS

Thanks to my Beta readers, Fran and Rachael, to my editor, Kitty Kladstrup, and to the family members and readers who have done so much to support and promote this trilogy. Thanks also to all the people who were patient with me through the messy process of growing up as a young woman.

BIBLIOGRAPHY

For a sense of the geography and ecology of North America just after the Last Glacial Maximum, I used David J. Meltzer's *First Peoples in a New World: Colonizing Ice Age America*, University of California Press, Berkeley, CA, 2009. I made changes to accommodate the story, and of course his book does not mention giants or dragons.

For Zillah and Ninshi's herbal treatments, I used *Prepper's Natural Medicine by* Cat Ellis, Ulysses Press, Berkeley, CA, 2015. What Zillah used to induce labor in Klee was a tincture of comfrey, because comfrey can cause miscarriage. I have no idea whether it can be used safely to induce labor in real life. Probably not. <u>Do not try this at home</u>.

For the viability of performing a C-section with stone age technology, see chapter 8 of Richard Rudgley's *The Lost Civilizations of the Stone Age*, Touchstone, New York, NY, 2000, which describes a successful C-section performed in Kahura, Uganda, in 1879.

Poverty Point is a little-understood archaeological site on Bayou Macon in northern Louisiana. About 3,000 years old, it is a large complex of mounds laid out in concentric half-circles, intersected by aisles which sight toward the setting sun at the solstices. There is a large mound immediately to the west of it, and the whole thing faces Bayou Macon on the east. Endu's Snake City is similar in layout to this Poverty Point site, though the fictional Snake City is much smaller in scale, farther back in time, and is located right on the Mississippi River. Also, the speculation about the uses of the "ribs" and the "temple mount" is my own. My source for Poverty Point was pp. 108 – 115 of *Mysteries of the Ancient Americas*, Joseph L. Gardner et al, The Reader's Digest Association, Inc., Pleasantville, NY, 1986.

For historical and archaeological evidence for red-haired giants living in ancient North America, see *Giants: Sons of the gods* by Douglas Van Dorn, Water of Creation Publishing, Erie, CO, 2013, and *Lost Race of the Giants* by Patrick Chouinard, Bear & Company, Rochester, VT, 2013. These two books have very different analyses of what exactly the giants were, but both are good secondary sources with bibliographies that establish the presence of giants in North America. Unfortunately, the giants' reputation for engineering prowess, cannibalism, and sexual assault is well-established in myths, legends, and even histories worldwide.

Some practices of the Snake People are intended to foreshadow those of Mesoamerican cultures such as the Maya. These include feathers as battle dress; the importance of maize; snake worship; a roof comb on the temple; and ritual bloodletting to induce a trance. LIDAR technology has recently begun to reveal that Mayan civilization was much more extensive than previously thought. Though there are many other sources on the Maya, I used a basic one: *The Magnificent Maya*, Thomas H. Flaherty et al, Time-Life Books, Alexandria, Virginia, 1993.

ABOUT THE AUTHOR

Jennifer Mugrage as a young woman was just as foolish and awkward as Klee, possibly more so. And now look at her! She is a schoolmarmish middle-aged author with interests in anthropology, linguistics, missiology, and ancient history. Don't miss her next novel, *The Bright World*, which will be set even farther back in time.

Visit her web site: https://outofbabel.com